Advance Praise for *Muses Over Mumbai*

"Today's Mumbai is a city with a dark side, in thrall to sectarianism, money and power, but the spirit of its people – the affluent as well as the marginalized, the selfish as well as the selfless – is still a rich subject for the probing storyteller. These fine stories set that spirit against the darkness, to original and powerful effect."

Salman Rushdie, Booker Prize winner and author of *Midnight's Children*

"Murzban Shroff's new collection of stories beautifully manifests all that I have long loved about his work. His consummate artistry not only gives us a ravishingly vivid portrait of Mumbai but it turns that city – as only literary art can do – into a portrait of the universal human condition in every large city around the world. *Muses Over Mumbai* is a brilliant work and Shroff is a very important writer indeed."

Robert Olen Butler, Pulitzer Prize Laureate for *A Good Scent from a Strange Mountain*

"Murzban Shroff writes with exceptional clarity and humanity from a place in desperate need of both."

Jonathan Franzen, National Book Award winner and author of *The Corrections*, *Freedom*, and *Crossroads*

"Ignoring the demarcations separating the personal, the epic, and the humble, these plangent but life-loving stories throw new light on the life that surrounds us."

Amit Chaudhuri, Sahitya Akademi Award winner and author of *Sojourn* and *Finding the Raga*

"A fitting companion volume to *Breathless in Bombay*, these stories ring timeless and true."

Jeet Thayil, author of *Narcopolis*, shortlisted for the Booker Prize

MUSES OVER MUMBAI

Stories

MURZBAN F. SHROFF

BLOOMSBURY
NEW DELHI • LONDON • OXFORD • NEW YORK • SYDNEY

BLOOMSBURY INDIA
Bloomsbury Publishing India Pvt. Ltd
Second Floor, LSC Building No. 4, DDA Complex, Pocket C – 6 & 7,
Vasant Kunj, New Delhi, 110070

BLOOMSBURY, BLOOMSBURY INDIA and the Diana logo
are trademarks of Bloomsbury Publishing Plc

First published in India 2024
This edition published 2024

ISBN: HB: 978-93-61313-87-5; eBook: 978-93-61314-58-2
2 4 6 8 10 9 7 5 3 1

Typeset in Minion by Manipal Technologies Limited

Printed and bound in India by Thomson Press India Ltd

For sale in the Indian Subcontinent only

MIX
Paper | Supporting responsible forestry
FSC® C010615
FSC www.fsc.org

To find out more about our authors and books visit www.bloomsbury.com
and sign up for our newsletters

Muses Over Mumbai

To my uncle *JIMMY*.
For the many illuminating hours
spent in his care and company,
and for the guiding role he played
in steering me to a love of literature.
To him, my dearest uncle,
I remain eternally grateful.

Call it Bombay or call it Mumbai,
my city remains the story capital of the world.
There are no limits to the inspiration it delivers,
no end to its generosity

— Murzban F. Shroff

Contents

Publication History

Grateful acknowledgments to the publications in which the following works first appeared in a slightly different form:

"Ruffled Feathers" in *Bryant Literary Review*; then in *Asia Literary Review*.

"The Mochi's Wife" in *Weber – The Contemporary West*.

"All That We Own" in *Catamaran Literary Reader*.

"Hafta: The Price" in *LitMag*.

"Conversations with a Terrorist" in *India Abroad*; then in *Mid-Day*.

"Mehrunissa's Story" in *Hawaii Pacific Review*.

"Mind Over Matter" in *Washington Square Review*; then in *Rockhurst Review*.

"Something to Think About" in *Chicago Tribune*.

"The Lady at the Bank" in *The Capra Review*; then in *Jotters United*.

"Mental About Mumbai" in *Transnational Literature*.

"Black Friday" in *The MacGuffin*; then in *Meniscus Journal*.

"The History Lesson" in *Tiferet Journal*.

"Neighbors" in *Panorama*.

"Scent of a Meal" in *Weber – The Contemporary West*.

"Auntie Elena's Revenge" in *Mid-Day*.

"The Earth Shall Be Enjoyed by Heroes" in *Manoa: A Pacific Journal of International Writing*.

Introduction

THE UNSPARING MATHEMATICS OF progess has gripped my city, and you can see it everywhere. In the insolent edifice that slices zigzag across the ocean, destroying a view and an expanse that was once the pride of the city. In the metro-3 construction that rises phoenix-like, impeding traffic, claiming trees, and driving temperatures to bristling heights. In the roar and rumble of earthmovers that replace old buildings with eager high-rises and bring to quaint neighborhoods the insularity of gated communities and the lure of super-luxurious amenities. Then, there are the giant water tankers that choke the roads, transporting thousands of gallons of water sucked out of fast-depleting wells. "Mumbai is upgrading," or so they tell us; but at what cost to its heritage and stability? Can a carefully pieced jigsaw of seven islands take all this relentless development? Can it withstand a double whammy of underwater reclamation and overhead pounding? Can a city that's growing vertical at supersonic speed meet its requirements for broader roads, smoother traffic flows, adequate parking, clean air, and a consistent supply of affordable water? And these are not the only concerns. One must ask the custodians of the city: How, in proportion to the thousands of building projects under construction (over 6000 at the time of writing this, I am told), how many public hospitals and schools have been planned, how much taxpayer money has been set aside for healthcare and education? It is my guess that the answers would disappoint, if not shock.

I, for one, have not seen a single public hospital under construction. (Which raises the question: Is this to be a city for merely the affluent?) But even in the midst of all this commercial anxiety, even while the body of Mumbai is being slowly dismantled and its face botoxed, there is one thing that remains steadfast. And that is the soul of the city. Its spirit, its ethos, which brings its diverse citizens under a single canopy of perseverance, a will to live and resist and triumph over their circumstances. To be a citizen of Mumbai is to be conscious of a larger design of life and illumination at work. It is to know of a city that can support your goals and aspirations, perhaps, your most feverish dreams. It is to be aware of a silent, flowing humanity, beyond the distinctions of caste and class, where the greatest progress is that which happens within. It is this enterprise of humane understanding that I have attempted to capture in this collection of seventeen stories. The soul of Mumbai is, indeed, the soul of a mother-city that nurtures its own, often at its own expense.

Ruffled Feathers

IT WAS ONE OF the finest buildings in South Mumbai. Not a fly could enter unnoticed. It had been constructed on slum land, but today bore an elite address. The affluent and the successful aspired to stay here. And stay they did, after paying a fortune for their apartments. There were twenty stories in all, with three levels of parking, three elevators for the owners, and a separate elevator for the domestic help.

The security in the building was watertight. Five sturdy guards in uniforms patrolled the premises, maintaining vigil twenty-four hours a day. Not that the neighborhood was dangerous, but every precaution had to be taken. That's why the maintenance charges were high: fifty thousand rupees a month. But no one minded, no one complained. And there was CCTV, too, eagle-eyed scanners that snapped up every movement.

The male servants were frisked before they entered and left the premises. The maids got away with a bit of flirting: they knew how to soften the men in uniforms. But the chauffeurs were checked morning and evening, and this would annoy them, for they had their pride, these men of spotless appearance.

There were strict rules. Every visitor would have to enter his name and address into a logbook and whilst leaving would have to sign out. This would annoy the visitors, but rules were rules, and the security could not be compromised.

It was surprising then that a pigeon got into the shaft. This was the long vertical enclosure that ran outside the bathrooms, carrying the plumbing pipes all the way from the first floor to the twentieth. It was a wonder how the bird got in, considering that the shaft was covered with a special bird mesh. It could be inferred that the pigeon had been looking for a safe place to lay her eggs and, in her quest for childbearing privacy, had torn through the mesh.

The bird was unbearably noisy. It cooed without pause, its cooing growing louder with every passing minute. Sometimes, as though seized by some terrible impulse, it would flap its wings and fly up, beating its wings so furiously that feathers from its body would dislodge and float into the bathrooms.

Fed up with the noise and the feathers, the women of the building decided to take their complaint to the property manager, Major Anirudh Sood, who had his office on the ground floor. The major was a broad-chested man with a thick, jowly face, alert eyes, and a faint, ironic smile. He ordered tea for the ladies, who had begun to talk among themselves. They discussed for about ten minutes matters of the home and kitchen, before remembering they were there for an important reason.

Kamal Suchanti was the first to speak up. She was a glum-faced woman, seventy years of age, residing alone on the third floor. She said that the bird had added to her constipation problem. As it is, unloading at her age was such a problem. And just when she would get the urge the damn bird would start its song of oppression – *hootoo, hootoo* it would go, and she would freeze up. Then the bird would rise to a higher level and, going *hootoo, hootoo*, would excrete sticky green droppings onto her bathroom window. She felt the bird was mocking her.

The other women offered some solutions. Had she tried bananas, papaya, prunes, or black grapes in her battle against constipation? Then someone asked: Had she tried throwing water at the bird before she began her business?

"Not just water," said Major Sood firmly. "Piping hot water! To shock, to stun!"

"Of course not!" said Kamal Suchanti, horrified. "That would be cruel. Horrendously cruel."

"Maybe we can fumigate the shaft?" said Mrs. Vyas helpfully. "That should get rid of the bird."

"No," said Mrs. Bansal. "That pigeon is pregnant, and we don't want to harm her babies. That would be like the Bhopal Gas tragedy. We don't want that on our conscience."

"No, surely not!" said Mrs. Venkatraman. "Whatever we do, we shouldn't endanger the bird or its eggs. After all, we are civilized people."

"What about tempting the bird with some seeds?" said Mrs. Thakore. "We could place some on the ledge of a toilet window, and when it comes to eat those, we could try and trap it."

"No, no," said Mrs. Kashyap. "Once the bird knows there is food available, it is never going to go. It will simply stay put."

"Which reminds me—" said Mrs. Adenwalla stiffly. "I must bring it to your attention, Mr. Sood, that someone has been feeding the crows every morning. They throw bread and chapattis on the ledge below my apartment, and the crows flock there and make a terrible nuisance. *Caw, caw*, they go all morning, which disturbs my meditation. May I request you to send a circular to all the flat-owners requesting them to stop this at once? And if that doesn't work, perhaps you could focus a CCTV upward, to catch the culprit."

"There is nothing wrong in feeding crows, Mrs. Adenwalla. In case you didn't know, crows are nothing but your ancestors reborn, and when you feed them, they shower you with blessings," said Mrs. Doshi. Short and stout, Sheetal Doshi had a grim, unsmiling face that belied her thirty years of age. She sucked in her lips and glared at Mrs. Adenwalla through round, severe glasses.

But Mrs. Adenwalla was not to be intimidated by a woman twenty years her junior. Coldly she said, "I can assure you, Mrs. Doshi, that if my ancestors *are* reborn, they are certainly not going to be crows. They are going to be civilized, cultured human beings, residing in London or Paris. In fact, I find it insulting that you'd think my elders to be scavengers. I will have you know, that we, the Parsees, have excellent taste in food."

"Oh, we know all about your tastes, Mrs. Adenwalla; don't remind us. You eat the brains and the liver and the kidneys of goats, and their private parts, too. Why, just the other day, the whole lift was stinking when you returned from the bazaar. I could tell it was some awful flesh you had brought back. So don't talk to me about your fine tastes. We know all about that."

"Well, if you know that much, Mrs. Doshi, perhaps you would also like to tell us who is feeding the crows. Who is following this uncivilized practice, day after day?" Mrs. Adenwalla's eyes glinted. The room bristled with tension.

"Ladies, ladies!" said Major Sood, stretching out his hands in a pacifying gesture. He felt like a man who had been invaded on his turf, drawn into a battle not his own. Yet he smiled patiently.

"Please stay out of this, Major," said Mrs. Adenwalla angrily. "I think Mrs. Doshi and I have something to settle, and it might as well be here and now."

"Well, first let me tell you, Mrs. Adenwalla, that you have no business bringing all your foul-smelling meats into the lift. Most of us here are religious people. We go to the temple; we do puja daily; we don't even allow our servants to eat non-vegetarian food. And you just walk into the lift with your stinking meats and pollute it. That is not proper. You should think of our feelings, too."

Mrs. Adenwalla crossed her legs elegantly. At fifty-two, she had the body of a gymnast. She brought her hands over her knees, and said, "I don't believe it, Mrs. Doshi. You are acting as though being non-vegetarian is some sort of a crime. You are trying to make me feel guilty, make me feel small. Well, you are not going to succeed. Let me tell you what it is like to bite into tender, flavored meat. It makes your palate sing, your senses soar. You eat not just to fill your stomach but to celebrate life, to feast on it. Something that nature *has* intended for you. But you can't imagine that, can you? How can you? You are so closed to the idea that you don't even know what you are missing. And another thing, please stop saying 'lift.' The correct word is 'elevator.' If you must use the English language, use it correctly."

Mrs. Doshi flushed red. Incensed, she brought her chair close to her opponent; then, through clenched teeth, she spoke. "Well, what do you think non-vegetarianism is, if not a crime? Let me ask you one thing, Mrs. Adenwalla, just one thing, huh? And you try and answer me. You think you are very clever, no, with all your fancy airs and your ideas about the English language, then you answer me one thing from common sense. My guruji told me this, and now I am asking you, and if you answer me, I will acknowledge you in front of all these ladies. If human beings are meant to eat flesh, then why we don't have claws and fangs like other flesh-eating animals? Why are we made differently? Come, answer me; I am waiting."

"I don't see why I have to justify myself to you, Mrs. Doshi," said Mrs. Adenwalla. "As far as I am concerned, non-vegetarianism is a matter of individual choice, and you had better learn to respect that. We live in a cosmopolitan society and, if you have a problem with that, then move out. Go somewhere where you can be with your own kind."

"Hah, you are trying to change the topic because you can't answer my question. How can you? You don't even know what you are stuffing into your body, what you are serving your family. If you really loved your family, would you give them dead offerings? Tell me, would you?" Mrs. Doshi turned and looked at the other women in the room, her face thick with victory.

"Ladies, ladies, please! We have strayed from the main issue. We need to decide the fate of the pigeon." Major Sood was polite and pleasant, but his smile was fast disappearing.

"Well, what are *you* here for, Mr. Sood, if you can't solve this problem? Our duty was to bring it to your attention. Now you decide how you want to solve it. All we know is: it has to go! The bird has to be removed gently, without hurting it. I am told a pigeon's breath is bad for the health. It can lead to asthma and lung infection. And we have many children in the building, and old people, too. So you must act promptly. Wouldn't you agree, ladies? Major Sood is the best man for the job. We should leave it to him."

This was Minoti the painter, who was known for her exquisite depictions of old Mumbai. It was a beautiful day, full of warm natural light, and Minoti was keen to return to her canvases.

The other women agreed. Yes, the major was the right man for the job. It should be left to him.

Major Sood shot Minoti a grateful look. He had a busy day ahead and liked to maintain an efficient pace. He rose to his feet and assured the women that the pigeon would be removed. Within twenty-four hours it would be evicted. They had his word on that.

Alone in his office, the major thought what a close shave it had been. It could have turned nasty, could have been unpleasant. Mrs. Adenwalla and Mrs. Doshi were old foes, their animosity having begun over a parking spot. Not their fault. In Mumbai, parking space was always in short supply. In the building, for instance, each flat-owner had been allotted two parking spots on the podium. But how was that to suffice when almost every person in a family owned a car? The space along the driveway was an open parking lot – anyone could park there, if they got in early. Yet, there was always a scramble for the spots and, sometimes, arguments, which invariably got resolved.

But one night, things had gotten out of control. Sheetal Doshi's husband, Chetan, had steered his BMW into the place where Soli Adenwalla usually parked his Jaguar. Now, you don't do that to a man like Soli, a big man, a successful man, with an ego as big as his belly. Not for nothing was Soli paying the security guards an additional ten thousand rupees a month. For that price, they were expected to keep an eye on his car and discourage other flat-owners from occupying his spot. But that night Soli was out, and Chetan Doshi had arrived from Pune, having driven three hours nonstop to get home in time for an India–Pakistan cricket match. Chetan was tired, and although he had two reserved spots on the podium above, he thought, why not make use of the open parking?

The security guards had protested. This was Soli Sahib's spot, he always parked there.

Where, where was it written? Chetan Doshi had demanded. And before his incensed gaze, the security guards had withdrawn.

Two hours later, Soli cruised in from a wedding, where he had knocked back four large single malts and gorged on chicken farcha, patra fish, salli par eedoo, and a spicy pulao dal that reminded him of the one his grandmother would make. Craving the luxury of his four-poster bed, he was aghast to find his parking spot occupied. Calling the security guards, he let fly at them, and all they could do was listen stupefied. "What could we do, sahib?" they said. "We tried explaining, but Doshi Sahib just would not listen."

That sent Soli into a frenzy. He ordered them to call Chetan Doshi and tell him to remove his car that very instant, before he, Soli, did something drastic. And Silla Adenwalla, standing beside her husband, tall and regal in her fineries, pleaded, "Soli, please, calm down, my darling. You know what Dr. Balaporia said about your blood pressure. You don't want to take chances. You don't want to ruin your health. You have to take care, my sweet potato."

The guards called up Chetan Doshi, who was equally furious at being asked to abandon an exciting match. Slipping out of his shorts, into his trousers, he swore that he would teach that arrogant Parsi a lesson; he would take him down a peg or two. And listening to him was his wife, Sheetal, who decided to accompany her husband, just in case things got out of hand.

Facing each other, the two men had argued, had stood their ground, and, when that failed, they had traded insults, then blows. When the security guards had tried to intervene, they had been ordered to stay out of it. And soon the wives, too, had joined the fight, screaming and railing abuses.

Just then a police van passed by. It had stopped, and three cops had alighted and questioned the men. Why were they brawling like hooligans and why were their faces bloodied, their clothes torn? The cops had asked the men to accompany them to the station. And, naturally, their wives went too, angry and shrill with accusations.

Complaints were registered, criminal complaints. On the basis of these, cases were filed in the Bombay High Court. If one of the complainants alleged threat to life and property (meaning car), the other said he had been subjected to a communal slur; he had been insulted to the point where he had suffered a loss of self-esteem.

Each complainant offered the security guards a bribe to testify in his favor. The guards reported this to Major Sood, who thought it wise to transfer them to another site and bring in a new lot.

The matter came up for hearing in the Bombay High Court. Justice Sundaram clubbed all the cases and brought them to a single hearing. The court didn't have time for petty matters, he said, matters that sprang from the ego.

Hearing both arguments, the honorable judge delivered his judgment. He said, the fault lay not with either party but with the civic authorities who had allowed builders to build indiscriminately without taking into account the number of cars. He fined the two complainants five thousand rupees each for wasting the court's time and suggested that they collectively file a public interest litigation asking the civic authorities to provide a complete report on how they planned to provide parking in the new development projects sanctioned by them.

The case made headlines in the Mumbai newspapers and brought Soli Adenwalla and Chetan Doshi into the limelight. Overnight, they came to be known as civic-minded citizens who had brought to light an important issue. Working together on the public interest litigation, Soli and Chetan discovered a mutual love for cricket. Which, for them, was reason enough to declare a truce and forge a friendship. But, somehow, their wives could not forget that the two men had traded blows, had inflicted insults and injuries, and been whisked away, in the dead of night, to the police station, like common criminals. The women were too proud to forget that night.

And that's how matters had come to a boil this morning, thought Major Sood. The argument was simply a fallout of the main issue. But that was not his problem, he thought. He had important work to attend to.

First, he had to get an estimate for installing a sewage water treatment plant in the building. The plant would recycle and treat wastewater, then utilize it for flushing, gardening, and washing cars. It was his idea, the plant, and would result in huge savings on water bills. He was sure that this would impress the flat-owners. It would show them the foresight he could bring to his job.

Then he had to visit the municipality and request them to level the pothole-filled road leading to the building. For that, he would have to withdraw some money from the bank. Because those jokers at the municipality would surely want a bribe.

While at the municipality, he had to complain about the stray dogs who kept up their barking all night. Recently, they had attacked Mrs. Sippy's pug, and Mrs. Sippy had refused to pay the monthly maintenance charges until the strays were removed.

He also had to get the water tanks cleaned, the main gate painted, and the chandeliers in the lobby polished. And, besides all that, there was that matter of the damn bird.

At the municipality, he was made to wait for two hours outside the chief engineer's office. Seated on a wooden bench, he could see the chief engineer – a small, wiry man with a foxy face – through the swiveling half-doors.

In passing, a peon suggested to him that he stand up and remain standing. If the chief engineer saw him standing outside his office, his ego would be appeased. The peon paused and lingered, and the major sighed and reached for his wallet.

Whilst waiting, the major wondered if he missed army life, if, in some way, he still hankered for the thrills of action. For him, it was never about the glory but the need to be of service to his motherland. Even as a teenager he had wept over patriotic songs and felt something stir in his throat and chest during the singing of the national anthem. A twitch in his hip reminded him why he had left the army and, as though to get away from the memory, he began pacing up and down the corridor.

Operation Lone Star it was called, and it was a clandestine operation. An operation that saw him venture across enemy lines and take risks that would have been considered a breach of treaties and peace pacts. The mission was nowhere to be found in any army records. Not as much as a word. They had been told that even their families would not know their location and, should something happen, their bodies would be declared missing in action.

There were five of them on the strike force: Pushpinder Sinha, Banwari Lal, Vivek Mathur, and Rajindra Singh Khosla. He was the senior-most, the man in charge, and together they were known as Sher-e-Parbat, Lions of the Mountain, because it was their job to move out after dark and comb the mountains for hidden bunkers and snipers and render them inactive.

It was almost midnight when they had come upon the house on the mountain, a solitary hut that looked deserted. And then he had seen a flash and knew that it was occupied. They were being watched, yes! Targeted, perhaps.

And he knew, too, that his men were exhausted. They had been on the move for days, walking along treacherous ledges, across mountain walls ripped by shells and mortar.

Their feet and fingers were stiff. Their boots and weapons felt like a burden. They were low on sleep, low on rations, and their breathing was slow and heavy.

So he had decided to check out the hut himself. Ordering his men to cover him, he had begun his climb, one hand cupped over a torch, the other holding a rifle.

On the way, he had seen the flash twice, and knew he had to get there quickly. But the hut was at a greater height than what it seemed from below. At five thousand meters, the eyes and the mind could play tricks: that he knew.

Glad for his bulletproof jacket and for the sheltering dark, he had inched his way up, expecting any moment to catch a burst of gunfire. The Lions always lived with that feeling: the tacit presence of death. Like knowing they could be consumed anytime by these jagged white peaks, where nothing in nature survived.

Luckily, he had found a path that led to the house, and had brought out his pickaxe and lurched forward, man against nature, and nature allowing itself to be conquered, slowly, grudgingly.

Finally he was there, outside the hut, breathing heavily, in short, hard spurts. He did not care if someone were to shoot him now. He was that tired, that numb.

Mustering all his strength, he kicked at the door, and the first thing he saw were the whites of eyes, startled, and a rifle pointing clumsily at him.

Then he felt a searing pain in his thigh, the ground wobble under him, and he, falling, had emptied out his rifle.

When he was sure that it was over, he had swung his torch around and was gripped by a terrible panic. What had he done? What, indeed? The figure before him, slumped against the wall, was that of a boy no more than eight or nine years in age.

He crawled across the room, wondering how the boy had come to be there. What was he doing here, at this height? And who was he? An Indian or a Pakistani? Or the son of a terrorist?

Under the torchlight, he had gazed at that face – a sweet, angelic face with long, feathery eyelashes – and realized it was not a face he would forget.

Removing his gloves, he touched the boy's forehead with his palm. It was still warm, and the hair was soft and moist.

He felt his thigh swell and his hip and groin throb agonizingly. But it was the pain in his heart that seemed unbearable.

He had shouted to his men that it was all over, and even as the peaks echoed his voice back to him, he knew that it was, indeed, *all over*. He had done his bit for the country, but it was life that had tripped him. He would have to live with that face now – and a bad leg to remind him.

Heavyhearted and numb, he had lifted the boy's body and carried it outside. And whilst he struggled with the weight, something fell to the ground. Something, he felt, he could ignore.

He had buried the boy, but did not have the heart to cover the face. Who was he to cover anything so beautiful, so pure? He left that to the mountains and to the gods above.

And then he had said a silent prayer and asked the mountains to forgive him. But the mountains, as usual, were cold and unresponsive.

And then he remembered the fallen object and went back for it.

The light from his torch fell onto a mountain-runner's badge. A badge worn by the brave men who carried news in this part of the world, who trod the narrow paths and the slippery slopes to deliver letters and parcels.

The boy was using the badge to signal someone, to tell him that he was alive and well.

It made him sick to think of what he had delivered to the boy, instead. His leg felt heavy now, heavy and unmovable.

On the way down, his leg had given way twice, and then he had fainted, and when he had woken up, days later, it was in a military hospital at the foot of the mountains.

There he had been told he was finished as an army man. He would never know about the fate of his men and was instructed to forget about the mission. To simply erase it from his mind.

As though it was that easy. But then he was a bachelor and used to silence. So getting back to civilian life was something he took in his stride. Besides, the army compensated him well. He was given a one-bedroom apartment in Colaba, a membership to the army club, and a card that entitled him to subsidized rations and free train travel across the country.

He got the first job he applied for. It was with an international property management company where the pay scales were world-class. And the first building to which he was assigned was one of the best in South Mumbai. So, in a sense, life had worked out for him. It had made him a bed as comfortable as he could expect at his age. And here, in his job, no one considered him handicapped. With a little bit of effort, he got around and made himself useful, valuable.

The chief engineer called him in. He had two of his assistants with him. They noticed his limp, but said nothing. One of them pointed to a chair.

The room smelled of freshly consumed lunch. Pickles. Onions. Papads. It reminded the major of what had been enjoyed while he was waiting, standing and pacing.

He explained why he was there. If the access road could be repaired and leveled, that would be helpful.

They laughed and said that was for their bosses to decide, their big bosses.

Looking at their faces, the major was tempted to throw a chair at them. It would be so easy, he thought, to topple the desk and crush them like insects. Instead, he bit back his anger and said, "Sahib, is there any way you can do some basic repairs? All our flat-owners have expensive cars. And they have important guests visiting. It doesn't look good for a premium building to have this kind of an access road." He brought out an envelope from his pocket and placed it on the desk.

Without looking at it, the chief engineer said, "Tell me, sir, what would be the total value of all the cars in your building? I hope your gift is in proportion to that. You see, our own tank is very large, it has a very big capacity." And then he had laughed, and his assistants had joined in, and the major, too, was forced to laugh. And in that, they had all seemed united. At least for a while.

No sooner had he returned than there was a call from Mrs. Sippy. She said her maid had refused to walk the dog, she was petrified of the strays. So could Major Sood come and walk the pug? He could carry a stick and teach the strays a lesson.

And Major Sood had felt a swamping anger in his heart. What sort of job was this that denied him his rank and his twenty years of service? And what had the country come to, that it chose to subject a man of his background to petty bribes and tawdry humor?

At 5.30 P.M. that evening a circular went out to all the flat-owners. It said: "You are hereby requested to cooperate in the matter of the pigeon eviction. The pigeon is known to cause breathing problems and lung infections. Hence, please don't take this lightly. Please switch on your exhaust fan in the toilet at 9:00 P.M. sharp. With all fans on, this will force the bird to seek refuge at the bottom of the shaft, from where it will be removed by the housekeeping boys. I have personally instructed the boys, who will work as per my instructions. All we need is your cooperation and support. So help us help you." – By Order of the Property Manager, Major Anirudh Sood, Sher-e-Parbat. He hoped that someone would ask him about the last bit, so he could tell them precisely who he was.

A security guard went around handing out the circular. In most places, it was collected by a domestic helper, the lady of the house having gone out or engrossed before the television set.

Minoti collected hers, only to wipe her paint-stained fingers on it and crush it into a ball. This was a distraction in the face of some serious art-in-progress.

Kamal Suchanti, heavy in the stomach and compelled to skip her lunch, peered at it sullenly and said, "How, how will this help? If nothing else, there will be more feathers, more nuisance."

Sheetal Doshi took it absent-mindedly at the door, while in conversation with her neighbor. "Tell me, Mrs. Venkatraman," she said, "tell me one thing, huh. About these non-vegetarians! Why do they call other animals wild animals when they themselves eat defenseless animals? Animals who can't protect themselves, who can't fight back. Is that normal, you tell me?"

And Mrs. Venkatraman replied, "You are so right, Mrs. Doshi. You were right this morning, too. But I could not say that openly. You know how that Mrs. Adenwalla is. A real fighter-cock! She would have fought and made us feel small. My husband always says, 'A human being is what he eats. You eat satvic food and you will be calm and pleasant, but eat spicy food and you will generate heat and anger.'"

"Why," said Sheetal Doshi softly, "that is exactly what my guruji says. Only, he explains it so beautifully.

Why don't you and Mr. Venkatraman come one day to one of Guruji's discourses? You will enjoy, I tell you. It will change your lives."

Mrs. Venkatraman stiffened. She said, "Why, thank you, Mrs. Doshi, but we don't need our lives changed. We are very happy the way we are. Simple living and high thinking: that is what we practice. And never to harm others or to speak ill of them. Even if they are different from us. Now, if you will excuse me, I will go and start preparing dinner. Mr. Venkatraman likes to eat early."

And so the two neighbors went to their respective duties and, of course, they forgot to switch on their exhaust fans. As did many others in the building.

The next morning all the housekeeping boys were called to the property manager's office. There they stood gazing at the object on Major Sood's desk and listened to him speak.

"The pigeon, by and large, is a dirty bird, a noisy bird," said Major Sood, standing erect, his hands behind his back. "But, in times of war, it has its uses. During World War I, for instance, it was a pigeon, Cher Ami, who, despite being shot in the eye and breast, continued its flight and delivered a message that saved the lives of a hundred and ninety-four British soldiers. And, again, during World War II, it was a pigeon who saved the lives of a thousand British soldiers. It flew twenty miles in twenty minutes to warn the soldiers that the town they'd occupied was going to be bombed. But that was in war, mind you, and those were special pigeons."

From the giant cage on his desk, a plump, overweight pigeon let out its first coo of the day, cocking its neck upward, then sideways, to reveal a curious orange-rimmed eye. Later, it would be given finely chopped almonds and pistachios, and the thick, battle-grazed finger of Major Sood would enter its cage and rub its head and neck gently. And that evening the bird would be removed to the one-bedroom apartment of Major Sood, where it would be positioned on a balcony facing the sea, the balcony on which Major Sood enjoyed his three rum-and-Cokes of the day while listening to old Hindi songs from the sixties and seventies, his fingers drumming away on his white wicker armchair. And once he was finished with his drinks, and the ocean before him had turned dark and foaming, dark and noisy, the major would rise, stand before the cage, and whisper softly, "Mother, little Mother, are you ready? Will you be ready soon?"

The Mochi's Wife

A STRANGE TRANSFORMATION CAME over the mochi's wife a few months after the mochi was arrested. During his working life, the mochi had been some cobbler. He'd sit in a shed, on a jagged pavement, repairing shoes, slippers, handbags, briefcases, and umbrellas. This part of Mumbai was a madhouse. The traffic was endless: a cacophony of competing horns, a sheet of hot metal chaos. Old buildings stood in art deco modesty, while new buildings wore flashy facades and grand, sweeping entrances. And in the midst of this was a whirlpool of commerce. You could see the commerce everywhere: in the long, noisy bazaar, in the supermarkets, the sari shops, the stationery shops, the sweetmeat shops, the chemist shops, the jewelry shops, the plywood shops, and the home decor stores. Of course, none of this mattered to the mochi. He was an illiterate man, meant to serve at people's feet. He was meant to work in all kinds of weather. He had to live, eat, survive. He had to feed and educate his daughters, the twins, who were growing up fast. Too fast for his liking.

As a father he was strict; he kept the girls in check. At the most, he would let them watch a movie that would be screened during the festival months. This would be at night, when the bazaar would empty out, and there would be this giant screen put up, and both sides of the screen people would sit, waiting for the film to start. The projector would roll, the picture quality would be diffused, but the audience would be absorbed, for every line delivered emotion, every scene promised a climax. The girls, watching, would bite their lips and wonder whether such a life was, indeed, possible. A life of uncontainable excitement.

On the other side of the bazaar was the railway station, and outside the station was a ladies' bar, where women danced to Bollywood songs and men gaped at them longingly. The ladies' bar was called the Red Stallion, and next to it was an adda, where laborers and migrant workers drank. The mochi was a regular there. Every night he went to the adda and stayed there till he had exhausted his earnings. He often ended up drinking on an empty stomach, wincing at the pain that stabbed at his sides. But it was the walk back from the adda that was difficult. The bazaar would swim before his eyes, and the scurrying rats would startle him, challenge him with their greedy little eyes.

During the festival time, the walk got even more difficult, for the idol of Lord Ganesha would dominate the lane. For ten days the Lord would preside, fresh and milky-white, his trunk curled over his belly, his one hand raised in blessing. For ten days, the residents of the neighborhood would flock to pay homage. They would leave their wishes at his feet, their wishes and their prayers.

In the queue, would be Shraddha, the mochi's wife. She was a short woman, so she had to stand on her toes to see the idol. But when she reached the head of the queue, she would place her head on the Lord's feet and whisper, "Please, my Lord, make him stop drinking before it is too late. Before something bad happens and our lives are ruined." And she was sure her Lord was listening; he had noted and filed her request.

Shraddha was a noticeable woman: fair, firm-bodied, and many years younger than her husband. She had come to the mochi as part of a debt settlement.

Her father owed the mochi's father a sum of money which he could not repay, and so a bargain had been struck. And a fine bargain it was. For the mochi, given his drinking habit, could not have done better. His young wife was a hard worker, she ran his house with the meager amount he gave her, and she never nagged about his drinking. The mochi had enjoyed Shraddha's youth and freshness, while maintaining a silence that kept her in awe of him. And she had given him two daughters and slipped into the routine of a housewife. She loved her daughters like crazy and could not bear it when the mochi spoke to them harshly. But she knew it was a man thing, so she did not say anything.

During the day, the bazaar crackled and roared with life. Under old beach umbrellas, the wares were laid out: flowery-white cauliflowers; rosy-cheeked tomatoes; dark, velvety brinjals; crisp, green cabbages; red, yellow, and green capsicum; sheaves of spring onions, coriander, and lettuce; and pyramids of fruit, all so ripe and inviting.

Seated at the entrance, Shraddha sold ginger, garlic, coriander, mint, basil, and parsley. She started late morning, after the girls left for school, and she worked till evening, till the sun had set and it was time to prepare dinner. Then she would bring out two vessels, partly burnt and dented, and an old kerosene stove, which she would pump at, till it was ready to flare and smolder.

Her first impression of the mochi was that he was a shy man. He would bring her the shoes he would make, gleaming like they were machine-made, or would hold out the shoes he had repaired, looking like new. She could tell that he wanted to impress her, and impress her he did, with his craftsmanship. His customers, too, were admiring of the way he would restore torn articles. He would repair them so artistically that you couldn't tell they had been damaged.

But over time, he began spending more and more time at the adda and giving her less money to run the house. The money for the girls' school fees, their school uniforms, and study books came out of her earnings, and this she did not mind. And in him she saw the devil of greed rise. He began to use thinner threads for the footwear, and cheap-quality soles, and inferior polishes. All that was okay; she accepted it as part of his business wiles. But then he began to accept shoes and slippers stolen from outside temples, and these he would retouch to a point where they were beyond recognition and could be sold for a fat profit. And this she flinched at, thinking about the sin it would incur. How it would lower them in her Lord's eyes.

Then once a week, he would bring home a piece of luggage, a suitcase of expensive leather, and he would work on it at night, after taking his dinner. The strange thing was he would not work in his shed, his workplace outside the bazaar. He'd work, instead, in the enclosure where they stayed: the large, roomy shed in the quadrangle. He would ask her to light two candles and leave, ordering her and the girls to sleep outdoors. And she did not like that, because there were rats in the quadrangle, large gray rats with plump, hairy bodies and long, pointed mouths. But after a while, she remembered that the rat was Lord Ganesha's vahana, his vehicle, and that her Lord rode it as a way of controlling his ego. So she started placing carrots and cucumbers for the rats, and in the morning would be thrilled to find them gone.

A little before midnight, the mochi would start out, carrying the suitcase he had been working on. He would go down the road, past the traffic signals, past the eateries, past the chemist shop. Turning left at the crossroads, he would take the bridge to the east side, where there were brothels, guesthouses, and dealers of drugs and women.

On his return, he would wake up Shraddha and show her his earnings: a thick, crisp bundle of hundred-rupee notes. He would flap the notes in her face and expect her to express surprise, to show delight. Seeing none, he would rise and leave, set out in the direction of the adda. And he'd stay there drinking, till the last order was taken and the shutters were rolled down halfway.

Waking up next morning, he would order her to prepare a big breakfast, which he would gobble. Then he would whistle and sing an old Hindi song: *Saala main to sahib ban gaya*. Or he would start off in that lofty voice of his. "You don't know how lucky you are, woman, that you have married an artist, a man with a gift in his fingers. Just think! You could have been married to one of those donkeys from the bazaar. Those donkeys who are going to remain here all their lives, shouting to compete, shouting to make themselves heard. But you and I and our girls are going to see better days; we are going to be rich soon, I tell you. Just wait and see. You will thank your lucky stars you married me."

She hated it when he spoke like this, for the "donkeys" were her friends. They – the onion vendor, the tomato vendor, and the flower vendor – worked beside her in the bazaar. They kept her amused with their jokes and their stories, and when the vans arrived, would rush to help her unload.

After some time, the mochi bought himself a cell phone. When it would ring, he would stare at it warily, then walk around the quadrangle, speaking loudly. He would pace the quadrangle, shouting that he was too busy, he couldn't come right away, where was the time, with all the work he had. What did they think? That they were his only customers, that he didn't have any other work? He would look like he was enjoying himself, refusing them. But invariably he would go, wearing a clean white shirt and trousers and, before leaving, he would instruct her to mind the shed, which she hated doing. She hated the fact that a customer would remove a piece of footwear and leave it under her nose, waiting for her to pick it up and repair it. She felt like throwing the footwear out onto the main road, where it would be crushed by the traffic. But it was not in her nature to do that. She would move to the shed, instead, requesting one of her vendor friends to mind her baskets.

With a screech of tire, they stopped their jeep outside his shed. He barely had any time to look up, to understand why they raised him by the collar, slammed him on the ear, on the cheekbones, on his temples, until his head reeled, his neck felt severed. *Wait! Wait!* he shouted. There was some mistake. But, no; they dragged him like a common criminal, a thief. His cell phone was left behind, his body was off the ground, his one chappal was missing, his heels were scraping the road. He felt humiliated, helpless. But did they listen? Did they stop? "Shraddha, Shraddha!" he screamed at the top of his voice, as they pushed him into the back of the jeep and snapped on the handcuffs.

At the station, they had so many questions. *Where was the hashish going? How was it going out? Who was the mastermind behind the false bottoms? Had he met him? What did he look like? How much was he paid for his labors? And: When was the next consignment?*

He said he knew nothing about the hashish. His customers had told him nothing, and he did not think it proper to ask. How could he? He was just a poor mochi; it was not within his right to ask.

The police did not believe him. They beat him so badly that his own daughters could not bear to look at him.

He was missing four teeth in front; his fingers had been broken, had been twisted back to the point where he'd never hold a hammer again or thread a needle; and his right eye could not open: it was a dark, puffy lump of purple. Their father must be a bad man, thought his daughters, for the police to have done this to him.

In spirit, too, the mochi was broken, and now he behaved like an old man. For every little thing he would call his daughters. To give him his meals. To heat his bathwater. To pour the water on his back. To soap him, dry him. To make him wear his clothes. To wash him after every toilet. Returning from school, the girls were expected to wait on him, and if they were busy with schoolwork, he would threaten to burn their schoolbooks. He would fight bitterly with Shraddha. Why did the girls need to study? What were they going to do with all this education? All it would do is fill their heads with foolish ideas. Instead, he was going to teach them his trade, make artists out of them. He had fed them for long, and now it was their turn to deliver. She understood what he was trying to do. Keep them illiterate, make slaves out of them, so that they could serve him lifelong. Well, she was having none of that. Not if she could help it.

She had always imagined Kalyan Babu as a demon who preyed on his customers' weaknesses. Why else would he own an adda, where men destroyed themselves on alcohol? Not just themselves, their families, too. And why would he run a ladies' bar, where pretty young women danced before rich, drunken men? But the man who emerged from the entrance of the adda was pleasant-faced and neatly dressed, in a spotless white kurta-pajama. He had large sympathetic eyes and deep features, and on his forehead was a red tikka. They couldn't talk at the adda, he said. It was not the right place for a woman. Tapping her on the shoulder, he pointed to the Red Stallion next door.

She was amazed how large the place was. It had thick silver-plated columns, a dance floor with black-and-white squares, elegant tables and chairs, and long red sofas. There were those large, funny-looking balls hanging from the ceiling, balls that winked at her with a million eyes. The place was not yet open, said Kalyan Babu. So they could speak freely, without being disturbed.

He had led her to a corner and ordered a nimbu paani for her. And then Shraddha had opened her heart to him. She spoke to him like she had always known him. She told him her troubles and asked if he could help her. She had heard that he was a powerful man, that he had contacts and connections everywhere, and was like a brother to women like her. Women in need, in distress.

And Kalyan Babu heard her and said, "I understand, sister. I understand how much of a burden it must be for you … on your young shoulders … and with two young girls, in this day and age … not easy, not easy at all."

And she had looked at him and said, "Yes, I want my girls to continue their schooling. And I want them to stand on their own two feet. I want them to be beauticians, have their own beauty parlor one day." She hesitated. Then said shyly, "I know the name already. I have seen it in my dreams. Riddhi-Siddhi Beauty Parlor. I want that for them, and I am prepared to do whatever it takes."

The names Shraddha mentioned were of Lord Ganesha's consorts. Did she know … could she have known … that he, Kalyan Babu, sponsored the Ganesha idol in the bazaar every year? The idol that cost two lakh rupees to make and another thirty thousand to immerse. But, no; how could she have known that? It was perhaps a sign from his Lord, thought Kalyan Babu. A sign that he must take this woman under his wing, protect her and her dreams, which were not for herself but for her daughters. Looking at her, he said gravely, "Yes, it's important to earn, sister; important to be secure in life. Not just for yourself, but for others." And Shraddha had felt a load lift from her neck and shoulders. She felt a wave of calm wash over her heart.

And now: a strange transformation came over the mochi's wife. She wore her hair loose and her sari below her waist, so that the folds of her navel showed. And she applied kohl around her eyes, so that they appeared deeper and darker than they actually were. And she fluttered her eyelashes and laughed aloud when speaking to her male friends at the bazaar. And when she walked through the bazaar, every night, after dinner, clutching her handbag, her face taut, shoulders erect, she looked like a woman who knew her value, her worth, a woman who knew where she was headed and why.

By the time she returned, the mochi would be asleep, snoring out his hangover in the quadrangle. Entering the enclosure, she would slip off her bangles and payals, trying not to make a sound, trying not to disturb her girls. But, invariably, they would wake up and come to her.

Half asleep and yawning, they would sit beside her and, with their tender little hands, would rub her shins, her calves, her ankles, her feet, all so tired from dancing. And Shraddha would feel the fatigue leave her, and something in her heart would snap, and a warm delicious feeling of sleep, of contentment, would overcome her, making her smile, making her feel like she was the most loved woman in the world. Smiling to herself, in the dark, she would listen to the sound of rats scraping, sniffing for breadcrumbs, carrots, and cucumbers, and she would think: how much better life was once you had overcome your ego. Once you had learned to let go your pride.

All That We Own

Anuradha Singhal, Anu to friends, curled her toes and tensed her feet, inching forward on the light, tensile diving board, from where she peered into the shimmering blue softness of the Presidency club pool. It was May, a hot day. The sun played on Anu's back. She felt its glow on her neck and shoulders, she felt its persistence on her backbone. Anu felt the sun would burn her, brand her, it would leave a mark, like a birthmark, on her translucent white skin, if she didn't take the plunge quickly. She knew she would eventually, after a bit of hedging, as she had in school days, at the pool where she and her classmates were herded to, an army of schoolgirls clutching their floats nervously, with their coach, a dark, stocky man in speckled trunks, yelling, "Come on, jump in. The water is not going to swallow you. Don't fear it! Make a friend of it!"

Anu liked watching her reflection in the water. Her slim, bronze body, well maintained at thirty-two; her coffee-brown hair, cut shoulder-length; her cheekbones, flushed with health; her smooth facial skin, ready to reveal two symmetrical dimples the moment she smiled; and her chin, small and delicately chiseled, which her husband described as "infinitely kissable."

Anu was a striking woman, dark-eyed and radiant. Her lush, black eyebrows were the most erotic part of her. Men found it irresistible, the way she raised her eyebrows, then smiled slowly. In courtship days, her husband would stroke them, feel them, tails of soft velvet, and he would marvel at the defining lines and pledge his love by bringing his lips over them. Anu had that kind of effect on men. She was the kind of girl you would want to curl up with, the kind you would want to hold and smother. There was something sleek and inviolable about her beauty. Something eternally youthful.

Her feet left the diving board. Air met body, body heaved, and took the full impact of the water. Anu felt the air in her lungs rush to her head. Her lungs felt inflated, overweight. She pushed herself up. And in one cyclical motion she landed on her back.

The waiters at the side of the pool broke from their duties. Old men with sunburned scalps looked up from their newspapers and then away, the warmth spreading to their ears. Sparrows, startled by the splash, left their abodes and flew to less noisy habitats. Crows, navigating the white, wooden tables in search of leftovers, glared and cawed out of habit. The late morning heat bristled all over.

Floating on her back, Anu tried to imagine herself as a rudderless boat. She tried to submit to a liquid utopia, an imagined freedom, but "not true!" an inner voice chided. Anu knew she was kidding herself. Her mind was not half as light as the soft swaying water.

She *had* tried to forget. She *had* tried to usher in distractions. Like fixing a leisurely lunch with friends, who'd liven up her afternoon with spicy bits of gossip, or she'd attend fashion shows, where she'd be shown the picks of the season. Or she would go to art shows, where the new masters would be unveiled. There were book readings, baby showers, brunches … but none of that made sense anymore, none of it felt real. The only thing real was the issue she was facing, and that seemed to be bigger than her.

Not so long ago, Anu ran a fitness center, her very own. "Hands up, hands down! Faster, faster! Knees straight, elbows straight! Move, move! Now bend, left to right, right to left. Don't look up! Don't look back! Feel the tension in your neck. Feel your spine stretch. Are your legs wide apart? Are your calves straining, hurting? Good, good! Sweat it out; burn it off, I say!"

What a sense of power she'd felt, working out with her girls. Then, onto the stage, where she'd boom in a voice she didn't know she owned, "All right, you back there, you have skipped four counts, I can tell. So let's start again. Let's see some real energy. And don't think you can fake it. Save that for your husbands, okay?"

The fitness center was her life's purpose. It had started with a batch of six girlfriends who shared an interest in looking good, in staying supple on the dance floor, in feeling less guilty for all the margaritas and tequilas they imbibed. They had asked Anu to show them some exercises, which she did, at home, in her personal gym, overlooking the sea.

Her friends realized that Anu was a natural instructor. They started asking her questions. What could they do to reduce on the hips and thighs? How could they firm up their stomachs and buttocks? Later: what they should eat, drink, avoid.

Her status as a Singhal placed Anu in a position of power; it singled her out for leadership. For she was married to one of the wealthiest men in Mumbai, the construction magnate Jai Singhal.

It was Jai who suggested Anu take up physical training as a vocation. He had said to her one morning over breakfast, "Why don't you start your own gym? You can use the Singhal Charities bungalow next door. It is under litigation, but that should resolve soon. The bungalow's got a great view of the ocean, and there is plenty of parking."

"Are you serious?" Anu had asked, shyly.

"A fitness center will work marvelously in our neighborhood. The time is right, people are big on healthcare, and they will pay well to belong to an upmarket gym. All you need is a catchy name and some good publicity."

Anu saw his mind flying over details. And she realized this was not a husband speaking out of emotion but a magnate who liked seeing a new enterprise come to light.

"I'd love to start," she said. "I know I can make a go of it. But won't it be expensive: the equipment, the trainers, the overheads? Besides, I know nothing about how to price myself."

"Don't worry about that; we can figure that out. And I wouldn't worry about the investment; it won't be much, anyway. Around ten million rupees … I think."

Anu had to stop herself from whistling out. Although she had been married five years, been part of a family where abundance was the norm, where millions of rupees were plowed daily into projects, and where properties were bought and sold in different parts of the city, still, it took her a while to digest figures like these. Her heart raced; her hands felt moist. All that money to be invested into her fitness center? What if she were to fail? What if things didn't work out? What would Jai think of her?

But he seemed excited and carried on, "I would spend five million on doing up the place, give it a really plush decor. And I'd spend another five on equipment, the best you can get! And we need a really good name, something modern and trendy."

He started pacing, thinking, thinking hard. And had come up with Body Talk, Body Rhythms, and Second Look. Then with Curves Ahead, which Anu thought was perfect. "It's got attitude and promise," she said, her eyes shining.

So Curves Ahead was born, there, in that long, mirrored dining room of theirs, in their home by the sea, their sixteen-room mansion, with white columns, green lawns, and marble fountains.

Anu had looked at Jai gratefully. To think she would finally start something of her own. It had bothered her that most of her friends were doing something: designing clothes or jewelry or image consultancy, whatever that meant. Moving her face close to his, she had sought out his lips expectantly. Her eyes had darkened and she had kissed him, lightly at first, then with vigor. If he didn't have to get to work, she would have led him to the bedroom.

The fitness center opened one Sunday morning with a lawn party, a bright, sparkling champagne brunch, a table full of breads, cold cuts, and pastries, and bright, fluttering parasols, and white tables and chairs.

Anu had waited for all her guests to arrive before she started on a tour of the bungalow.

The exterior of the center was white, like a Goa-style beach house. There was a lawn in front, and around it ran a jogging track. A thick hedge separated the bungalow from its larger cousin, the Singhal mansion at the side. Occasionally, the guests would glance from house to house and wonder how a single family could own so much prime property in such a plush neighborhood.

Inside, there were red Chinese screens, shuttered changing rooms, and a sleek, oak-finish wooden floor with exercise mats. There was space for a hundred and fifty to work out, and in front was a semicircular stage with a fifty-two-inch television. The ceiling was high, and on the walls were black-and-white pictures of Hollywood actresses in supple, athletic poses.

A little after noon, a well-built youth in a sleeveless T-shirt and shorts rode up on a sports bike and whipped off his helmet to reveal the face of a famous Bollywood actor. The women swooned; the men declared they were impressed; the women whipped out their cell phones and rushed for a picture.

Anu led the actor onto the stage, where he popped a bottle of champagne. Then he lifted up Anu and proclaimed that here was a lady who was the living embodiment of Curves Ahead, a lady who would show others the way, and that he was not going to put her down until they all agreed. "Yeah, yeah," the guests had chorused, breaking into a song "For she's a jolly fit fellow."

The actor had posed for a few pictures with Anu, gulped down two fruit juices, kissed Anu on the cheeks, then gotten onto his bicycle and zipped away, much to the disappointment of the other women. The center was then declared open to memberships, at eight thousand rupees a month, three months' fees payable in advance. Wives insisted that husbands draw their credit cards and sign them up right away. If the husbands wanted to see curves and not tires, they joked.

So, Curves Ahead came to be born on the refurbished premises of a heritage bungalow owned by Singhal Charities. And there was nothing to suggest *charity* about the way it was done up.

Here women sweated and persevered. Here they shed weight and complexes. Here they toned their muscles and saw a healthy glow appear on their faces. And they felt a joy in their veins and limbs, and they saw this joy in the eyes of their husbands and boyfriends.

After their workouts, the women would retire to the lawns. Seated on benches by the sea, they would share their problems with Anu, who would chide them or guide them, depending on what she thought was required. And as they spoke, a bearer would wheel out a trolley with fresh fruit and vegetable juices and herbal tea and loaves of fresh multigrain bread.

Soon Curves Ahead became the buzzword at colleges, pubs, and nightclubs. Also at beauty salons and fashion stores. Long waiting lists were recorded, and women who were less influential asked those who *were* influential if they knew Anuradha Singhal and if they could secure them a place in her class.

Anu got written up in the fitness magazines and got featured on the health channel, and it was not uncommon for her to walk into a restaurant or a nightclub and have someone yell, "Watch out, curves ahead!"

She ran three classes a day. An early morning one for college girls and working women, a midmorning one for housewives, and a late morning one for those with health problems like diabetes, hypertension, and obesity. On Saturdays, she took an advanced class, giving count and keeping pace so unflaggingly that even the younger women would marvel at her fitness.

At the end of her first year, Anu was approached by a healthcare company that wanted to buy out her brand name. Politely, she declined.

In her second year, she was approached by an international cosmetics company to train girls for the Miss India contest, with the promise that she would train the winner for the Miss Universe edition and be free to use that association to her advantage, in the media.

The fitness center did wonders for Anu's social standing, too. While earlier she was dismissed as a trophy wife, a woman who had charmed her way into the upper echelons of society, she was now seen as a self-made success, independent of her husband's wealth.

Now at parties when women spoke of things like clothes, jewelry, and gourmet cuisine, Anu spoke on health-related topics that got others to sit up and listen. She no longer had to grope her way around. She no longer felt inadequate and helpless. She was the support other women craved for, reached for. She liked that feeling.

A splash. It overwhelmed Anu. Then another, and another, lurching blue waves that slapped the chlorine straight into her eyes. And a series of wild screams and laughter. What on earth! What was happening? The pool had been invaded by four young boys, slim, dark, and wiry. By God, were they noisy! Shouting and screaming, they threw a ball at each other with great force.

The ball splashed next to Anu. She recoiled.

The boys smirked with delight.

Rich, spoiled kids, thought Anu grimly. With strong strokes, she began to swim away, putting some distance between herself and the boys, who had fanned out, taking over a part of the pool.

She retired to a corner from where she looked at them disapprovingly. Her heart was beating fast, and she realized why it was so. She had been displaced from her comfort zone, evicted without a warning. She knew that feeling.

It was a December night, Anu remembered, windy and starless if you were out on the lawns, and snug and safe if you were in the genial embrace of the Singhal mansion, which is where husband and wife were, in Jai's study.

Coiled on the sofa, Anu was flipping through an issue of *Fitness International*. Jai was reading some papers at his desk. He looked greatly involved and, in between, would reach for a bowl of cashew nuts and help himself.

"Darling, must you have so many nuts after dinner? You know they are not good for you," said Anu reproachfully.

"I know," said Jai, sighing. "But we always veer toward things not good for us, don't we?"

"Something wrong?" Anu asked, looking up from her magazine. There were so many things on her husband's mind, things she knew nothing about. He had projects all over Mumbai. He was constructing an expressway, a biotech park, a mall, a seven-screen multiplex, a stadium, and all those skyscrapers that needed an awful lot of negotiation.

"Let's go for a walk, shall we?" said Jai. "There's something I need to talk about."

"What is it?" said Anu, sitting up. It wasn't like her husband to involve her in his problems.

She followed him onto the lawns. On the way, she picked up a shawl and draped it around her shoulders. She asked Jai whether she should switch on the lawn lights and get a servant to lay out chairs. But he said he'd rather walk, later they'd go to the beach. She found this surprising. He always said he found the beach threatening at night.

They walked in silence.

After a while Jai said, "Let's sit," pointing to the parapet at the edge of the lawn.

Anu removed her shawl, folded it, and placed it on the parapet, before seating herself.

Jai swung his long legs over the parapet and, leaning back, rested his weight on his palms. The sea before them was dark and foaming, a boom rising from its depths.

"It's nippy. Put your arm around me," said Anu to Jai, glancing over her shoulder to see if any of the servants were around.

"You should cover yourself with the shawl. The ledge is quite clean," said Jai, drawing her into his arms. "We are lucky to have this view, aren't we? It's the best in the city."

"Best is where you are," said Anu softly, burrowing into his arms and slipping her fingers through his. "Honey, what is it you want to talk about?"

Jai drew in his breath and began. "You know, love, there are things in life you get attached to, because they are what you always wanted. They represent you, reflect you. So when those things are taken away, you take it to heart. You feel cheated and let down. But that is when you've got to be strong, hold it together. You need to realize that there might be another choice, a better choice, if you give it enough time."

"I don't understand," she said, stiffening, and thinking, Could there be someone else?

Jai continued. "You know the Curves Ahead bungalow has been under litigation all these years. Originally it belonged to my dad's elder sister, Channan Auntie, who was a tough old bat. She was married four times, and each time she was the one to leave her husband. She was one of those women who could do everything a man could; hence, she was always impatient with men. She thought none of them were good enough for her, none could live up to her, expectations. After her fourth marriage broke up, my grandfather built a bungalow for her, and he gave it to her, along with a stake in some of our other businesses. She was a director in several of our companies and, although she wasn't allowed to take any decisions, she'd get her share of the profit. One thing my grandfather was clear about: she would be in charge of Singhal Charities. She had the temperament for it, was tough when she needed to be, and could see through people. I remember we would have a long line of people queuing up on Saturday mornings and Channan Auntie would hear their appeals for clothes, food, rent, medical help, and children's education. I remember my aunt used to be so rude to them that I would feel ashamed. I was only a boy then, eight years or so. One day I asked her why she did this, and she just smiled and said, 'Jai, beta, you are a real child. You don't know the world we live in.' She asked me to come to her bungalow the following Saturday.

"When I reached there, she made me wait by her side while she heard people's problems. Some of them would weep; some would fall at her feet and stay there pleading. She would listen and say things like: 'Arrey, arrey, how sad! Did you think of this when you invited your husband to mount you? Did you think who would feed your third child?' Or she would say: 'Oh, you haven't eaten for two days? No problem! Our freedom fighters didn't eat for weeks in jail. You also do *bhook hartal.* Go on a hunger strike and become a hero.'

"That day, around midmorning, there appeared a woman who was so distraught, so shabbily dressed, that I could not help but pity her. She spoke to Channan Auntie of her problems: her husband losing his job after a long illness, the bills piling up, and no money to pay for their children's schooling, her children who were in their final year of school. At that point she choked, and Channan Auntie leaned forward and offered her a glass of water, which she gratefully accepted. My aunt waited for the woman to finish drinking; then, turning to her secretary, a man named Lehri, she ordered him to throw out the woman, to use force, if necessary.

"I was shocked. I thought the woman had a genuine problem. I looked at my aunt pleadingly, but she was looking straight at the woman, who said that my aunt had been her only hope and now, with that gone, there was nothing to keep her alive. At the door, she stopped and mumbled something under her breath, and I went cold, thinking, this woman is surely going to do something to herself.

"Moments later, my aunt asked me to follow her. Taking my hand in hers, she ran along the hedge, tailing the woman in a way she could not see us. The woman kept turning and looking behind. Reaching the main road, she stopped beside a new Austin Minor car, opened the door, got in, and drove off. 'See Jai beta,' my aunt said. 'Let this be a lesson to you. Don't ever take human beings at face value, for the face they wear may not be the face they possess.'

"Seeing this, I felt so stupid. I asked my aunt how she had guessed the woman's status. 'By her fingernails,' my aunt replied. 'When I gave her the water, I saw they were varnished. She had forgotten to disguise them.' While I agree that my aunt was right in chucking her out, I think that perhaps that woman had cursed us and that the curse has affected our family."

A strong wind started and swept Anu's hair into her face. She brushed it back slowly, but some of the strands fluttered right back.

Jai continued. "As Channan Auntie got older, there were some issues that came up between Dad and her. I am not sure what these were, but I think she had a problem with Mother. She said a few things that hurt Mom. As a result, Dad and Channan Auntie stopped talking altogether. And after Granddad's death the gap became wider, and when Channan Auntie passed away she willed the house to an old manservant who had been looking after her. She said things in her will that really hurt Dad, things like she had seen more kindness from the manservant than from her own family and that she had learned more from observing the manservant's life than from all her days in the Singhal home. She said that we – the Singhals – were too caught up in our game of accumulation, and to show the world that at least one of us was different, she was giving her property to a man of humble means. She wanted to create an opportunity for someone who had none. We were sure the manservant had taken advantage of her. He had played up to her and got her to sign the will in a moment of weakness."

"What a bastard! I hope you threw him out … got him arrested," said Anu.

"We tried. We even filed a case of manipulation and fraud. We contested the will, and the case was fought by Diwan Sahib and his team, who did a splendid job, but—"

"But what?" said Anu indignantly. The ocean seemed to roar at her feet. The waves were rushing in, foaming and frothing.

Jai looked at the beach. It was high tide now. There was no way they could take that walk.

"But," he said softly, "we lost."

Anu fell silent. She could feel the salt on her lips. The salt and the dryness.

"Lost! But how? Can't we appeal it? Can't we fight this in a higher court?"

"Honey, we lost in the Supreme Court. We lost the appeal. The Curves Ahead bungalow is gone. We have only a month to vacate, to hand over the place." Jai tightened his grip on her.

"But can't we do something? Can't we speak to the old manservant? What will he do with a bungalow this size? How will he afford the taxes, the maintenance? Can't we buy him out?" There was a tremor in her voice. Her eyebrows were furrowed – dark, like the clouds overhead.

"I tried my best, but he refused. He seems to think he would be unfaithful to his memsahib if he sold the place to us. He doesn't want that on his conscience. He says he will sell it to anyone but us. So we will have to shift Curves Ahead to another location."

Anu fell silent again. After a while she began shaking her head and saying, "I don't believe it. I just don't believe something like this can happen. Not when things are going so well. This is unreal; tell me it is." Leaning against Jai's chest, she began to cry, and Jai let her, for he too felt a sense of loss akin to heartbreak. But what could he do? The highest court in the land had decided.

It turned out that the manservant had struck a deal with Talreja Builders, a rival of Jai's, who had borne the manservant's full cost of litigation, and, who, eventually, bought the bungalow. The Talrejas made it their home, but before that they made some changes to the place. They added two new stories to the existing structure and painted it a brick red. They put up porch lights along the hedge and built a pool, in the shape of a figure eight, right in the center of the lawn. At the edge of the lawn, facing the sea, they installed a statue of the founder, old man Talreja, with his forefinger raised defiantly to the sky.

The sight of that tormented Jai. It appeared as though his rival was mocking him. And to make matters worse, Anu had become stubborn. She refused to see other places, refused to consider other locations. How could she settle for less? she said. Would Jai compromise on his sites? Or on his design plans? Or on the amenities in any of his projects? And Jai didn't quite have an answer to that.

A week before the evacuation, Anu addressed her girls. She said she was closing the center for personal reasons. There were other things she wanted to do that were beyond the realm of the body. Things like yoga, meditation, and social work. "Your health, ladies, is in your hands," she said. "Make sure that nothing hijacks it." She had tears in her eyes when she said that, and one by one they came up and hugged her warmly.

A bell: light, tinkering, and persistent. Someone was ringing for the waiter. The sound came from the foyer, over the lawn, over the white wicker chairs, over the water, and into Anu's ears. She felt a flush of annoyance. This primitive way of summoning the waiters had always annoyed her.

The ringing persisted, louder and more urgent.

Anu's temper rose. She raised herself out of the pool. The water shimmered off her. Luminous drops of sunlight clung to her back and thighs. She felt the youths' eyes on her as she walked toward the foyer, to the thick, white column, behind which her tormentor sat.

"Who do you think...?" she spluttered, hands on her hips.

The face that looked up was that of a round-faced man, eighty years or so, clean-shaven and with bulbous eyes. Dressed in white, he sat in his chair, shaking uncontrollably. A bell dangled from his pink, age-spotted hand.

Anu shuddered with embarrassment. Old Mr. Vajifdar, once a leading constitutional lawyer, was now afflicted with an advanced form of Parkinson's. He stayed alone in a 3000 square foot apartment, while his children – two sons and a daughter – were settled in the U.S. His chauffeur brought him to the club every morning, where he stayed until teatime. Then he was taken back to his apartment, with only his television programs for company.

Mr. Vajifdar looked at Anu with large, wet eyes. He spoke with effort, with difficulty. "They don't listen. People don't listen anymore." His voice was plaintive, almost pleading. The veins in his neck flickered against the underside of his throat, which was grazed from faulty shaving. The hand holding the bell trembled.

Kneeling, Anu reached for his other hand and slipped her fingers into his. "Uncle," she said softly. "You are right. People don't listen anymore. But tell me what you want. I will get it for you."

Mr. Vajifdar shivered. Then jerking his head, he summoned Anu to come closer.

Not minding the fact that passersby were staring at her, that she was not supposed to be there, in the foyer, wet and scantily clad, Anu brought her face close to Mr. Vajifdar's lips. "Go on, Uncle," she said, "I am listening."

She could feel his hot breath and see his chest heave slowly, heavily. His face turned red. Then he said in a whisper, "I forgot. Forgot what I wanted."

Anu looked at him, the hesitation in his eyes, the fear and uncertainty of a mind that had given up its preserves of knowledge and memory, all that it had achieved and accumulated, all that it had assiduously built up over a lifetime. And she thought: Was there nothing one could own? Eventually, nothing? Not the space between people, nor that in your own mind?

She looked at the face before her and said, "Don't worry, Uncle. It will come back. It always does. Trust me." And with that, she slipped her other hand over his, the one that held the bell, and she held it firmly, to silence the tinkering, to still the shaking.

Hafta: The Price

"KAI RE, SUSHILA?"

"Kai re, Tiwari?

"Why the glum face, Tiwari? You look like you've come from a funeral."

"What to tell you, Sushila? The life of a constable is hard, hard. Look at me! After ten hours of duty at the station, I have been given another eight hours in this chowky. Sometimes I feel like I am in a prison – from one prison to another, that's all I am doing – and there is nothing to look forward to. Not even a good night's rest."

"You need a woman, Tiwari; someone to take your mind off all these hardships. Here, admit me into the chowky and I'll give you a neck-and-back rub. There is strength in these hands, magic in these fingers; I will make you feel better, I promise."

"You know I can't do that, Sushila; I have to respect my uniform, my job."

"You look like a boy when you frown like that, Tiwari. And you are frowning so hard because you are unsure of yourself, of what you want. I am not offering to be your wife, re baba; just some relief." Sushila's eyes glinted, she grinned. She was all of twenty-two, a lively twenty-two. Anyone else in Tiwari's shoes might have been tempted, might have relented. But, no, Tiwari was proud of his job and proud of his caste. He would not allow himself to yield, to give in to this dark attractive girl who visited him in the chowky every time he was on duty. How she knew he was there: that was baffling. She just showed up like a devi. He knew she did not visit his colleagues, only him. And that pleased him, it flattered him. He would not have liked her to visit his colleagues. That would have made her a loose woman; he wouldn't have spoken to her then. He hated women like that. Just the thought of them made him frown heavily.

"Your eyebrows will fall off one day," said Sushila, lifting, with two forefingers, the skin of her forehead, just above the eyebrows. "Then you will look like those Nepali men who work at the Red Stallion." She cocked a thumb at the ladies' bar on the opposite side of the road.

"How do you know about those Nepali waiters, Sushila? Have you been inside the ladies' bar? If that Kalyan Babu has been tempting you, I will, I will …"

"You will do nothing, Tiwari; you can't do anything. You policewallas get so much money from Kalyan Babu. And food and alcohol and God knows what other favors. You people are dependent on him for your hafta. You know that, too."

"Not me, Sushila, not me. I don't even take the food he sends me. Every time I am on duty, he sends me a tray from the ladies' bar. At first, he sent me non-veg, which I refused, because I am pure vegetarian. Then he started sending me a vegetarian thali; his man Surdev would bring it personally. And I always refuse. I tell him, Brother, I have just eaten dinner, but thank you. And Surdev knows that I am proud, that I don't want to eat his food, that I consider it polluted by the kind of work he is doing. So what do you know? He walks back with the tray and, before my eyes, knowing that I am watching, he scrapes it all into that litter bin outside the ladies' bar. And he knows that I don't approve of his action. Such wastage! Such arrogance! He does that only to spite me. To show me that's where he thinks my pride belongs – in the litter bin."

"But you *are* proud, Tiwari. I know that, even you know that. We could be so much closer if it weren't for your stupid man-pride. I know you think yourself to be superior. I don't know whether it is your caste or your morals. I don't know you well enough to say. But you give off this feeling: it's like you have a wall around you. But I can see behind that wall. And I see a boy who is too good for this city, who shouldn't be here. And I want to do something for this boy. Something … anything … but he won't let me." She looked at him with eyes full of warmth.

Tiwari sighed. How to explain to this silly girl? She was young, ignorant, full of impossible dreams. She did not know the ways of the world. She did not know how unforgiving the world could be. Why, he himself would never be able to forgive himself if he did something stupid. Like: if he were responsible for taking her innocence, for spoiling her. Why did she keep offering herself to him? Did she not know a flower is best when it blooms in a garden? Plucked, it withers and dies. And yet, how beautiful she looked standing under the golden streetlight, leaning on the windowsill of the chowky, and speaking to him as though he were the most important man in the world. Tiwari felt the blood rush into his face. He felt a stirring in his loins, and he lashed with his boots at the wooden wall of the chowky. He kicked at it savagely; then, slowly, rhythmically – *tap, tap, tap* – as though testing how strong it was.

"You *are* nervous, Tiwari," said the young imp facing him. "What is the matter? You have something on your mind. You can speak to me freely. I know I may not be good enough for you, but I have two ears and they are open. And I have a heart that feels for you, that cares." She looked at him with unflinching tenderness.

"You must go from here, Sushila," said Tiwari, lowering his gaze. "I can't be seen speaking to you.

I am on duty, remember. You will get me suspended, if someone sees us."

"Let them, Tiwari; let them. What sort of job is this, anyway, that you have to be on your own all night. They haven't even given you a TV, nor a kettle to make chai. How are you expected to keep awake?"

"You are no one to talk about my job, Sushila. No one!" said Tiwari angrily. "Look what you do for a living. Scrape through garbage, collect waste, earn your living from that ..."

"But so do you, Tiwari; so do you. What makes you think you are any better? You policewallas live off the scum of the earth. You arrest petty criminals and drunks but protect rich businessmen, politicians, and underworld people. Don't get me angry, Tiwari; you haven't seen my anger yet." Her eyes blazed, her face shone with an incandescent beauty.

"Now that you have told me what you think of me, perhaps you should go," said Tiwari. He was fighting hard to contain his feelings. Every inch of his body cried out for her, every cell craved to hold her. With both legs he kicked at the walls of the chowky.

The sound alarmed Sushila. She backed off, saying, "I am sorry for you, Tiwari, really sorry. You are not happy, and it's nobody's fault but your own. You don't want to give yourself a chance. You love only yourself and your stupid, obstinate beliefs. That is why you are so miserable."

"Go, go!" he hissed, his eyebrows coming together like an eagle in flight. "You don't know what you are saying. You are just a silly girl pretending to be grown up. You are a foolish girl who lives in the clouds. You don't know this city, don't know the sort of people it has. You don't know anything, in fact. I don't ever want to see you again. I have been kind to you so far, but I can't bear you. That is the truth of the matter."

And he looked so angry, that Sushila turned and ran. She charged across the road; then stopped, swiveled around, slapped her thighs, and pushed out her tongue at him. That's what she thought of his anger: it was only good for a laugh. And he too smiled and thought, what a child she was, a real child.

The two had met one night when there was a brawl in the gypsy enclosure. The gypsies – a group of twelve families – had come from North Gujarat and settled outside the railway station. There, in the quadrangle outside the station, they had camped with their belongings: moldy old bags of plastic, a scattering of mattresses, some blankets, some buckets, a rusted kerosene stove, half-burned utensils, a broken stool, and a clothes line that now hung between two electric poles.

The gypsy men were all skin and bones, with long unwashed hair, red sleepy eyes, and stained teeth. They looked older than their wives, who seemed too young to be mothers. And yet they were mothers, with bare-bodied infants running about and babies suckling their breasts. The children were ordered by their mothers to stay inside the quadrangle, within the railing that fenced it off from the main road. During the day, the main road was thick with traffic, and the pavements, too, were lively with vendors of fruit and vegetables and carts of street food.

The gypsies would fight like starving animals. It was always the men versus the women. The men were lushes, wastrels, and wife-beaters. They would snarl abuses and rush at the women. It was almost always over money. The menfolk lived off the women, who made baskets and garlands or rode the trains, selling combs, trinkets, hair clips, and ribbons. Since the men refused to work, the women had to bring in the moolah, which the men would spend on alcohol. By night, the men would be drunk and slurring, and the women would be resigned.

When the gypsy men would beat them and relieve them of their earnings, the gypsy women would fight back. They had loud, thick voices and more anger than the men. The fights would last an hour or so, shattering the peace of the neighborhood, after which the women would slip under their blankets, pull up their saris, and wait for what they knew would happen: a truce between two parched and willing bodies.

Sometimes, a drunk gypsy man would lie with a woman other than his wife; he would do so by invitation. Or he would sneak up to a young teenage girl who was asleep and who had caught his fancy; approaching her, he would take his chances.

But if the girl woke up, all hell would break lose. Then the whole community would stir to life, sides would be taken, screams and threats would rend the air, lights in neighborhood buildings would come on, residents would flock to their balconies, passersby would stop and stare, a riot – it seems – was imminent. And that's when the policeman on duty, the keeper of the chowky, would have to rise and intervene. That's what he was there for: to maintain law and order, to keep those unruly gypsies in place.

But that night things had gotten out of control. Bhoomi had refused to give her husband Dhanu any money, and to spite her he had taken their daughter's schoolbooks and sold them to the raddiwalla. It was cruel what he had done, and now the girl would have to suffer. She would be scolded by her teachers, perhaps even sent back home. How could she admit that her father had sold her books to fund his drinking habit? Bhoomi knew the real reason Dhanu had done that. He did not want his daughter to go to school; he hated the fact that he was stuck with the daily chores – the fetching of water from the public toilet, the washing of clothes and utensils – while Bhoomi rode the trains, selling her wares. But Bhoomi wanted her daughter to be educated, to attend the municipal school, mix with girls of her age, and enjoy the free midday meal that was served to them. Dhanu would resent that his wife and daughter would be gone while he had to slave and toil. What he wanted to do was play cards with the other men, or pull at a chillum and enjoy a dreamlike state, or comb the railway platform for things he could find and sell so that he could be assured of his next glass of hooch. But seeing him work, the other men would taunt him. *What a fellow you are, Dhanu. Truly, the wife's slave you have become!* And this would burn him up, enrage him. He would brood about it while working. And, if he didn't find the money for his evening quota, that would incense him even further.

A vicious fight had ensued and Dhanu had denied the theft. He called Bhoomi a whore and accused her of grooming their daughter in the same fashion, and Bhoomi had called Dhanu a namard, meaning impotent.

At this, Dhanu had raised his hand and advanced. And Bhoomi had caught him by the collar and pulled at his shirt, and the shirt had torn and some notes had fallen from the pocket, which were scooped up by Bhoomi. Then Dhanu had caught Bhoomi by the hair and whirled her around, and Bhoomi had scratched Dhanu's face, and Dhanu, blood flowing from his cheeks, had cursed and looked around wildly. His eyes had fallen on a large chopping knife glistening in the moonlight. He had grabbed at it and lunged at Bhoomi, who stepped aside nimbly, then dropped her sari, exposed her stomach, and challenged him to use the weapon, to prove he wasn't a namard, after all.

His teeth clenched, his lips curled in a half-smile, Dhanu swung his hand back, then forward. The knife would have found its mark had Sushila not jumped in. She was at hand, rummaging through the garbage dump outside the public toilet, looking for articles that could be salvaged and sold. Something told her that Dhanu meant business, that he would not let Bhoomi's insult pass unavenged. And she had leapt forward boldly and clutched at the knife as it lashed in midair, inches away from Bhoomi's stomach. And she had held on, while Dhanu tugged at it, savagely. And though the tears welled up and her lips quivered and her hand trembled with searing pain, she held on, till the policeman arrived and swung his lathi across Dhanu's face, and the gypsy man was thrown back by the sheer force of the assault. Then, while the other gypsy men rushed forward to vent their fury on the fallen Dhanu, the policeman had reached gently for Sushila's palm, dripping with blood from the knife embedded deep in its folds, and said, "Oh sister, you shouldn't have … it was brave of you, very brave, but anything could have happened. Anything!"

The constable had flagged down a scooter and rushed Sushila to a nearby hospital.

The emergency room was next to the lobby, on the ground floor. There, two male interns had attended to Sushila. They pressed wads of cotton against the wound and daubed at it with a yellow disinfectant. All this while, Tiwari sat upright in his chair, his hands resting on the lathi which balanced on his knee. He watched this brave girl as they first gave her a local anesthetic and then stitched her up. And he marveled at her courage, the fact that she was smiling throughout. And something stirred in his heart, something like respect.

She would need blood, said the doctors. Three bottles of A+ to compensate for what she had lost. He wondered why they were telling him this, what he was doing there in the first place when he should be at the station booking Dhanu for assault, for causing grievous injury. But there was something called insaniyat, humanity, and this girl, Sushila – she didn't seem to have any family at hand. She said she stayed near the garbage dump, was a goniwalli, a ragpicker, who made her living by scavenging from the waste of the city.

A rebellion rose in his mind. *Why should he care? What did he have to do with her?* He was just a havildar on duty. Besides, this girl was very likely from a low caste – why else would she be doing the kind of work she did? But then, she could have stayed away too; she didn't have to jump in to save Bhoomi's life. But she had – and now she was here – with three bottles of blood drained from her body and fourteen stitches in her palm.

And yet she was smiling. She smiled at the doctors, and at the elderly nurse who came to give her the injections, and at Tiwari, her legs dangling from the high bed on which she sat.

And he made up his mind then. He *would* give her some of his blood, his precious blood, the blood of a Brahmin. That would cleanse her, elevate her, assure her a better birth in her next life. The thought gave him the courage to say the words that were stuck in his throat. "I am of the same group," he said to the doctors gruffly. "I will give, I will donate; but make it quick."

After the transfusion, they had to rest for an hour or so, flat on their backs, in adjacent beds. Then, the girl had spoken nonstop. She had questions for Tiwari. Where was he from? Why had he come to the city? Did he like it here or in the village? Was he married, planning to marry? Was he happy in his job? Did he like his bosses? What were the most exciting cases he had handled? Had he shot anyone, killed anyone? How exciting would that be! Before he could finish answering a question, she would be ready with the next; such a motormouth she was.

On discharge, she said she was hungry. So Tiwari led her to the hospital canteen and ordered some chai and two plates of batata vada. The bowl of chutney, she raised to her lips and slurped; then she wiped her mouth on the sleeve of her blouse. When the bill came, she insisted on paying, but due to her bandaged hand was unable to get the money from her salwar pocket. Seeing her frustration, Tiwari laughed. This girl was so funny and so stubborn.

The next night she was back at the garbage dump, rummaging with one hand, while holding her bandaged hand upright. When Tiwari reminded her that the doctors had warned about the risk of infection, she asked him how she would eat if she did not work. Then coyly she said she would not mind if he supported her whilst her hand healed. And Tiwari had blushed and said, "I can give you some money, sister, if that is a problem?"

"Forget that," she said, "I am only joking. But have you seen our friend Dhanu? He is so terrified of you, thinking you might arrest him, that he has moved house." And she pointed discreetly to the overhead skywalk, where Dhanu lurked behind a column, peeping down at them. And the two of them had giggled feverishly and pretended not to have noticed him.

And so a friendship had been struck, in the way life brings certain strangers to your door to whom you feel connected. And Tiwari began to feel for this girl. What it was, he could not say. She had no family, from what he could see, and she lived off the streets, picking up the waste of the city, making her way through its main roads and back lanes. And he told himself that he should stop thinking about her. But each time he came on duty, he found himself searching for her bright little face to appear at the window and enliven him with her nonstop chatter.

Once Sushila left, Tiwari could focus on the matter that weighed on his mind. Just that morning, he had received a phone call from his mother who lived in the village. His father, it seems, had gotten into trouble with the panchayat. A month ago, his father had visited a cattle fair in town, from where he had bought a large white bull. According to his father, the bull had looked upon him, Shivkumar Tiwari, in the same manner Nandi the bull looked upon his lord, Lord Shiva. The bull had a proud, sturdy bearing and long circular horns, and when Shivkumar had moved away from the enclosure, the bull had raised his head and bellowed loudly. This, Shivkumar felt, was a sign from the Lord. And so he had purchased the animal, saying he would guard their home against evil, the way Nandi stood watch at the gates of Mount Kailash, the abode of Lord Shiva. And bringing the animal home, Shivkumar had refused to keep him fenced in or tied. He said the bull was his brother and that he would earn the Lord's wrath if he confined him. And his wife did not object, because it was not in her nature to contradict her husband.

Thereafter, the father went around happily, inviting his neighbors to come see the new addition to their family, this magnificent gift from the Lord. He forgot to mention that the gift hadn't come free, that he had paid five thousand rupees for it.

After a few days, a strange thing happened. People would swear they had seen the bull standing outside their cattle enclosures at night. And it was discovered shortly afterwards that his leanings were not all that divine; he would jump over the fence and impregnate the cows. Shivkumar was asked to contain the bull, but he refused. He would not show such disrespect to his brother, he would not imprison him, he said. The bull continued his nighttime forays, seeking out fresh pastures each time.

A panchayat meeting was called. Shivkumar was summoned. The villagers were furious. One by one, they came up and complained. Theirs were not ordinary cows but high-yield breeds like Red Sindhi, Deoni, and Sahiwal, which could only be mated with a pedigreed bull.

After hearing them, the panchayat members conferred in low voices. They asked Shivkumar if he had anything to say. The old farmer got to his feet and said that the villagers were making a big mistake by going against his brother, it would only bring the curse of the gods on their heads. He reminded them how, in the Ramayana, Nandi had cursed Ravana that his kingdom would be burned to the ground by a forest monkey. Did they want that? he asked. That kind of fate for their farms?

A shrewd farmer who had stood and won against Shivkumar in the last panchayat elections, rose to his feet. "We did not know you think us to be like Ravana, Brother Shivkumar," he said. "This is news to us: that you think so badly of us." And before Shivkumar could reply, all hell broke loose and the villagers demanded that he be penalized. And the panchayat had no choice. They estimated the damage to be around fifty thousand rupees. That was the sum Shivkumar would have to pay his neighbors. He was given a fortnight to come up with the amount.

And so the mother had called Tiwari. "Ramkumar, my son, you must help," she said. "You must do something. Your father is old and stubborn; he does foolish things. You must come down and speak to the panchayat. I am sure they will listen to you. And you must bring the penalty money, at least half of it. That will pacify them. For the rest, you can request some more time."

The call left Tiwari fretting. Didn't his mother know that he earned barely twelve thousand rupees a month? And he could live on that only because he had no vices, and because – unlike his colleagues – he refused to take any hafta, his share of the protection money that came from illegal businesses in the neighborhood: the bars and the gambling dens. His refusal made him a laughingstock at the station, with his colleagues, but he did not care.

Besides, he was not due for any leave. Even if his sahibs were to grant him some days off, it would be cut from his salary. How would he manage then, and with what face would he visit the village? He couldn't go empty-handed, without gifts for his parents, uncles, nephews, and nieces. All this pressed on his mind, made him irritable and miserable. And poor Sushila: she was the one who had paid the price, borne the brunt of his ill temper. Well, he could always apologize and get her those jam biscuits that she loved. Such a child she was!

He considered the options before him. He could, of course, put his hands up and say that he was not in a position to raise the money. Or he could suggest selling a few acres of their farm, which would break his father's heart. Or he could take loans from his uncles, who wouldn't miss out on a chance to gloat about it and taunt his father. Or he could ask Surdev to arrange a meeting with Kalyan Babu, where he could admit that he was open to some kind of an arrangement; yes, to taking hafta. But could he do so separately, discreetly, without his colleagues knowing, without anyone knowing, especially not Sushila, who held him in such high esteem? He peered out from the chowky and felt a wave of guilt wash over him. His eyes fell on the ladies' bar opposite, onto its silver door, and he waited for it to open and for Surdev to emerge. For once, he was eager to receive the henchman.

After leaving Tiwari, Sushila entered a narrow side lane that could not be seen from the main road. The lane had gray somber buildings and puddles of black sewage and some wooden carts left by vendors who had retired for the night. There were only two shops in the lane – one that belonged to a raddiwalla, the other a chicken shop – and both had their shutters drawn. Sushila stopped outside a blue wooden door and pried it open. Fumes of alcohol and clouds of cigarette smoke enveloped her and, through that, the scene before her suggested that the place was an adda, a drinking joint for poor laborers.

Any other woman in Sushila's place would have swooned, but not she who had endured the worst smells of the city, she who scrambled through its garbage, morning and evening, making her living from that. "Good, good that you have come," said the manager at the counter, smiling. "It is getting rowdy in here. Those customers on the last table: they are on the verge of a fight. So it's better we get started. Before there's any trouble." He brought out a mic from under the counter and switched it on. Then tapping it for a sound check, he announced: "Okay, haraamis, you don't deserve this, but we are going to give you some entertainment. So shut up and listen."

Sushila had her back to the crowd. The men present were hard drinkers, laborers mostly. You could see the struggle in their faces, the despair in their eyes; but to her, it was all the same, all those faces. She removed a lipstick from her pocket and ran it over her lips. She could feel the thick red coating, the pasty feeling she did not like. But she knew it was necessary, the only touch she needed. "*Hai re, diwano*," she said, taking the mic from the manager and turning to the crowd. "Are you ready for some music? To remember the wife who waits for you at home, or your mistress?" The men stared at her with surprise, and then with longing; but that lasted only till her voice came on, soft, clear, and melodious.

Beqaraar karake hamen yuu na jaaiye, aapako hamari kasam laut aaiye she sang, and the men listened, enrapt. And when that was over, she sang *Aap yahan aaye kisliye, aap ne boolaya isliye*. She sang joyously, wriggling her shoulders and rolling her eyes, and then she took some requests. And while she obliged, two waiter-boys went around with boxes, saying, *Come on, come on, don't be a kanjoos. Open your heart and contribute like a man*. At the end of the session, which would last for thirty minutes or so, the boxes would be full of small change, of five- and ten-rupee coins. The man at the counter would pour these into a plastic bag, which he would hand over to Sushila, saying, "May Goddess Laxmi never take her eyes off you, sister. May your talent always keep you prosperous." Then he would gesture to the waiter-boy Salim to go with her. The two of them would step outside, into the dark, silent lane. There, they would perch on a cart and count the earnings. Then, Salim would go to the Red Stallion, where he would exchange the coins for rupee notes. These he would hand over to Sushila.

That night, after Sushila had emptied the bag of coins onto the cart, Salim looked at her curiously. "Tell me," he said. "Why do you do this every night? Why perform before men who are barely in their senses? Who look at you with eyes of lust and longing?"

"Why not, Salimbhai?" she replied. "Why should I *not* sing before these men? What is wrong with them? Why should only the rich enjoy? Even the poor deserve to relax and forget their worries. Besides, I am not pretty or fashionable, like our sisters at the Red Stallion. I can't dance and entertain the way they do; I can't make that kind of money. But I have my voice, and I know it is soothing, and besides, singing is important to me. It reminds me of my childhood; it helps me keep alive some memories."

"Who says you are not pretty?" said Salim, grabbing her hand and holding it to his chest. "To me, you are nothing less than a heroine. Nothing less than Kareena Kapoor. You have the same eyes, same lips, and your skin is smooth, like chocolate." He loosened his grip on her hand and looked at her anxiously. Had he said too much? Would she report him to the manager? But no; she was not like that; there was no meanness in her.

"Have you gone mad, Salimbhai?" exclaimed Sushila. "Have you been drinking or smoking charas? Me, like Kareena Kapoor? You need to see an eye doctor and have your eyes checked. Have you not noticed how dark my skin is? Like charcoal!"

"No, I don't see anything, Sushila; I don't *want* to see. I only see you, and I see us, you and I together in this big, mad city. I love you, Sushila; I can't live without you. I think about you all the time, and I wait for you to come, and when you come and start singing, I forget everything else. And then I see the way other men look at you, and I want to kill them. I want to reach out and smash their bottles on their heads. That's how much I care for you, Sushila." He withdrew his hand and looked at her imploringly. And what he saw in her face assured him that he wouldn't be misunderstood or rebuked; that he had done well to release the storm in his chest, the storm that had raged in him for weeks.

She smiled at him with teasing eyes, and said, "You had better not go killing your customers, Salimbhai; I don't want to see you in jail." Then softly she added, "I just don't see you as a boyfriend. I see you more as a younger brother, someone I can depend on."

The waiter-boy frowned. "Is it … is it because I am a Muslim?" he asked. "I know in this city these things matter."

"No, Salimbhai, if I liked you in that way, I wouldn't care which community you belonged to. Besides, what do you know about me? About my background and my caste, which I am trying so hard to forget."

"Then tell me, Sushila, tell me. I want to know everything about you: where you come from; how you came to be in this city; if you have family; someone waiting for you back home?"

"You are mad, Salimbhai, mad," she laughed. "Why would you be interested in *my* life? I am just a girl who lives in the dumps, among all the germs and infections."

"Yes, I am mad for you, Sushila, mad. I have seen you perform every night, and I know what happens when you sing. You light up from inside, and that light, it spreads to others. The men inside: they forget their drinks, they forget their worries, they look at you and wonder what it is you have found that makes you like this. And I wonder too, Sushila, how you can carry so much joy when life is so hard. And then, after you have left, I carry that light in me. It stays with me, it burns and it grows, and it waits for you to come back the next day. And till then, it's just me and that light, *your* light! And even when the manager screams and rains abuses on me, he calls me all sorts of names, I don't mind. Because I have *your* light with me." He looked at her wide-eyed, and Sushila could have sworn she saw a glint in his eye, like a small flame.

She hesitated, then began. "I come from a small village in Bihar, from a community which is the poorest of the poor. We are so poor that we are not even listed in the government registers as a tribe. We live on the outskirts of the city, without electricity or water. We are not allowed to go to school or enter temples. We are not allowed to visit hospitals for treatment. We are not allowed to wash clothes in the river or draw water from wells. We don't get rations or jobs, and for our meals, we have to catch fish from the drains, or live off what we can find in the forest. Many of our menfolk, they work in a brick kiln, in the next district, and there too the mukkadams exploit us, because they know we are from a low caste and that we need the money.

"My father was no exception. He, too, worked in a brick kiln, where he made fifty rupees a day. But then because of the dust his lungs got weak, he would become breathless, and could no longer carry the bricks from the pit to the storehouse. One day, he fell, and most of the bricks broke. So the mukkadam refused to pay him. My father begged and pleaded, but the mukkadam, he refused. And so my father picked up a brick and did what any wronged man would do: he pushed it into the mukkadam's face and broke his nose. Naturally, all hell broke loose. The mukkadam ordered his men to beat up my father; they beat him till he couldn't stand, couldn't walk, he had to be carried back home. And the mukkadam declared that he would no longer hire any member of our tribe.

"This was a big blow for us. How would we eat, how would we survive? There were children to think of. In my family itself, there was me and my brother. He was twelve; I, only eight. The menfolk would have to steal a chicken or a goat from some neighboring farm if their families had to eat. But how often could they do that, and, besides, once the villagers got to know of the theft, they would inform the police. The elders of our tribe begged us to leave the village. Only with us gone, could they approach the mukkadam and appeal to him to take back his decision. And they were kind, our elders; they even collected some money and bought us our train tickets to Mumbai. They said we should try our luck in the great city.

"Two days before leaving, we had another shock. My mother, Kanta Devi, said she did not want to go to Mumbai. What would she do there? This was her life, her home. She said she had made up her mind: she was joining the Maoists, she was going to take up arms against the upper castes, against those who had exploited us. She said she had only one life to live and that she was going to live with her head held high. And she also wanted that for her son, my brother.

"I knew why she wanted this; I knew the real reason. She had been seeing this young Maoist commander whilst my father was away at the brick kiln. My father would be gone all week and return only on Sundays. So my mother would visit the commander at night, in the forest, and would return toward dawn, thinking no one had seen her. But I knew … because I had followed her on more than one occasion.

"My father reasoned with her, but she was adamant. She said she wanted to bring up her son like a hero, spare him the oppression of the upper castes. My father said he would do anything to stop her. He threatened to tell the elders her plan, he threatened to go to the police station and file a complaint. He said he was not going to give up his son without a fight. She could leave if she wanted, but he was not prepared to lose his son.

"That night, four men with their faces covered came to our hut and placed a gun at my father's throat. They warned him that he had better leave, if he knew what was good for him. And he shouldn't think of taking the boy, who was theirs now. They hit him in the chest and stomach till he coughed and spat blood. My mother did not say a word, and nor did my brother. My father knew then that there was no reason for him to stay back.

"We left with a heavy heart, Baba and I. We came here, and sure enough, Mumbai took care of us. It made sure we could eat, and that there was always some work available. And here no one was bothered about caste; everybody was too busy just surviving.

"At first, my father pushed a handcart; but then, because his legs were giving him trouble, he picked up the goni, the sack. Over time, his limp got worse, and he developed these lumps on his legs, which became very painful. The doctors at the government hospital said he would need surgery. He would also have to take some medicines lifelong.

"My father rubbished the idea of the surgery; he said he was not going back to the hospital. These doctors were like butchers, only waiting to cut you up. He took to the bottle instead, and would spend all his money on daru, and when he was drunk, he would sing old Hindi film songs, and when he would do that at the adda, people would come and leave money at his table.

"Soon he realized that he could earn more from his singing than from rag-picking. It seemed that one door had closed but another had opened. So we would set off riding the trains, all morning, all afternoon, till just before the peak hours, before the trains got too crowded. And when my baba would sing, I could see that he would forget his pain.

"Then one night he got this terrible fever. It made his whole body burn, and he began raving, asking for my brother. He rambled on and on, saying how much he missed his son. I told him I was there by his side, but he was scarcely aware of me. He kept calling for my brother.

"After some time, his breathing became heavy and he lost consciousness. I grew afraid and asked some of our fellow ragpickers to take him to the hospital, where the doctors rushed him into intensive care. He stayed there for two days, and when he came out, it was with a white sheet over his head. I was only twelve and did not know what to do. Except to pick up the goni and follow in his footsteps."

"And so you sing, in order to remember him and keep his memory alive?"

"Well, yes, Salimbhai; but there is another reason too. I will tell you, but please don't laugh."

"I swear, Sushila; I would never laugh at anything that is important to you."

"I sing because I am saving up money to learn driving. I want to become an Uber driver. I am told a lot of women prefer a female driver, especially at night, because they feel safer."

Salim straightened up. "That is such a good idea, Sushila. But how much have you saved? You've been singing at the adda for quite some time now. I am sure you have saved enough."

"Well, yes, it's all thanks to Kalyan Babu, who gave me this opportunity. He is like a father to me. He might be making money from daru, from both his bars, but he does so much for women like me, who would, otherwise, have no one."

"Ah, yes, he is a good man, Kalyan Babu; we are lucky to have his hand over our heads. And one day soon, I am going to go over and tell him that I want a promotion; that I want to work at the Red Stallion, be one of his security guards. Like that Surdev, who looks at me as though I were a beggar."

"No, Salimbhai, you must aim higher than that. As a security guard, you will still be serving someone. Is that all you want from life? To be at someone's beck and call?"

"I don't know, Sushila; I really don't know. For now, that is all I can think of. But if you think of something better, let me know. Perhaps I too can drive an Uber. Then one day, we will have our own car, and on our days off we can go for long drives to Pune and Mahabaleshwar. What say?"

Suddenly, a loud voice broke through the night, startling them so that the cart lurched and the coins slid to the edge. "What do you two think you are doing? Are you fucking or what? I try and help you, I try and be considerate, and this is how you repay me, by keeping Salim away from his work." It was the adda manager, and he was fuming. He advanced toward them with his one hand raised. But before he could reach them, Sushila sprang like a panther between him and the cart, between him and Salim. "Don't!" she warned him. "Don't you dare! I will scream and bring the policeman here. Then you will be in real trouble."

The manager stood glowering at her. He glared at her for what seemed like a very long time. Then he said in a low voice, "Okay, but know this. You can stop coming from tomorrow, you can take your singing elsewhere; I will inform Kalyan Babu how irresponsible you have been. Irresponsible *and* ungrateful." And then, stepping forward, he scraped the coins off the cart, into the plastic bag, and holding the bag in his hand, he turned and walked back toward the adda. He walked slowly, with a swagger, whistling *Beqaraar karake hamen yuu na jaaiye, aapako hamari kasam laut aaiye,* as though mocking the woman he had just sacked.

It was an angry, disconsolate Sushila who returned to the main road, and there, next to the garbage dump, she entered the public toilet. She went into the ladies' section and stared moodily at the floor: at the clumps of hair and the footmarks. Her eyes rolled over the surroundings: the sagging basins with red paan stains; the foggy mirrors with scratches; the broken taps; and the water pipes, green and mildewed. The stench was unbearable, but she was used to it, for this was where she did her daily ablutions. She swung open the door of a cubicle and went inside. She bolted the door, dropped the lid of the commode, and sat down. Lowering her head into her hands, she wept, her upper body lurching in deep hacking sobs. Oh, why could she not speak the truth? Why, after all these years, could she not blame her father for what he had done to her? Daily he would take her to the adda, where he drank and sang, while strange men would approach her, touch her, hold her by the chin, and say how pretty she was. She could still recall their faces, feel their callused hands and their hot, fetid breath on her cheeks. And her father was too numb to realize that, to see the wild thumping fear in her eyes and rush to her protection. Then one day, Kalyan Babu had walked in and, seeing her sitting in a corner, trembling, had roared: "What is this child doing in here?

She is too young to be here." And he had lifted her up and taken her next door, to the Red Stallion, up a flight of stairs, to a large office, where, onto a soft leather sofa, he had lowered her, and said, "Sleep, my child, you will be safe here. Once your father has finished, he can come and collect you. Till then you sleep soundly, huh."

And on Kalyan Babu's orders, daily she had slept at the Red Stallion, and daily there would be a treat waiting for her: a bar of chocolate, a packet of jam biscuits, or a bowl of ice-cream. But after her father had died, Kalyan Babu had called her to his side and said gently, "I can't have you coming here anymore, my child. The world outside is cruel. They will say things … accuse me of keeping an underage girl. You will have to stop coming here. But, if you should need anything, or if anyone bothers you ever, let me know. I am always there for you."

And so: when she had this idea of becoming an Uber driver, she had walked over to the Red Stallion and asked Kalyan Babu for help, and he had promptly offered to pay for her driving lessons. He had insisted she take the money as a gift, but she refused. She said she wanted to earn herself, earn from her talent, and if he could allow her to sing at the adda, she would make that amount in no time. And he had hesitated, and his brow had clouded, and she could see how much he hated the idea. "I am grown up now," she had persisted. "I can look after myself. Besides, your manager will be there, and the waiters, so the customers won't try anything funny." And Kalyan Babu had grudgingly given his consent, thinking, this girl was so very stubborn but she had that spark, that fire, what it took to succeed in this city.

And now that manager would ruin it all. God knows what lies he would tell Kalyan Babu, and if Kalyan Babu would believe him. She hoped Kalyan Babu would not vent his anger on Salim. The waiter-boy needed this job. Like

Sushila, he was alone in the city, he had no family; from his job at the adda, at least he could eat. And it also gave him a place to sleep. She would have to meet Kalyan Babu and explain that things were not the way they appeared. The manager was being vengeful. Why, Salim was like a brother to her. And, besides, she was not the kind of girl who'd stoop to indecent behavior. Nor would she ever be ungrateful to Kalyan Babu.

She rose and patted down her churidar. With the end of her dupatta, she wiped her tearstained face. Then, holding onto a water pipe, she raised herself on the commode, so that she faced the overhead flush tank with the broken chain. She raised the cover of the flush tank and, with her free hand, she fumbled inside. Ah, she found what she was looking for. Slowly, she withdrew her hand and set the cover back in place. Then she jumped down, steadying herself so as not to slip on the wet, greasy tiles.

Seated again, on the lid of the commode, she stared at the object in her hand, a thick gray pouch of plastic. Opening the pouch, she drew out a wad of notes and began counting it. On finishing, she counted again. Yes, there were eight thousand rupees in all, enough for her to enroll in the driving school and buy some decent clothes. Today's was a big loss, she thought ruefully, but then nothing good ever lasted.

Feeling like a man about to commit a murder, Tiwari entered the Red Stallion. And murder it was, he thought, the death of his conscience; with one move, one decision, he had killed it. Crossing the road, his shoes had felt like they had rocks in them, and yet he had to hurry lest he ran into Sushila. Oh what was it about the girl that made him never want to fall in her eyes? Thinking of her made his heart pound, and he felt the blood rush into his face. With a slight bow and an ironic smile, Surdev held open the door for him. Tiwari looked at him reproachfully; under a different set of circumstances, he would have nothing to do with him. And the smile on Surdev's face showed that he knew what the constable thought of him. He had known that even when Tiwari had smiled at him unctuously and accepted the tray of food, when he had mumbled his thanks and asked Surdev if he could meet with Kalyan Babu urgently. And Surdev had said, "Let me see, brother; let me see. Sahib is a very busy man. Important people come asking for his help. When a project is held up, they ask for his help, and sahib is so kind, he never refuses. You wouldn't be in any trouble, would you? If that is the case, I can ask sahib. He never says no to anybody. He says: you are brought into this world not for yourself but for others." And Tiwari had replied, "Yes, please; I need a favor from sahib. Not for myself but for my family." He felt better the moment he said that. He felt exonerated.

On entering, Tiwari saw that the place had two levels. One level led to a heavy wooden door on the ground floor; the other, to a flight of steps leading upward. Surdev pointed to the door facing them. "Wait in there," he said. "Sahib will finish his meeting and join you. It might take a while, but he will come. Till then you eat, drink, enjoy." He winked at Tiwari conspiratorially. Like they were old friends about to share a secret.

Surdev pushed open the door before them; from inside, a blast of music hit them. Tiwari stepped into the room and promptly Surdev shut the door after him. Tiwari found himself looking upon a dance floor with flashing lights, men in Safari suits standing around, and other men seated before low knee-level tables, with glasses of booze before them. The room was long and rectangular, and along the walls were plush red sofas. The walls had end-to-end mirrors, and at the front of the room was a giant-size TV that showed a Bollywood actress gyrating wildly. But it was the occupants of the dance floor who drew his attention: they wore welcoming smiles and were so young and pretty. Their hair was loose and flowing, their faces were rouged, and they wore long backless gowns of chiffon that showed their firm backs and flawless skin. The blood rushed to Tiwari's face. Hai Ram, he thought, this *was* a den of vice and these *were* women of low morals; all that he had heard about the ladies' bar *was* correct.

A man in a Safari suit came up and asked him if he would like a drink; they had foreign liquor too, he said. He could feel the eyes of the others on him: the security guards, who stood around like hawks, and the women, who had now turned away from the other customers to face him. It was almost like he was the chief guest there. For a moment he thought it was a conspiracy to shame him, and then it dawned on him that the attention was all because of his uniform. But should that not make them nervous, make them fear him? Apparently, not! he concluded. So confident were they of their racket, so sure of the hafta they were paying.

Tiwari sat rigid and uncomfortable, choosing to avert his face each time one of the dancing girls set her eyes on him. And they did that quite often, looking at him and winking, then shaking their hips invitingly, in sync with the music. No respect, he thought. No consideration for my uniform. And what about the other customers? They were busy flirting with the girls and showering them with rupee notes.

Thankfully, the customers were not allowed to touch the girls. It was all verbal, the flirting, and money talking, money enticing, setting up dates for later. And there was no dancing, either. At least not in that vulgar way, like it was earlier, before the ban. This was all thanks to that home minister who had banned the dance bars on the grounds that the dancing was obscene and that the bars were, in truth, pick-up points for girls who came to the city in search of work and had no other means of survival. And looking at the girls, Tiwari could believe it. They looked like models, like actresses. There was one who was fair, like a Rajasthani princess, and another who reminded him of the actress Deepika Padukone: she had the same kind of dimples and the same dazzling smile. The girls stood in a row, jiggling their hips and pouting at the men. And the men: they were so young and flamboyant, so drunk and excited.

Every few minutes, Tiwari would be approached by one of Kalyan Babu's men who'd ask him if he would like something to eat or drink, and each time he refused. He was polite, of course, and quick to clarify that he had just had his dinner, which was sent so kindly by Kalyan Babu, and the men just smiled and moved away, knowing they had done their duty.

Finally Surdev entered and said that Kalyan Babu would see him.

Tiwari got to his feet, a wave of relief sweeping over him. On his way out, he heard the sound of laughter, and someone smacking their lips and saying he should come again, he was always welcome. And then it dawned on him that he would have to get used to this place, to coming here often, if he decided to work with Kalyan Babu, if he sold his soul to him. And trudging up the flight of stairs, holding onto a brass railing, Tiwari felt like an old man, old and tired, beyond his thirty-odd years.

They stopped at the top of the stairs. Surdev pushed at a door on the left and said to Tiwari, "Look, take a look inside. We have twelve rooms here, twelve dance floors, and today only one is functional. The one where you sat, down below."

Tiwari poked his head in and was astonished by what he saw. A long corridor with six rooms on either side. Looking at the bar from outside, he wouldn't have thought it had so much space.

"At one time, each of these dance floors was alive and flourishing. We had the best of girls, the best of dancers; people would come all the way from the suburbs to see our performances. You won't believe if I told you the kind of people who would visit. Well-known businessmen and politicians and municipal corporators, and once, even, a famous actor with his friends." His eyes darkened. "That ban spoiled everything – everything! It ruined Mumbai's nightlife, and put the girls out of a livelihood. Seventy-five thousand women unemployed overnight! You can imagine what that did. It drove them to drugs, alcohol, suicide." His voice lowered. "We ourselves lost two of them. And till today Kalyan Babu is taking care of their families."

"Yes, but it also ruined homes, didn't it? It led men to leaving their families and squandering their savings on these girls. It was prostitution under a different name, and an easy flow of black money, with everyone involved: from politicians to corporators to the underworld bosses and the police. It was an epidemic of greed, and everyone was a part of it. It was just as well that it was banned. It had no right, no right!!" The dam had burst, the sluice gates had opened, there was no stopping the flood now: all that had welled up in him, all that he had tried to suppress.

Surdev looked at him with surprise, then his face tightened. "You have some strange ideas, my friend; very strange. And I don't know if you are ready to meet with Kalyan Babu yet. If you even understand the good work he is doing ..."

"Good work, my foot! He is making money out of people's weaknesses. Man's weakness for sex and woman's for security! He is creating a breeding ground for lust and corruption: that is what he is doing. He is nothing but a dalal, an agent, and an opportunist."

The security guard's face bristled with rage. His fingers curled into hard smoldering fists, and Tiwari could almost smell the heat off him. In that tiny space, between two doors, Surdev suddenly seemed enlarged, he seemed like a demon who had sprung up to protect his master. The next moment, he punched Tiwari on the shoulder; he punched him hard and said, "Go on! Move! Before I forget who you are and do something drastic. And don't let me see you here again. Here, or in that chowky!"

And suddenly Tiwari was afraid. Not of Surdev but of himself. Of what he was capable of. He began his descent, while Surdev stood at the top of the stairs, his arms folded and glowering.

Suddenly, the door on the right opened and out stepped Kalyan Babu, a man in his fifties, with a broad face, deep searching eyes, and thick wiry hair. "What, what is going on?" he asked Surdev, who replied, "Nothing, sahib; nothing you should bother with. This haraami policewalla thinks he can come in and insult you, insult us … the kind of work we are doing. He says we are doing prostitution, corruption…" The henchman almost choked with rage.

"Arrey, Surdev, the problem with you is you take offense too easily. Our friend here has probably got some wrong information. He is misinformed and misguided; it becomes our duty then to correct him." He placed one hand on the security guard's shoulder and, with the other, he beckoned to Tiwari. "Come, my friend, don't leave like this. Whoever comes to these doors is always welcomed; no one should leave unhappy. That is what I have always believed, always practiced. Come, let me see how I can help you." He gestured to Tiwari to return, and what the constable saw in his face was a genuine need to help, to be of use, almost like a craving.

But then something else caught Tiwari's attention. Someone who had crept up behind Kalyan Babu and lurked in the doorway. Hai Ram, what was *she* doing here? She, the only one whom he trusted. Whom he cared about. What was she doing here, in this accursed place? And Sushila's mouth dropped too, and she held out her hand, as though to explain, by which time it was too late. Tiwari was rushing out, rushing down the stairs, as though it were his fate he was running from.

Conversations with a Terrorist: Reflections on 26/11

On 26 November 2008, my city of Mumbai – trusting little insomniac that she is – watched disbelievingly as ten lethally armed terrorists, young, smiling, and high on speed, targeted key locations on its southern side. These included: the CST railway station, from where millions of people commute daily in large dusty trains that snake their way across the city and across the country; the Hotel Taj Mahal, heritage host to the wealthy, the genteel, the dressy, the showy, the well-heeled, the elderly (who must be seen as examples of good taste), and the young who, well, simply must be seen; The Taj, where marriages are plotted as feverishly as mergers, where flavors settle fluently on taste buds, where architects and aesthetes celebrate the ambience of another day, another age, without doubt, the grand old dowager of monuments; Leopold Café, Mumbai's own nook of bohemia, teeming with tourists, music, chatter, beer, the romance of marble-top tables and elegant black chairs, and foreigners in light summer clothes and waiters swiveling in between, tiptoeing to their tables, nimbly; Hotel Trident, the end-of-the-road glitter in the Queen's Necklace, where the city sparkles before an endless ocean, where lovers turn their backs on the city and gaze at the horizon, where vendors stroll purposefully, their wares in hand, hope and expectation alight in their eyes, and where people of all ages and all communities arrive to shed their frustrations: job cares, family cares, money cares, health cares: Who cares as long as they have a seafront to wash these away? Here they sneaked in, here they attacked. How do you think we felt? We, the ones who belong to this city, in as much as the city belongs to us.

They came in from the choppy seas
Accompanied by a traitor wind
Dark-eyed monsters with a collective spine
Abject orphans of a mastermind

No God they knew
No fear, no guilt
Their purpose was clear:
Kill, kill, kill!

They blazed with fury
They bristled with rage
They shot to pieces
Our heritage

No parent they saw
No mother, no child
The victims that fell
Fell to their bile

He who feasted
And he who served
And he who never made it
To a fair dessert

With sweat on our lips
And terror in our hearts
We watched the places of our youth
Fall apart

Let me tell you, Mr. Terrorist, these places *are* the arteries of my city. Life happens around them, through them. They are our lifelines, pounding with blood and business. By delivering on their promises of livelihood and sustenance, they assure us that Mumbai won't stop working, what is sought shall be delivered, be it a train that leaves on time from the CST, or a creamy cold coffee at the Sea Lounge, or a delectable Peking Duck at the Golden Dragon, or a plate of chicken tikkas at Leopold Café. In a world of inconsistencies, these places are our constants, our absolutes. They are our institutions, the pillars on which we base our hopes, our expectations, our memories, our trust. They are the worlds we inhabit. So many worlds in a single city.

But when these places get shot at, blown up, eroded, when you see them smoke and smolder and fall to the virulence of an intemperate age, when you see them reduced to graveyards of annihilation, you are reminded that it is not life who is the villain as much as human beings who fail to interpret it.

Why were you here in the first place? What brought you here? Please tell us, Mr. Terrorist.

How they make cities like yours stand tall, stand tall,
When we are reminded that our mosques must fall, must fall?

How they make your children think free, play free,
When ours are meant to be jihadis?

How do we forget unresolved crimes and unpunished leaders?
Think: Are we not human? Are we not bleeders?

Now excuse us if our untreated wounds boil and fester
And the blood that spills out is not warm but cold
Not a trickle but a flow
Not ours, but yours, alone.

So they told you that you will have access to a hundred blushing virgins in heaven. And that you can have your way with them. Did they tell you why those women died as virgins? And what their ages were? God, they say, is in the details. So how come they forgot to share with you the details? Did they share that Arabs once ruled the city of Mumbai? Surely, the Prophet must have been worshipped then. In every house, his name would have been invoked, his tenets of tolerance taught. But once again they chose to forget the details, and God, as they say, is in the details. Tell us, Mr. Terrorist, what were you thinking of when you played out your dance of death? What was in your heart and mind?

Cold coffee
Cold blood
Sea Lounge
Death hounds

Shamiana
For you, Osama!
Golden Dragon
Cooked its wagon

Wasabi
Out of Sushi
Peking Duck
No luck

Zodiac Grill
Had your fill?
Crystal Room
No room

Chandeliers
Frozen tears

Chambers
Embers

I spare no woman
I spare no child
The smell of Kaffir blood
Makes me smile

And if you must,
join me in the Ballroom
Where the last waltz plays on,
plays on ...

You are, indeed, the lowest form of life on this planet, Mr. Terrorist. Your mother doesn't want you, your father regrets you, your brothers deny you, your friends disown you. You sell yourself in the name of religion, and you hurt God's people. You did not even spare that good kind lawyer who pleaded the last case of his life. He pleaded for others younger than him. You did not spare the Jewish priest who served God under a different name. You severed him from his only child. You shot the chef who led his guests to safety; he paid the price for facing you. You blazed through policemen in the line of duty, guests who had no idea of their fates. The bravest and the best fell to your rage. You severed children from their mothers, fathers from their sons, friends from enemies, who will surely miss them, as all of us, human beings, eventually do. And you parted us, the lucky ones, from all sense of reason, all sense of understanding, that we, as humans, are all created equal. By destroying the rules of order, by reducing well-gathered orderly lives into shrill voices of fear, you have denied the Almighty. Denied Him his right to manage his world his way. Denied Him the power of life over death. Now, perhaps, in death, you shall tell us what you see.

Voices,
I hear voices now:
"Why did you separate us from our loved ones?
Why did you deprive us of them?"

Voices,
I hear voices now:
There a mother, there a child
There a father without a shoulder
A child without a mother

Voices,
I hear voices now:
Here a mother without breasts,
No mother at all
Here a child without milk,
No child at all

Voices,
I hear voices now:
No sweet virgins
To call me to their tender embraces
No nymphs to fan me
While I wheeze out my fears, in starts

Voices,
I hear voices now:
Not those of my friends laughing
Nor those of my masters teaching

Voices,
I hear voices now
I have just been told we shall be returned to earth
All ten of us
A pig in a well

A chicken in a coop
A goat destined to bleed on Bakri Eid

So where is the heaven you promised us, my masters?

And, now, you had better know what really happened, Mr. Terrorist, the facts as were found later. While one hundred and seventy people fell to your evil, there were over six hundred saved. They made it, despite your bullets, your bombs, your fury, your jihad.

Maybe Allah wanted them alive. He certainly did not give *you* the numbers you wanted. He did not tilt the scales in your favor. And He did not want *you* to be among the ones who got away. He preferred you dead than alive. And He made martyrs of the brave cops who died for us. And of the brave commandos who saved our people. (They are the ones who got all the candle marches and the memorials, and they will get these every year, as long as memory survives.) And He, merciful Allah, showed our politicians that at some point they had better start taking life seriously; that is, lives apart from their own. But here is the irony of it. We don't hear anyone talking about you, do we? How can they? Who will own up to you, claim you? Not your friends, nor your family. Certainly not your masters who thought you would be more useful to them dead than alive. So they kept themselves for the speeches, the bile, and the hatred. And cleverly they left you for the virgins.

Mehrunissa's Story

ONCE UPON A TIME she was free. Like you and me. Once upon a time she went to college. With me. Once upon a time she wore churidars and salwar kameez, and plotted with a girlfriend to slip into jeans, T-shirts, high-heel shoes, a dab of rouge on her cheeks but no lipstick. She made this transformation early morning, in college, before classes began, and she discovered what she had suspected all along: that she could attract guys from all communities. It was nice just to talk to her and have her smile at us. But ask her out, to a movie or a prom, and she would refuse, gently, in a way we wouldn't mind. Joy, kindness, piety, grace: the many virtues of the human heart would shine in her face, and we would make it a point to note every expression, for we knew we wouldn't see her thereafter, in later life, this ethnic beauty, with her dimpled cheeks, her small, bony chin, her quaint nose, her brown eyes, her thick, flowing hair, waist-length, her laugh, like a gurgle.

We were warned by our professors that she came from a highly orthodox family and was in college only to boost her matrimonial prospects. In all likelihood she would be married off before she got her degree. But any interest from us – any familiarity, so to say – and it could be earlier.

We didn't want that to happen. So we met her discreetly, behind the canteen, or in the library, or in the chapel. She liked the silence of the church, she liked its grandeur and its peace. The steeple gave her hope, she said, and the hard wooden benches reminded her of the ground rules of life.

Also, she liked the idea of kneeling before a man who had given up his life for humanity. *Did he succeed? Did he wipe the slate clean for everybody?* she asked. She couldn't read about it herself, because that, as per her religion, would be blasphemy. But could someone please tell her how it had all panned out? Were people any better than what they were? Were they more tolerant, more accepting?

Later, she found a good man for herself. She'd talk about him. He was older, dignified, soft-spoken. Nice teeth, a neat beard, large twinkling eyes, gentle and honest. He could quote Kabir as easily as he could recall Ghalib, and he cheered for the visiting cricket teams as happily as he did for India. That assured her that he was balanced, he liked fair sport. She wished, though, she could invite us to her wedding. She lowered her eyes when she said this, when she expressed her regrets.

We understood why she could not. She was not expected to have male friends. Not expected to mingle with the opposite sex. That was her part of the deal for being allowed to go to college. Our presence might raise questions where there were none. She changed the conversation. Told us about her hubby-to-be, her Habibi, as she called him.

He was self-assured, quick-witted, and enjoyed a good joke long after the punchline had been delivered. For family and friends, he'd put himself out on a limb, go that extra mile. What luck she had found him, she said. She could at least hope for a modern upbringing for her children. And hope for a larger degree of freedom for herself. She wanted four kids, she said, two boys and two girls. But four boys are better, said her Habibi. They would travel, he promised. Take a holiday twice every year but, en route, he would stop for business in Muscat or Dubai. Then she'd have to amuse herself, at the malls or in the gold bazaars. In Mumbai, she could drive her own car and go visit her family. Cookery classes she could attend, and aerobic classes, too, where the dress code was *decent*. Meaning? Nothing tight or revealing. No pubs, no late nights: that sort of thing did not wash well with Habibi. But she could work from home or from his office. That was fine with him. Jewelry designing? Yes, good idea! He would set her up, and his agents in the Middle East would help market her designs. He wouldn't mind her meeting her male cousins as long she remembered to address them as Bhaijaan. It was all about tehzeeb, he said, all about the right etiquette and never ever forgetting herself in public.

She seemed comfortable with this arrangement. It was a reasonable compromise, she said. Her older sisters weren't so lucky. They were not allowed to choose careers or decide on holiday destinations. And they were compelled to wear a burqa. But Habibi had promised her she wouldn't have to wear one. She felt, in his own way, he was proud of her looks and wanted to flaunt them. Of course, he would never admit that.

Having shared her situation, she took leave of us. It was probably the last time we were seeing her. There was no point in having a farewell party, she said; she wouldn't be allowed to attend. And there was no point in us inviting her to alumni reunions; by then she would be a fat, boring housewife, she joked. She came up and hugged each of us, her male friends. Not a hurried, remote hug, as we'd have imagined, but a long, lingering one.

"It *has* been wonderful, guys," she said eventually. "I wish it could have been different. I wish I could have completed all five years of college." The flatness in her voice was chilling. And then she turned and walked away, without looking back. In subsequent years, we wondered whether she thought of us, missed us. And what of her beauty? Would it be as fresh and enticing? Or would it have diminished, in managing kids and home, in managing the needs of her Habibi?

Twenty years later, I am at a bookstore, deep in thought and browsing. This is the one at Kemps' Corner, where books call to me from every rack. By then, books have become the pivot of my existence. I would spend hours leafing through the latest releases and new imprints of the classics. Sometimes, I would talk to the manager, a glint-eyed intellectual who knew more about literature than anyone I had met. During these discussions, we would wax eloquent about our favorite authors: Baldwin, Bellow, Carver, Camus, Chekhov, Coetzee, D.H. Lawrence, Dostoevsky, Flaubert, Fitzgerald, Steinbeck, and Yates; then, some of the contemporary ones: Jennifer Egan, Aimee Bender, Ben Fountain, Cynthia Ozick, Jonathan Franzen, Junot Diaz, and Ron Rash. In between, our eyes would trail the chic, well-dressed women who'd walk around with bags of books in their hands. The women would buy mostly bestsellers or romance, and would have kids in tow, pleading to be taken to the toys' section. But that day I was distracted by an unusually exhilarating sight.

"Mehrunissa," I said, looking into those eyes which stared at me through the racks. "Mehrunissa, I am so happy to see you." I drank in the progress of time. She was much the same: the same dimpled cheeks, the same warm eyes, the same quaint nose and shapely chin. Still, she could light up a place with her presence. But, wait, all was not what it should be. She was now wearing a burqa.

"For you I risk censure," she said, smiling and touching the raised veil on her head. "But I couldn't resist – and neither could I resist picking this up." She held up my book of short stories, my debut collection on Mumbai. It did not escape me that she held the book delicately, like it were an object of art, of value.

"Well," I said, "you know I always wanted to write. That was the only thing I was serious about."

"Among other things—" she said teasingly.

An impish smile played on her lips. It was the confidence of a woman protected by her garb and, perhaps, by the distance of time. I wanted to reach out and hug her. I wanted to tell her how delighted I was to see her. And, probably I would have, had it not been for the garment that covered her. It stood between us as a reminder of the time lapse, of the person she might have now become.

"You are looking well," she said. "You've gained some weight around the waist, and your cheeks have filled out, but the gaunt look is gone. Thank God for that!"

"That's because I stopped smoking," I said, grinning. "I had a bitch of a time giving up. Tried yoga, meditation, hydrotherapy, nicotine patches … could only succeed after seven attempts."

"That's great! I remember you saying your cigarette was your sixth finger and what doesn't bother you won't kill you."

God, she remembered! I had a ready stock of lines those days, which I used to pull for effect. I never missed a chance to have the last word. But, at this moment, all I wanted to say was: "Mehrunissa, *what* has become of you? Why the burqa? You said that Habibi had promised he wouldn't curtail your freedom." She might have sensed my discomfort, for she quickly dragged me to the coffee shop upstairs. But before that, she introduced me to her son, Aahil. He was eight years old, fair, good-looking, and tall for his age. The most striking part of him was his hair: it was reddish brown and soft and fluttery. He appeared aloof and distracted, and did not seem interested in knowing me. "He has his father's nature," said Mehrunissa apologetically. "But my looks, I think."

The boy demanded money from his mother, saying he wanted to buy some computer games. She pulled out a five-hundred-rupee note, which brought a sneer to his face.

She gave him another note of the same value and he stared at her sullenly. She had to give him two more notes with a "That's enough now!" before he left. She gazed after him pensively, then said, "Shall we go up? I don't have much time and we have so much to share."

We chose a corner table and ordered two coffees. From there we could see the display of books and the shoppers below. She asked about our friends – Gentle Rox, Exotic Gool, Delicate Diana, Crazy Charmaine, Horny Harsh, Meaty Melissa, Simple Savio (we had names for each of them) and about the two handsome Rajput princes who were always stoned and oblivious to the effect they had on women. She asked where they all were and if I ever met them. I caught a wistful note in her voice, and she heard me intently, while I provided an update. Then she asked about our English professors: Eunice de Souza and Nisha da Cunha. And about our principals: Father John Correia Afonso and Emil D'Cruz. Eventually, she came around to me, and I told her how I had thrown off the yoke of advertising, my earlier profession, and taken to writing, and she said, "It was always your calling. I remember your stories in the college journal. I remember reading them and thinking, one day you will be counted. I would wonder why you took so long to get down to it." She asked if I was married, how I had come to meet my wife, and she heard about my courtship with dignified patience. It must have sounded childish to her, for by then she was married twenty years. She said she lived a boring life, and used words like *settled*, *domesticated*, and *uneventful* to describe her routine.

She said she had a large house, five servants, three dogs, two cats, and a garden, which was her pride. Her husband traveled frequently. He manufactured perfumes and traded in semi-precious stones. He had business interests all over the Middle East. He also did a lot of community service, sending pilgrims to Haj at his own expense. She helped with that, interviewing the applicants and choosing the ones who were genuinely needy and deserved to go. "He is a good man," she said, "my Habibi. The one I am worried about, though, is Aahil. He doesn't mix, has no friends, is given to mood swings and outbursts. The only time he is happy is when he is spending money, and he has no idea what it takes to earn it. He wants the latest gadgets and the most expensive brands of clothes and footwear, and Habibi and his grandfather simply spoil him." She said *that* was her only grouse with Habibi; she wanted him to wield a firmer hand with Aahil. But Habibi said that the boy had a mind of his own, that he had good taste; they had named him Aahil, meaning prince, after all. She said, when it came to her son, she had failed to convince her husband.

I thought that was the perfect cue to ask about the burqa, how she came to adopt it.

She fell silent, locked her palms before her face, and rested her chin on them. She looked like a schoolgirl pondering over an examination paper. Then she began.

It was the night of 26/11, the night the city went into shock. Her father-in-law had arrived from Jeddah, where he stayed, and Habibi had booked him into the Taj Mahal hotel.

Her father-in-law was a proud man. Although he had three sons in the city, he would refuse to stay with them. He liked his privacy and, more than that, the luxury of the Taj. He would insist on a sea-facing room, in the old wing, and, if he didn't get one, would throw a fit. He was a self-made man, stubborn, imperious, and used to getting his own way. His family was in awe of him.

It was Habibi who had requested her to wear the burqa. It would be an exception, he said. His father was visiting for just four days, and all the women in the house – his aunts, sisters, nieces, and brothers' wives – would be wearing one, out of respect for the old man. Her husband had asked so politely that she couldn't refuse. Not that she was thrilled about it. She found the burqa confining. She found it difficult to walk in, breathe in. Besides, it just wasn't her. But then, she thought, her father-in-law visited only once a year and it pleased him to see the women in his family maintain traditions. She could easily do that for her husband, she thought. And so she had consented.

There were going to be twenty of them at dinner and Habibi had booked a table at the Indian restaurant in the Taj. Barely had they sat down when Aahil said that he wanted to visit the restroom. She asked him to wait until they had ordered, but he was insistent, said that he wanted to go right away. His grandfather – from where he sat at the head of the table – said to Mehrunissa that she *should* take the boy, they would wait to order. "*Jao, beta*," he said to his grandson tenderly.

No sooner had they left the restaurant than Aahil began to act up. He ran down the corridor and into shops, where he would order the salesmen to show him various clothes. The moment the sales person would show him something, he would lose interest. Only when Mehrunissa threatened to summon his father did he leave.

She sent him into the men's room, while she waited outside. After a while, she got bored and began staring at the window displays. She was not much interested in the jewelry and the saris but was fascinated by the photographs of celebrities who had stayed at the Taj. There were gorgeous black-and-white pictures of The Beatles, The Stones, Jacqueline and John Kennedy, Princess Diana, Prince Charles, Ben Kingsley, Sir Richard Attenborough, Alfred Hitchcock, Zubin Mehta, and the Dalai Lama. She stood admiring these legends and the quality of the photographs. Suddenly, she heard some explosions, like muffled blasts, and then the patter of feet and shouts and screams.

Aahil emerged from the men's room, buttoning his fly. Mehrunissa grabbed him by the shoulders and led him down the corridor, into a passage, where they heard the rattle of gunfire, then glass shattering and shouts and screams and the sound of footsteps running away.

Then, suddenly, they were face to face with three men: one, young, stocky, and clean-shaven; the other two, tall and bearded. All of them had a blank look in their eyes and carried rucksacks on their backs, and they held machine guns, loosely, expertly, like trained soldiers.

They looked at her, then at Aahil, and tightened their grip on their guns. Then one of them said to her, "Go! Go through that door! This is not for you, nor for him. It is Allah's war, against them." Turning, he sprayed a showcase with bullets, and laughed when the glass splintered.

Screams rose from somewhere and she wasn't sure if she had added hers to them. Her heart was beating madly; blood pounded at her temples; under her burqa she sweated; her hands and feet felt numb, paralyzed …

When she found the courage to look up, she saw that the terrorist who had addressed her had shredded his arms and neck and was bleeding in places, but he didn't seem to notice. Meanwhile, the other two gunmen stalked off. Like phantoms, they disappeared into the smoke.

Aahil was shivering now. His head was shaking from side to side and a strange whimpering sound rose from his mouth. He kept looking at the man with the gun, who had a front tooth missing, a lush black beard, and blood running down a tattooed arm.

Slowly, she had inched Aahil away from this bloodied warrior, who gestured with his gun *Go! Go!* and then he looked away and went toward the lobby, while she fled down the corridor, keeping her son pressed to her stomach.

She felt the bullets whiz past and saw people fall before her eyes, people she was unable to distinguish as men or women. She just kept moving, moving. She did not know how she made it to a side exit. She only remembered seeing a police cordon, a police van, a policewoman grabbing her by the shoulder and pulling her to the side, just as she fainted.

In the same way, her husband and his family, too, had been lucky. The terrorists had burst into the restaurant and lined them up. They had ordered her family out, and her mother-in-law had remembered to flip her veil over her face and the other women in the family had done the same. And the terrorists had given way respectfully, while they filed out, their faces burning with guilt. Later, she learned from her sister-in-law that they had stopped Habibi, only him, and he had said in a trembling voice, "I am a practicing Muslim, circumcised, believe me, I can show you." And they had nodded and let him go.

"That broke my Habibi," she said, drawing patterns with a manicured finger on the table. "Overnight, he became a changed person. He kept himself glued to the television, watching the coverage. He refused to eat, refused to take calls from his friends, who were worried about us and about Abu Jaan, my father-in-law. Habibi told his brothers to look after his father, who kept saying, 'It's those damn Americans who are responsible. They are the ones who created Osama. They are the ones who trained him. You nurture a snake and this is what it does. It comes back to bite you.'

"And then, three days after it had ended, Habibi came to me and said, 'I want you to do one thing for me, Mehrunissa, and I don't want any arguments, I won't hear them, I tell you. I want you to throw away all the clothes you have, all those other Indian outfits, and I want you to start wearing the burqa. I have thought about this long and hard and know it is the right thing to do, the only thing left. Whatever happened that night was a sign from Allah that we must abide by our traditions. If all of us were saved, if Aahil is alive today, it is only because you women were wearing a burqa.'"

She gulped down the last bit of her coffee and reached for a tissue. Wiping her lips, she said, "So you see, in a sense, I was the last casualty of 26/11, the case that never got reported in the newspapers. The friend you knew in college died that night. And what you see before you now is a good Muslim woman who obeys her husband, who dresses and acts the way he wants her to."

"Mehrunissa," I said. "Are you happy? Are you okay? You can tell me, you know."

But she was on her feet and reaching for her handbag. "I have to go," she said. "He will be calling, he will want to know where I am. Besides, Aahil shouldn't see me here, having coffee with you. He is close to his father. Yes, very close."

I rose as though to follow her, then sat down. The weight of a twenty-year-old gap closed in on me. God, how I hated loose endings, particularly unhappy ones. How I hated to see beauty denied, freedom curtailed, youth truncated …

A few moments later, she was back, breathless and panting. Looking at me wide-eyed, she said, "Can you sign your book for me? But please don't write anything personal. No best wishes or anything of that sort. Nothing meaningful. Just sign your name. Nothing more, please."

Accidental Karma

IT WAS A LOCKED door meeting. Outside, it was business as usual: people flitting to and fro. Inside, it was serious business: money matters. I looked at the three of them seated before me and said softly, "Six hundred and fifty million rupees in six months is some achievement, don't you think? That, too, during a recession. We *should* share the profits with the team. Give them a bonus."

The boss tapped the floor with his boots. He was a big man, the boss, his giant legs spread out. For a man of his size, he looked nervous. That's what the tapping was about: a nervous tick, an uncontainable anxiety.

A frown clouded his wife's face; she was thinking hard. She looked girlish when she did that. It was easy to see what had attracted the boss to her: her range of expressions, piquant and childlike. Rare, in the corporate world.

The second man gulped. I could see his Adam's apple flicker. He had thin lips and small, wary eyes, the eyes of a finance man. He was the third partner in the agency but no one called him *Boss.* It was only the big man who was *Boss.* That's because he was the ideas man, the brains bank. His wife was the client handler, and the second man was the moneyman, he was there to save them money. It was a well-considered arrangement and worked well for them. They could play good cop, bad cop very easily, and navigate the tricky by-lanes of business.

The moneyman waited for the others to say their piece. It was protocol among them. Without the other two, there would have been no advertising agency, no clients, no profit, no perks; none of the privileges he enjoyed. He was smart enough to understand that.

The boss looked at me and said, "I am not sure about the bonus. I know you are a people's person, Gussy, but we don't want to spoil these guys, give them wrong ideas. Besides, we don't know when this recession will end. We have to be cautious, you know."

"Crap!" I said. "We can sail through this recession and you know it. Now that we have all this government business. The government won't default, it never does! Our money is safe. But we need to reward our guys. They've been working their butts off. They've done evenings, nights, holidays … without a word of complaint. I am not saying that we should hand out hefty raises, but at least some kind of a bonus. To show that we appreciate them."

His wife interjected. "Know what, Gussy? You are a fine creative guy, and so popular with clients and colleagues. They love you, same as we do! But you will never grow in your career if you keep thinking with your heart. You must think like a management person, get more business-minded. I say this for your own good."

The boss smiled and stretched his legs; his thighs hardened like surfboards. He brought his hands behind his head. His T-shirt pressed against his chest, and his biceps came into view, they rose like hillocks. Serious work had gone into that body, serious age-defying work.

The third partner flashed me a smile. His thin lips gave the impression of a motive lurking. "You don't have to worry about yourself," he said. "We know all this business wouldn't have been possible were it not for you. And we are grateful; we are not going to forget it. We are going to take good care of you, very good care." He smiled again, a jubilant smile.

The boss said, "We are not saying we are not going to reward the team. It's just that *now* is not the right time.

Employees have a different mindset. Reward them once and they will expect it every time we get new business. We don't want to create this kind of false expectation. As for you, we are thinking of a new car. Something premium, more your style."

I could see that the boss was treading cautiously. He did not want to upset me, and I could understand why. It was I who had notched up all that business during a recession. At a time when the private sector wasn't spending, when it was severely cash-strapped, I had gone out and acquired government business. Infrastructure, insurance, oil, pension funds, tax bonds, tourism: nine months of pitching, and we had it all wrapped up. The campaigns broke and our profits headed north. Our balance sheet was strong and robust, positively glowing. This, while other ad. agencies were struggling to stay afloat. The boss knew what they stood to lose if they lost me. But what they did not get was: it was not *my* well-being I was interested in but in that of my team. I was, anyway, on a fat salary with handsome perks, making more than I had ever imagined. It was the team that deserved to be rewarded. I tried to explain this to the three partners, I tried to reason with them, but it was like speaking to a stone wall. As I left the conference room, I heard the boss's wife say, "Really, he is so immature. I don't think he is ready for a management position, yet. I don't think we can trust him."

I left the office, fuming. It was the earliest I had left in the last twelve months. I felt guilty leaving because I had promised our petroleum client a campaign by the end of the day. The idea was ready in my computer, it had only to be printed out. Our client was under pressure from the petroleum ministry and the campaign was important to them. But right now, work was the last thing on my mind. I just wanted to get away. Away from this self-serving trinity.

On my way out, I saw people in my department working. They were huddled over their computers, absorbed in their tasks. They would be trying out different colors, different fonts, strong layouts to impress me. These were my people, my guys. I had trained them personally, and they had reciprocated with dedication.

A strange sensation rose in my chest, a feeling of helpless suffocation. The sensation grew in me and made my breathing heavy, my heart pound. It was tough to explain this feeling, for I was in my early thirties and too young to feel this kind of stress.

Emerging from the office building, I looked for my car. It was nowhere in sight. I was about to call my chauffeur when I remembered that he had said it needed servicing – he'd be taking it to the service center. I needed to find a cab, and saw one with its meter up.

I approached the cab and opened the back door. The cabbie asked me where I wanted to go; I told him. He shook his head and said no, he wasn't interested. *Here we go*, I thought, *the usual tug-of-war with a Mumbai cabbie.*

Placing a leg in, I reminded the cabbie of the law: if his meter was up, he had to take me.

He turned in his seat, and that's when I saw him clearly: a dark, sweaty man with a shaven head and bleak, insolent eyes. This man wasn't going to relent, I thought. He wasn't the kind to take the law seriously.

The next thing I knew was that he had started the cab and that we were moving. I, with my right leg trapped under his seat and flat on my back, was dragged along a rough, tarred road. The back wheel swerved close to my face, the exhaust pipe spat clouds of black fumes, the back door flapped open – powerless – like me.

A madman, I thought, *a fucking madman*! I must keep my wits about me, I must survive.

The cabbie swung the cab into a one-way street, where there were cars parked on one side. Behind me, I could hear shouts and cries of alarm. People – horrified – were running after the cab.

A moment ago, I had been sure I would survive this ordeal. But now the cabbie was going zigzag, zigzag, and although I couldn't see him, I could feel his rage. He was trying to shake me off, trying to slam me against a parked vehicle. He would approach a stationary vehicle, and I would flinch, drawing in my body, and feeling, on my face, the heat of the spinning tire.

He gathered speed and closed in to where a four-wheel drive stood in the line of parked cars. Among the other smaller cars, its rugged contours protruded.

I could see it coming, could see my head severed from my body … this was it, I thought.

OOF! I took the impact on my back, and at that moment my lungs gave up on me. I gasped, I writhed, I choked. And through that I realized that I had been shaken free of the cab, shaken free of the madman. But the pain was such, it made me want to curl up and die.

When I came around, I was in the emergency room of a hospital. I had been strapped to a respirator, and an oxygen mask covered my face. Over the mask I could discern some faces. Those of my parents, my sister, three office colleagues, two female nurses, two male interns, and a doctor whom I recognized as one of Mumbai's most respected surgeons.

I smiled weakly at my parents, who reached out and took my hands. I looked at my sister; her tense unsmiling face revealed to me the full extent of the damage. Bad, huh? I tried to say, but the pain engulfed my words.

My eyes circled the room and fell upon the cabbie. What was he doing here? I wondered. And why was he seated in a chair while the others stood? The surgeon was looking at some X-rays, holding them to a light box, and addressing the male interns in a low, tutorial voice.

One of the nurses bent and whispered at my ear, "Try not to look at the taxi driver. We have taken away his license and are waiting for the police to come and deal with him."

My office colleague, Vishal, whispered at my other ear, "We had to come here in his taxi. Because of the peak hour traffic we couldn't find another cab." I vaguely remembered being helped into the back of the cab and the cabbie's bullet-shaped head as he drove us to the hospital.

The pain stabbed at me from all sides. I was told that I had broken four ribs and that one of them was digging into my right lung. Because of that I was unable to breathe freely. My back and elbows were a mess. The skin had been scraped off.

I was in for a long stay. Three weeks at least, said the surgeon. "With ribs, there is nothing we can do but wait for them to heal. We can only help you with the pain. I hope you are ready to help us help you," he said genially. Then, without waiting for an answer, he said, "Good, good; that's decided then. That's the spirit."

Two policemen arrived, but the doctor asked them to wait outside. There were too many people in the room, he said.

My office colleagues went outside to speak to the cops and brief them on the accident. "Not accident," said my father. "Murder! Attempted murder!"

The oxygen mask dug into my cheekbones, making me feel stifled and suffocated. My mother and sister, standing on either side of my bed, gazed at me tenderly. I could tell, by their faces, that they felt my pain. I wanted to comfort them. But was numb myself.

The cabbie sat glowering at me. I could tell he was seething. *Why was I tied to his destiny? Why was I sent his way?* I could see these questions in his eyes; questions I, too, would ask myself later.

My colleague Vishal returned to the room and told the cabbie he was wanted outside. The cabbie pretended not to hear him and kept staring at me instead. There was something fixated about his gaze, something deeply disturbing.

Vishal went out, and moments later, returned with a policeman.

"Shaukat Ali?" asked the policeman, peering at a driving license in his hand.

The cabbie turned to look at the policeman, at the license in his hand. Then quietly he rose and followed the policeman out of the room.

Nurses and young doctors would enter the room and look at me. They would stare at me, shake their heads, and leave. I realized that the news of my accident had gotten around.

Soon after, the surgeon said, "We are going to sedate you while we strap up those ribs." He nodded to a nurse, who came up, rubbed an antiseptic on my arm, and injected me. I lost all consciousness.

It was dark when I woke up. I had been moved to a private room. A slow fan spun above my bed. The pain gripped me in a way I couldn't move, couldn't scream. The respirator had been removed, but I was connected, via a tube, to a bottle of saline. The bottle was half empty, which told me how long I had been asleep. My chest and ribs were strapped up with an elastic bandage that seemed to be tightening its grip by the minute. Next to me was my sister, fast asleep in a chair.

A low moan rose from my throat: *God, help me; help me, God.* The pain was unbearable.

My sister woke up and began to stroke my forehead. I tried moving from side to side, as though to get away from the pain, but that made it worse.

The pain persisted; I couldn't take it any longer. My sister went to fetch the night nurse, who came, looked at me with genuine pity, and said, "First night, no. Will hurt." She went away and came back moments later with a sleeping tablet which knocked me out.

Toward morning, the pain returned and attacked me in spasms. *The body as enemy, the body as burden, the body as serial offender*: I lived through each of these states, realizing how grievously injured I was. And yet it would be the body that would fight back; I just had to be brave and patient.

My family members took turns to stay with me. My friends would visit daily. My office colleagues would drop in after work. They would get me a dish prepared by their wives or mothers, and sometimes the security guard at the entrance would confiscate it, saying the hospital did not permit outside food. I would feel bad about that, the wasted labor.

The pain was such that I could barely talk to my visitors, and yet they came and ended up talking among themselves. Friends bonding with other friends – it gave me great joy to see this. But it also made me realize that people tend to lean toward the healthy and the normal; that a sick person is a liability, no better than furniture. He reminds you of a condition you don't want to be in.

My room was spacious. It opened onto a balcony, which opened to a view of the ocean. The balcony ran all around the floor so that every room had a sea view. In the mornings and evenings, a nurse would come and throw open the doors to the balcony. A crisp, strong sea breeze would sweep in and refresh me. I was eager to visit the balcony and gaze at the ocean, but I lacked the strength to rise and get into a wheelchair.

The strong medicines caused a reaction: I developed a facial rash. The resident doctor prescribed an application that first burned then cooled my skin. I suspected it was a steroid.

The wincing pain in my sides persisted, and this brought me the attention of the nurses. These angels – all from Kerala – would keep checking whether I had slept well or not, taken my medicines or not, needed anything for my comfort. Their large sympathetic eyes and kind touch became part of the treatment, part of the cure. And their sweet accents amused me, made me forget my pain, momentarily.

On Sunday morning, a barber came to shave me, and after he had left, a sweet-faced nurse came to change the bedsheets. Stroking my cheeks, she asked, "You don't want French? No French? I think French look nice on you."

On Sunday evening, the hospital corridor became unbearably noisy. I thought it was because of the weekend visitors; but no, I was told that a famous guru had been admitted and that his disciples had arrived in droves, to pay their respects.

Soon the disciples had taken over the balcony and I had to request a ward attendant to close the balcony room-doors. Yet I could hear their voices and then some chanting.

After a while, the chanting increased, it became almost frenzied. I called the reception and said this was a hospital, and I didn't care if the guru was a magician who performed miracles, his fans were a nuisance, they were treating the hospital like a temple.

The man at the desk heard me out. "I beg you to tolerate, sir," he said. "Visiting hours are almost over; they will soon be gone." Then, lowering his voice, he whispered, "We can't do anything, sir; can't say anything. He is the guru of one of our trustees."

"Fuck your trustees! And fuck their guru! What is the point of all your 'please-be-quiet' signs, if you are going to let these people kick up a row?" Even as he stammered his apologies, I hung up.

Instantly, the pain started again and did not let up all night. Toward morning I slept, but was awoken by the sounds of the hospital stirring to life: nurses taking the vitals of their patients; ward attendants readying the bathtubs; trolleys rolling down the corridor and breakfast trays being distributed; doors swinging open and doctors entering with a group of interns, saying, "Well, well, and how are we this morning?"

When I told my doctor about my unceasing pain, he turned to one of his interns and said, "We had better get some tests done. ESR, ECG, urodynamics, and multiple X-rays of the ribs and chest. And let's run him through a CT scan, too."

I groaned, thinking how I would cope with the movement. But the doctor said I should not worry, they'd give me a painkiller before taking me for the tests.

The CT scan department was on the ground floor. It had a large waiting area, with rows and rows of red plastic chairs. People sat, awaiting their turn. Some of them held a bottle of colored liquid in their hands; they were to consume this before their test. A bare-chested man in a lungi was wheeled in by two attendants. His forehead was smeared with streaks of orange paste. I inferred this was the guru.

I drew myself up in my wheelchair, and said, "Excuse me, sir; I am glad to have met you. I happen to be on the same floor as you, and am recovering – well trying to – from a terrible accident. And it so happens that your disciples are a real nuisance. They crowd outside my room, on the balcony, and talk loudly and chant. Can you please request them to maintain some order, some discipline? I would be much obliged."

The guru looked at me with warm, unflinching eyes. There was a youthful sheen on his cheeks and, below that, a lush, gray beard. Without doubt, it was an arresting face, full of vitality. He looked at me with interest and said, "Tell me about the accident. Was it serious? How did it happen?" I realized he had ignored my request.

I narrated the events bit by bit. I did not know what made me do that; it's not as though I have any affinity for gurus and godmen. He listened intently, nodding from time to time, and stroking his beard in a slow, downward motion.

On finishing, I asked him, "So what kind of a guru are you? What do you preach?" Promptly he replied, "I don't preach, I just lead people to God. To his door. So you can say I am a guide. No more, no less."

"And how do you explain God?" I asked, eager to engage him.

"Well, I have yet to see him, but, to my mind, he is like a great gambler who sits in the sky and deals out cards to us, humans. To some he deals a good hand and to others a weak one. My job is simply to help people see the cards they have got – the good ones *and* the bad ones. And I teach them to play with the good ones and to discard the bad ones, so that when they get up there and face him, He knows that their time on earth has been well spent. That they have understood the cosmic game."

"You are talking about karma?" I asked.

"Yes, that and Maya, the game of illusion. It's also important to understand that. But tell me, are you married? Are you a householder? With children … responsibilities?"

"No," I said, laughing. "I am a free man. Unburdened – out of choice!"

"Ah, good, good. These days I worry more about married people than about the single. They have more troubles, more difficulties." He lowered his voice. "The people who come to see me are mostly all married, with families. And families have big problems."

"Why is that?" I asked.

"Well, you know, everyone has high expectations from the other and egos to match. So, a father is displeased with his son for not following his ways, and the son challenges his father because he wants to be different, and the mother, who is trying hard to balance things between the two, is torn apart, and brothers are fighting among themselves, and the mother is further torn apart; then the daughter is fighting for her rights, wanting to be treated like her brothers, and that is not possible because she has a husband. And that's not all. Married women are unhappy because their husbands are running after money or after other women. The Indian housewife is, by and large, an unhappy soul. She feels cheated and shortchanged. And that is because she is not loved enough. Not in the way she wants to be. A man doesn't need love, he needs appeasement. He is like a child, always wanting to be told how good he is, how charming, how successful! But a woman? She carries the gift of creation inside her. She is born with that gift, which is a demanding one. It has to be fed, respected, and nurtured. Because that's how creation works. But Indian women are seldom loved that way. So they seek consolation in their role as mothers, or in God. In things that can absorb and distract them, make them forget their dreams and desires."

"Whew! You really know your women, don't you?" I said.

"They are not *my* women, my friend. But women who I observe and read." He paused, then said, "With your injury, you are not going to be able to have sex for a long time. That might be difficult, huh, at your age?"

"What *are* you? Some kind of a sex guru!" I was curious now, and suspicious.

"Well, if you hold that sex is a part of life, an important part, then I am that. Exactly what you say. And if you say that love, too, is a part of life, then I am a love guru. But right now, I see that sex is going to be your problem. So I must address that."

"But why do *you* need to address that? I don't recollect choosing you as my guru. Or are you running some kind of a sex racket in your ashram?"

He laughed. "Sex becomes a racket only when one person is exploiting the other. When one uses it as a way to feed the ego. But when one uses it for liberation, to dissolve the ego, to understand that sex is no different from other bodily functions and that we need not build a philosophy around it, like how we don't build a philosophy around other body functions, then sex becomes understanding, it becomes acceptance, and most important, love. Love of the self. Love of the divine. Love of the instincts we are born with."

"So, you *do* propagate sex in your ashram?" I prodded.

"I propagate nothing, my friend, nothing. I only state things the way they are. How they are meant to be seen. Without the veils of Maya, without the traps we fall into so easily. My role, as I told you, is to lead people to that great gambler in the sky and to lead them there with minimum collateral damage."

Just then, the door of the CT scan office opened and a doctor emerged. "Come, Guruji, this way," he said. "We are sorry to have kept you waiting." But the guru pointed to me and said, "He was here first … before me." Then to me, he said, "I will see you soon, my friend. I am sorry about the noise. You won't have to complain again, I promise."

In the week that followed, I had a stream of visitors: doctors from various departments, asking about my progress; the head of administration, checking if I was satisfied with the nursing; a smartly dressed nutritionist, who sat opposite me, holding a pen and a file, and asked me what kind of meals I would enjoy. Daily she would arrive, and daily we would set the menu. Delectable continental meals were now served to me in special crockery; the clunky hospital whites were removed. I was given a vaporizer which, I was told, would help clear my lungs. And I was prescribed physiotherapy twice a day.

At the end of the second week, the boss and his wife dropped in. They came carrying a bouquet of long-stemmed roses.

The boss had brought me a thick hardcover book with witticisms on various subjects. "You will love it!" he said. "It will help you forget the pain."

His wife settled into a chair and propped her feet up against the edge of my bed. Her feet were small and porcelain white; her toenails, a lustrous pink. Theirs was a strange match, I thought. He, big and brawny; she, delicate and feline.

The two of them spoke animatedly. They had just returned from a holiday in East Africa.

At Maasai Mara, they had enjoyed dozens of lion sightings and seen a pride of lions bring down a zebra. At Lake Nakuru, they had seen a cheetah swallow a flamingo. At Amboseli, they had seen the wildebeest migration into Tanzania, and gaped at the glacial majesty of Kilimanjaro. And at a pond, from a log cabin up in the trees, they had seen all kinds of animals – cheetah, elephants, leopards, lions, giraffe, bison, deer, rhinoceros, and zebra – drinking water like they were one big family, each respecting the other's thirst.

"And yet man, who is supposed to be a rational animal, fights over water," said the boss philosophically. "You must visit Africa, Gussy. That place has great beauty, which you won't see elsewhere. Next time, we are planning to go gorilla trekking in Uganda. Do you know you can actually spend time with a gorilla family?"

"I am not sure I want to," said his wife frowning. "Animals are okay from a distance but you can't trust them. You never know when they will turn hostile and maul you."

I don't think we can trust him. Her comment about me came sailing back into my mind. I wondered how she would have watched the kill. With fascination, with interest, reclining against the warrior chest of her husband, while the zebra – life oozing from its body – would have raised its head skyward and wondered when its agony would end.

And I had been there myself, flat on my back and almost dragged to death by a loony. *Why? Why?* I needed to know. I needed to understand the reason for the cabbie's hostility.

"Have you had any thoughts on the petroleum campaign?" the boss's wife asked abruptly. "I am asking only because you have all this time on your hands."

"There is no rush, no rush at all," said the boss hurriedly. "You should recover first. Recover fully."

"But it is good to be mentally engaged. Work will make him feel better," said his wife. I could see they were at it again, playing good cop, bad cop. It came so naturally to them.

The wife persisted with her suggestion. She offered to send one of the secretaries with a laptop, if I decided to work on the campaign. She gave me a dazzling smile and waited for my response.

And then it struck me. They were paying for this, my stay in the hospital, and had come to see if I could earn my salary whilst recovering. How convenient! How smart! Commerce over concern: so that's what this game was about.

"I will work only when I feel up to it," I said firmly. "Let me see, how much leave have I got accumulated? Eight weeks? Ten weeks? This might just be a good time to claim it all."

"I agree," said the boss. "The more you rest, the quicker you will recover." He smiled at me half-heartedly. A scowl appeared on his wife's face.

The boss said he needed to use the restroom. I pointed to the door next to the entrance. Rising, he disappeared into the restroom, leaving me alone with his wife.

An uncomfortable silence followed. Then brightly she said, "About gorilla trekking: it's crazily expensive, and you've got to train before the trek so you don't do anything to upset the beasts. I don't see the point of all that. But he is so keen … and I don't like to refuse him."

Just then the door of the room opened and a ward attendant entered. At least he looked like a ward attendant, but was dressed like a doctor, in a green surgical robe. He was short, dark, shaven-headed, and holding a knife in his hand. The knife was raised over his head.

The boss's wife turned. Seeing him, she screamed and hurled herself on the bed, beside me. The bed shook, and I felt a sharp jolt in my ribs. I coughed, and that made the pain worse.

The cabbie advanced, and just then the bathroom door opened and the boss stepped out. His fly was open, he was scowling, he had been alarmed by his wife's scream.

With the kind of speed that distinguishes a man of action, the boss moved, grabbed the cabbie's wrist, and yanked it so that the knife fell from his hand. Then once, twice, thrice, he rammed his bulbous fist into that round face. The cabbie dropped like a sack of potatoes.

The boss moved to the phone and punched at a button. "We have an emergency," he shouted. "A patient has been attacked. Send your security guards, right away!" He kept his eyes on the inert cabbie.

The security guards arrived and carried away the attacker. Doctors came to inquire how I was, and each of them checked my blood pressure and pulse rate. Within an hour, the police arrived and took my statement, and one of the trustees called to apologize. He said he did not know how this had happened, how the cabbie had gotten past Security, but someone was going to pay dearly for the lapse. The boss's wife was radiant. "If it wasn't for him," she would say to the visitors, "you would have seen two dead bodies today." Leaning over, she would kiss her husband's hand, and he would smile grudgingly, with embarrassment.

My parents arrived, breathless and frantic. My mother kept stroking my head and saying, "Thank God! Thank God you are okay." My father paced the room pensively. Finally he said, "This man came here today because I have filed a criminal complaint against him. He is obviously very dangerous and possibly even deranged. As though it wasn't enough that he tried to kill you on the road, he wanted to finish the job here."

I looked at my father with surprise. He was a reserved, soft-spoken man. It was unlike him to file a police complaint.

"Well," I said. "There will be other charges against him now, and, hopefully, they'll put him away."

At last the visitors stopped coming, the phone stopped ringing, and I was alone with my family. I felt drained, exhausted; my ribs were throbbing. Suddenly there was a knock on the door. My sister opened it, and there stood the guru. I realized I did not even know his name.

"How are you, my friend?" he asked. "What is this I hear: that you have killers after you? You must be an important man, after all."

"No, sir, just lucky," I said. "Someone up there likes me."

He introduced himself as Dr. Brahm Vasudevan. He had been a professor of interfaith studies at an American university, he said. Had retired ten years ago, and returned to India to start a meditation center, which, eventually, grew into an ashram. He did not know how this had happened and did not care to analyze it. According to him, it was God's will, His plan. He held out his hand to me. A bowl wrapped in cling film. "This is our special kheer," he said. "We make it at the ashram. Have it later; you will like it." I realized that he had dressed up for the visit. He was wearing a white, long-sleeved shirt and a rich silk lungi.

He started telling us how difficult it had been to start a meditation center. Just when the place was ready and he had admitted his first batch of students, a temple from a neighboring plot had begun to blare bhajans. On making inquiries, he found that the plot belonged to a local politician, who later called him and asked him to buy out his temple. The price quoted was exorbitant, but he had no option. The volume at which the songs were played would have made meditation impossible. And it was not even a proper temple, just a shed with some obscure deity.

But today the politician was his disciple, he said. That's because there were millions of people coming to the ashram, and the politician wanted to project himself as a religious man. "You should come and see the work we are doing," he said to my parents. "The ashram is run on gobar gas, in our fields we use only natural fertilizers, and we employ hundreds of men and train hundreds of women, including unwed mothers and widows." Then, rising to his feet, he said, "I just came to see my friend here. To see if he was okay and give him some prasad. It's time for my prayers now; I should be going." He came to my bedside, placed a hand on my forehead, and said, "You will sleep well tonight. The worst is over."

After he left, a sweet lemony fragrance filled the room, and a golden light, as though the sun had left behind its parting rays. My father said, "Nice man – genuine – I liked him." My sister remarked that he didn't seem like a guru, he was a rather cool guy.

At half past eight, my dinner was wheeled in: a cauliflower-and-broccoli bake, with salad, bacon-stuffed mushrooms, and garlic bread. There was also a cheesecake, on which was inscribed in raspberry sauce: *Wishing you a safe recovery*.

I gave the cheesecake to my sister and reached for the kheer. It was delicious: soft and creamy and full of almonds, pistachios, and raisins.

At half past nine, my family members left, and at ten o'clock a nurse arrived and gave me my medicines. Soon after, I dozed off.

In my sleep, I dreamed that I was nineteen and at a beach, a long way from home. There was a girl with me, around my age. We checked into a shack, one of those rent-by-the-day places, with nothing more than a bed, a fan, and a toilet. There, we made love and lost track of time. We broke for lunch, a seafood thali. Then, we smoked a joint and fucked some more.

It was well after sunset by the time we emerged. Seeing the beach empty, my girlfriend panicked. It seemed that her father was a strict disciplinarian; he wouldn't understand about her being late. We asked around and were told by the locals that the next bus was due after an hour but it could be cancelled. So I flagged down a cab and told the driver to take us into town.

Along the way, my friend was silent, thinking about her father. I reached for her hand and found her fingers ice-cold. I fell silent too, because I was worried about how I would pay for the long cab ride. After paying for the shack and the lunch, I did not have much money left.

It took us an hour and a half to reach town. I dropped my friend off, and she was so relieved that she rushed off without saying goodbye. I then took the cab to Chowpatty, where, outside a college, I asked the cabbie to wait, saying that I needed to collect a suitcase before carrying on with my journey. Then in through one gate and out through another, a side exit, while the poor cabbie waited for his fare. A fare he would never see.

And then a switch went off in my brain and I saw myself in recent times.

I was in a jungle, walking behind the boss and his wife, both in khaki fatigues. The boss was smiling, his wife was frowning, and through the foliage I saw a family of gorillas walking alongside. They were just a few feet away from us.

One of the gorillas turned and looked at me with red inflamed eyes. In a flash, he came charging, bouncing on webbed feet, his shoulders heaving, his nostrils flared. Trees gave way like straws, bushes flattened. He came up to me and started sniffing, his long-clawed paws resting on my shoulders. I stood still, very still, frozen by his hot breath and pungent body odor. The boss and his wife: they continued walking.

Then the gorilla wrapped his arms around my ribs and began to squeeze. One of his claws dug into my chest, deeper and deeper, till it pierced the skin and entered my lung. I couldn't breathe, couldn't scream, I was paralyzed. When I looked up, I saw it was the cabbie, not the one I had ditched outside the college gates, the old man with the tired eyes and sunken cheeks, but my recent enemy, my nemesis – and he was smiling, a gloating kind of a smile.

Just then my eyes opened and I saw that the bandage around my ribs had loosened. I could breathe again, breathe long, deep gulps of air. I reached for the napkin on the headboard and wiped my brow. Then I drifted off again, fell into a deep dreamless sleep.

The next day, after my morning physiotherapy, I was told that I could wheel myself onto the balcony and onto the terrace. I had never felt more elated. The sun was high in the sky and its rays fell on the water, making it sparkle like gold dust. Was there any limit to this beauty? I wondered. My work, my accident, and the attempted assault: it all seemed so far away. Seemed purged from my mind, like remote memories. The waves lapped playfully against the rocks, and I tried to sync my breathing to the sound. In the distance were the three sentinels of the city: two Hindu temples and a Muslim dargah, lofty against the morning sky.

A voice behind me murmured, "Hospitals and temples exist for the same reason: they are great places to cleanse yourself."

I turned to the smiling face of Dr. Brahm Vasudevan. He was sitting in a wheelchair, wearing a lungi. A shawl covered the upper half of his body. There was no sign of ill-health on him. He looked powerful and muscular, like a king who had come to inspect his kingdom.

"And what is *your* reason to be here?" I asked. "I know I am late in asking."

He shrugged. I noticed he was holding a lit cigarette in his hand. No, wait; it was too thick to be a cigarette. Damn, yes! – it *was* a joint. A marijuana joint.

He held it out to me. "Good for compressed lungs," he said. "We grow it at the ashram. One more reason to visit, huh. Unless, of course, you prefer hospitals."

I took the joint and inhaled cautiously. Seeing my hesitation, he laughed. "You still don't trust my prasad?" he asked.

I laughed. "I don't know about this one, but the kheer was very good; I enjoyed it immensely. Although it did some strange things to me at night."

"Nothing you might not have done to yourself," he said smiling.

I nodded. How did he know what I had figured out through my dreams? The dots, the gaps, the cause and effect, the action and reaction, specifically, the payback of my old bad karma. But then these gurus have their secrets. After years of meditation, they develop special intuition.

I pulled at the joint, savoring the rich stream of smoke that filled my mouth. It was the first touch of normalcy I had experienced since my hospitalization. The first sign that life, regular life, would resume shortly.

"You asked me why I am here," said the guru. "It's for the love of my disciples. They are worried about me because, these days, I don't sleep at night, sometimes not for five nights in a row; and they feel it has something to do with my health." He took the joint I held out. Seeing me glance furtively at the entrance, he said, "Don't worry; no one will come here. I have told them we are going to be meditating, that we should not be disturbed."

He took a drag of the joint, then continued. "So I agreed to get admitted and go through some tests, and it turns out that my heart rate is extremely low. I will need a pacemaker to keep me going; it will extend my warranty by a few years. And *that* could be one reason for my being here. The other being that I *was* fated to meet you."

I gazed at the ocean, a sparkling white bowl of eternity, sparkling with a million eyes, a million secrets, and I thought this is where it begins, my journey toward the spiritual. Not what is right or wrong or what I cannot change, like my bosses' attitude toward their employees. But what I most certainly can: my own karmic fuck-ups!

"Well," I said to Dr. Vasudevan. "If you are growing weed like this at the ashram, then you are definitely my man. As long as we are clear this is what it is all about."

Mind Over Matter

When Ramesh Malpani, racing magnate, film financier, takeover tycoon, and a lover of all things unattainable, gave up the back seat of his Mercedes Maybach and hoisted himself into the driver's seat, taking care to adopt the stoic expression of a chauffeur and the starched white uniform and cap that went with it, no one was surprised at his departure from normalcy. Not his friends at the racecourse, nor the scriptwriters and film directors who came to him begging for breaks, nor his family members who had long back given up trying to fathom his mercurial mind, least of all his real chauffeur, who, under the new arrangement, found himself transferred to the back seat of the Mercedes, fitted in a Versace suit and Burlington tie, holding a business magazine that made no sense to him.

"Overstressed!" exclaimed Jan Pastakia, executive secretary of the Greater Mumbai Racing Club, who, just that morning, at the club entrance, had been witness to the new arrangement. Jan said this sympathetically, digging her bony white teeth into a copious club sandwich, cleverly avoiding contact with her artfully painted lips.

"Genes," whispered Johnny Malingham, part of the same circle of billionaire punters. Johnny preferred to be frugal in his opinion; he expended most of his fury in the Bombay High Court, where he was known to be something of a genius, bringing judges and opponents into his web of verbal intrigue, his thrust and parry of shrewd God-given logic. Johnny's declaration implied that he'd stumbled upon the history of the Malpani family, and he knew something about Ramesh Malpani which the others didn't. But his tone was such that he was not to be questioned, he was not to be asked to elaborate. Johnny could afford such airs. He charged twenty-five thousand rupees an hour to deliver his addresses in court, to set his verbal traps delicately and insidiously, invariably at great profit to himself. In fact, Johnny never looked you in the eye. To do so was to admit to an equality he did not believe in.

"Renunciation," beamed Muktanand Swami, master of Kalyug-Yoga and fiery-eyed protagonist of the "say-no-to-life's-pleasures" school of thought, the austere part of this august gathering. Swamiji liked to spend his evenings at the racing club. He liked the open air, the cool breeze, the various shades of green that sprang around the race track. He liked watching groups of elderly men and women walking briskly and talking animatedly and young boys and girls jogging, sweat dripping from their toned, overheated bodies. He particularly enjoyed the cheese pakodas and the chili cheese toast that the club served as part of its evening menu. Swamiji was in a particularly expansive mood that day, for one of his disciples, Sushilkumar Maldaar, had expressed a desire to open an ashram for him in Darien, Connecticut. There would be a trust to manage the ashram and to take care of Swamiji's expenses when he visited the U.S. No more would Swamiji have to depend on the hospitality of rich Indians; no more would he have to settle into their guest rooms, looked upon, by their children, as some kind of a freak. Sushilkumar said they'd have to wait for clearances from the Indian government before transferring the funds; the formalities could be long and tedious, but he could short-circuit them if he had Swamiji's blessings, his sanction to grease palms and spread a little wealth around.

"The mind removes all barriers for the spiritual man," Swamiji had said to Sushilkumar, smiling. "And God expresses himself in many ways, mostly through man." Sushilkumar had bowed deferentially. He understood the status Swamiji was conferring on him. And for that he was grateful.

"Communism! It's a sign that it's here to stay," said Purobit Roy, chief executive of Kolkata Carats, his big black eyes gleaming with utopian fervor as he contemplated the ludicrous swap-act of Ramesh Malpani. But withering glances from the rest of the gathering told him that such loose thoughts about Mumbai's elite weren't to be entertained in this circle. What did a man have if not his self-esteem, his awareness of a superior hierarchy among God's people? And the communists were not known to support this kind of thinking. In this day and age of unbridled capitalism, they were considered spoilers. Purobit better understand that and fall in line. Otherwise, there was a provision that a guest was allowed admission to the club only three times a month. That rule could be invoked to keep him out of the circle. Purobit smiled nervously and said "Just joking!" drumming away on the handrest of his armchair.

"Misunderstood," sighed the wistful-eyed Lulu Aranha from deep inside her spinster-soft heart. No one bothered to ask her *how misunderstood*, thereby snuffing out the chances of a three hundred and sixty-fifth recital on how only *she*, with her intuitive charm, could fathom the quirky motivations of the rich and the famous. After all, she, Lulu, had grown up with them, played with them, dirtied her hands in the sands of their sprawling seaside bungalows in Juhu, then curled up in a hammock, the sound of the waves gurgling in her ears. This was when Juhu was not yet a developed suburb, it was merely a picnic spot and a location for film shoots.

These were more or less the responses at the Greater Mumbai Racing Club, a place where nothing surprised people anymore, a place immunized by its very location to shocks and upsets, to earthquakes of providence that saw winners lose by a distance and losers romp home, uncontested. The real consequences of Ramesh Malpani's quixotic act were felt by his employees: the clerks, accountants, executives, and managers, who watched, with growing unease, their boss's mental slide. Of course, there had been signs of this decay, some early signs....

Once a week, for instance, Bossman Malpani would make them sit on the ledges outside their office windows, so that they'd see how uncertain the future was, how transitory, and they'd realize why their salaries were delayed sometimes and why their bonuses were unexpectedly withdrawn. Business was like that, he would say firmly, as mercurial as the weather, as unpredictable as life.

And merely a month ago, he had made them take a meditation course in the office, over the weekend, where they were asked to concentrate on the untapped powers of the human mind. All through the day, the employees had to deny themselves food, water, and the call of nature. Bossman Malpani felt they'd bring this grit to their work. It would give them the will to work beyond office hours, to sit through meetings that stretched endlessly. Not surprisingly, his employees had chosen to meditate, instead, on various ways they could dispense with him. But such sweet thoughts could flourish only in dreams, not in reality, although they did become inviting when the employees were stuck with a bill for the course. Five thousand rupees for learning about self-control.

At the turn of the year, Bossman Malpani threw a party. He invited all his employees and their spouses to a lavish dinner, where a feast of international cuisines was unfurled. Just before the guests could dig in, Bossman Malpani put on a video of his vision for the new year, a four-hour-long address that made them feel trapped at first, then sleepy and surly, and which earned them the ire of their spouses, who were not used to eating dinner in the wee hours of the morning. Ironically, Bossman Malpani disappeared after the video was switched on. He was seen the next morning in the *Bombay Times*, a dark, fat man with an oversized belly and stubborn jowls; he was seen eating, drinking, and carousing elsewhere. The cost for the dinner was deducted from the salaries of the employees, and the explanation was that he wanted them to feel a shared sense of responsibility in the company's future, and that any employee who failed to see it likewise was free to resign.

With a series of loony acts to his credit, Malpani's latest caper brought forth exclamations of the "final flip," considering that all employees were now asked to take orders from the smiling, suit-clad Arangatal Kayasthami, the naïve-eyed chauffeur, who attributed his changed destiny to Lord Thirunghatam, the Lord of Delicious Irony, in whose name he had performed a three-day puja while on vacation in his village in south India.

The puja, it appeared, had worked marvelously. Bossman Malpani had started eating out of Arangatal's hand. So much so, that the bossman did not merely trade places with Arangatal, he also traded clothes, duties, manners of speech, airs, accent, bankbooks, and credit cards. The boss jumped to attention when he saw Arangatal; he publicly held open doors for him; he carried out boxes of clothes, shoes, and sweetmeats, which Arangatal bought on a new unchecked credit allowance; and he waited patiently, outside restaurants, while Arangatal dined with his wife, the voluptuous, erumpent Mrs. Malpani, eyeing, in between mouthfuls, her sloping, mountainous breasts, her corpulent lips, her manicured, diamond-studded fingers, the fleshy folds of her neck.

Arangatal was convinced that Lord Thirunghatam had given him the power to hypnotize and control whomsoever he wanted, that he shared a secret pact with his Lord, who had singled him out for a special destiny.

Therefore, he never took seriously the two men who came up to him at a traffic signal, who pointed their pistols at him, who sneered and said this is what he got for not listening to their advice, and who shot him through his Versace suit, once, twice, thrice.

And as Arangatal's body slumped forward in the back seat and his blood darkened the plush gray seat, Ramesh Malpani, looking through the mirror and pretending to incredulous, tremulous shock, did a quick mental calculation on the replacement cost for the upholstery. The back seat, the carpet, and a little compensation for Arangatal's family, who, he thought, would have to be told about the hazards of driving in Mumbai: the jams, the potholes, and the constant pitting of wills, which led to a snapping of nerves and to accidents like these. But that apart, it would be a lot less taxing, he thought, than the whopping huge amount he would have had to pay had he taken the extortionist's calls seriously, had he paid up without using his mind, endangering his reputation as the master of uncompromising wealth.

"Mind," said Muktanand Swami, to the same circle of billionaires, "is that phenomenon of nature as close to nature as nature itself. It sweeps like an irreverent force, to heal or to destroy, like wind, water, and fire. It is attracted unfailingly to matter, to all that the senses can see, smell, and savor. In this age of Kalyug, it is to be seen if the mind can be used to control matter or whether matter will consume the mind, eventually."

The rest of the gathering fell silent. To them it was obvious that Ramesh Malpani had lived by using his mind while Arangatal had died by filling it with all sorts of high ideas about himself. And so, what was common between these two was a love for matter, a love for the good things in life, which must be desired, pursued, owned, and fought over. The question was, what was more important: Mind or matter? And were they mutually exclusive, as some holy books would have us believe? Or were they in cahoots, companionable twins, as per some inexplicable law of nature? Or were they like husband and wife, locked in a churlish marriage, each testing the other's capacity for endurance? Or were they simply nature's conspiracy to keep us perishable when our time came? Fallible within ourselves, dispensable within our milieu?

None in the circle were sure of closing in on the answers. Not Jan Pastakia who, when placed in charge of the club repairs, claimed a slice of the pie from the contractor. Not Johnny Malingham, who seeking ways to harmonize his bank account with his brilliance, contemplated settlements between warring parties at some advantage to himself. Not Purobit Roy, who launching a new line of jewelry in the sparkle-thirsty Mumbai market, had settled on a grade of diamonds the Belgian market would find offensive. Nor Lulu Aranha, who saw her taut, well-toned body as a means to seduce captains of industry, proving herself mistress of their minds.

Not even Muktanand Swami was sure if he had the answer, for his own mind – disciplined as it was by satvic food and celibacy – seemed to be drifting, to verdant Connecticut, to the lush, rolling woods of Darien.

And so they all searched for the answers, and they grappled with the burden of their own lives – mind versus matter – how much to absorb, how much to throw out – to each their own limits of indulgence; call it survival, at the best of times, or call it being practical. And yet, every Sunday, the horses would thunder in and the same crowd that would applaud the jockey for winning would jeer him for losing. It did not matter whether he had lost by an inch or by a yard or by a hair's breadth. They would hiss vengeance at him, wreak curses on his head – *Bastard, you have eaten our money; you are building a house at our expense; you'd sell your own mother if you could, you scoundrel!* And the jockey's wiry little body would cringe with shame and his shoulders would droop and his legs would quiver, astride the warm, trembling animal he led in. But in the next race he'd be their hero. *Saala! What a rider! What a genius! Did you see the way he took that bend?* After all, where there were human beings, there was always hope of acceptance, always hope of redemption. And the only one constant in all this would be Ramesh Malpani, he in his box, clean-shaven and suited, a hat on his head, a cigar between his teeth, his binoculars raised and smiling, his sights firmly on the finishing line.

Something to Think About

THE BUILDER'S OFFER CAME in good time. I was broke, terrifically broke, having run through the royalties on my last book and my next book a few months away from completion. So when Friend Pramod, who had lost his job at the bookstore and was trying to set himself up as a literary agent, suggested that I meet the builder, I did not refuse. The bank balance showed an alarming low, and the builder had an offer in mind that could change that.

A thundering Mumbai local delivered me to Sewri, where the builder had his office. He had set up a two-story structure in the compound of an old defunct mill. The mill was in ruins; it had crumbling walls, broken windows, tall, rusted chimneys, and large, empty warehouses. In the distance, on a clear patch of land, some construction work was going on, and I assumed that the tall gray tower that presided over the neighborhood belonged to the builder.

We took a narrow staircase that led to the builder's office. Pramod whispered at my shoulder that there were only two offices on that floor: one occupied by the builder; the other, by his son. The father and son also shared a secretary. Their staff was housed on the ground floor, jammed into small white cubicles with florescent lighting.

The builder was a non-resident Indian from Dubai. He was into construction, hotels, infrastructure, and international trading. His was quite a success story, said Pramod. Virtually rags to riches. His son was U.S.-educated.

From which university? I asked. But Pramod said he did not know.

The builder's secretary was a dark, heavily built woman with thick, flabby arms and curly hair. She sat at a semi-circular desk, answering phone calls in a cultivated voice. Picking up the receiver, she informed her boss that "Mr. Pramod and his writer-friend" had arrived. Promptly, we were ushered in.

No sooner had I stepped into the builder's office than I was met with a barrage of expletives. Behenchod! Gaelchodya! Madarchod! Chutiya! A tall, slim man stood over his desk, grinning affably. He appeared to be in his mid-sixties and had a full crop of hair which was noticeably dyed. I wondered what I had done to merit such compliments when he clarified. "You are a Parsee," he exclaimed. "I love Parsees. I can be myself with them."

I wanted to tell him that I wasn't one of those Parsees from whose mouth swear words flow naturally. But he looked so delighted with his icebreaker that I thought I should not disappoint him.

He asked us what we would like to drink: Tea or coffee? We opted for two cappuccinos. He buzzed his secretary, gave her the order, and asked her to send his son in. She replied that he was in a meeting with the municipal commissioner and had asked not to be disturbed.

"Wah!" said the builder, still speaking into the intercom. "The municipal commissioner is here and no one even informs me. I think I should retire. There is no work for me, it seems." He looked at us with twinkling eyes. The secretary laughed and said she would send in "sir" as soon as he had finished his meeting.

The builder began to talk about his son. He had a civil engineering degree from MIT and a major in construction management from Virginia Tech. He had been raised in Dubai, and then gone to the U.S. for his grad and post-grad studies. But he was more Indian than anyone born here. He loved Indian food, Indian music, Indian films, and enjoyed visiting temples and pilgrimage sites. He was only twenty-four but already conceptualizing projects of his own. He had one planned in Goa, one in Kochi, and was starting with one in Mumbai. But he was naive, said the builder. He did not know how things worked here: the red tape, the corruption, the wheels within wheels, which could send your top spinning. So, when they'd first arrived from Dubai, he would send his son to the building proposals' department to get permissions. There were forty departments there, ranging from fire safety, water, and electrical to sanitation and environment. Your file could be stuck for months unless you knew how to lubricate palms and fast-track matters. Other builders had agents and touts doing this full-time, but he wanted his son to get a first-hand taste of Indian bureaucracy. The municipal commissioner, visiting them in their office, proved how well the boy had done. Oh yes, he was proud of his son, who was now overseeing the entire project himself. He paused and asked us if we knew what the project was.

We nodded *no*. Pramod tried to make some excuse saying he had tried to log on to their website but was unable to do so. "It's under construction," said the builder. "We don't want to give away too much information yet. Besides, most of our sales will happen anyway, by word of mouth." He was seated in his chair and swiveling from side to side. I could see that he was restless, he had the nervous energy of a go-getting businessman. Also, he was remarkably fit for his age.

He began. Kedia Celestial was a 50-story building where each of the flats would be designed like a villa, with its own swimming pool, terrace garden, gym, mini theater, and Jacuzzi. The apartments would be spacious, with a carpet area of 4500 square feet. "Nothing like this has been built in Mumbai before," he said, brimming with feathery pride.

Then he came to the point of our visit. His son wanted to commission a book on his life, which would capture his journey from being a small-time trader to an upscale builder. In Dubai, he had built hotels, IT parks, stadiums, theaters, and would shortly build a world-class township. He said he was very close to the rulers of Dubai, he even got invited to their homes on Bakri Eid. But when they visited him on Diwali, he would request them to leave their footwear outside the door and they would comply. No one did that to the sheikhs, he said. No one would have the guts to.

I asked him how he had come to achieve this closeness, and he said, "Good question. You see, I was the one who gave the sheikhs the idea of transplanting trees and introducing drip irrigation when the place was a desert, an arid wasteland. I grew up in a village in Rajasthan, where we got water only once a week. We had to buy the water and bring it back in tankers, and sometimes the tankers got attacked, the water was stolen, and our men got killed. I lost two uncles that way. So I figured that this element called water owed me a living. And when I set up drip irrigation plants for the sheikhs and they saw the change in their surroundings, they started giving me more projects. They opened up bigger opportunities for me and even helped with the finance."

I asked him why he had returned to India when he had such lucrative business prospects in Dubai and the support of the rulers. He said he wanted to raise living standards here. Life had been kind to him, and now it was his turn to contribute to his motherland.

I asked him whether, as a builder, he had any political patronage. At this, he laughed and said he had never faced any trouble. Not from the authorities, nor from the locals.

"Give me a few minutes and I will illustrate why," he said, smiling and rising to his feet. He disappeared into a small room at the side. The door to the room was invisible, lost in a facade of smooth, vertical panels.

Moments later, he reappeared. I could barely recognize him. He was wearing a brown leather jacket, snug-fitting shades, and a thick belt with a studded buckle. The transformation was uncanny. He looked years younger, and somewhat dashing, like a Bollywood star.

"This is how I show myself in the neighborhood," he said. "I stand outside my site and abuse my engineers loudly. Abuses learned from my Parsee friends. I say to them if they were in Dubai I would have them killed, have them buried alive. Sometimes, I even cuff them on the ears and deliver a kick or two. This way people think I have an underworld connection. And no one tries to fuck with me."

"Secondly," he said, "I am very close to RP, and I let this connection be known to all." RP was a politician of dubious origins. He was known to be a thug and an extortionist.

Seeing my strained expression, he asked, "It seems you have heard things about RP?"

"Well," I said. "RP's reputation does precede him; no one has a good word to say about him. I spend time at the press club, so I hear things … not quite encouraging."

"No, no, you misunderstand him, and I can't say I blame you. RP is the most misunderstood man on earth. It is the media and his political rivals who have painted him as a villain. I am not saying he is beyond reproach. Politics is a dirty game, after all. You have to swim with the sharks, and sometimes you've got to become a shark yourself. But, on a personal level, RP is a principled man. Trust me on this."

A snapshot went off in my head: of RP at the book launch and me in a photograph with him. I shuddered. I would never again be able to write about corruption, extortion, the usurpation of green zones, and the murder of civic activists, all that RP was capable of.

"Do you know," said the builder, "when we go for a vacation overseas, RP never allows me to pay? He foots the whole bill himself. For me and my family. Right from our air tickets down to our accommodation and food."

"Well," I said, feeling the blood rush to my face, "has it occurred to you that someone else might be footing the bill? Some industrialist or businessman brought under pressure."

For a moment the builder looked annoyed. But he quickly collected himself and said, "RP never asks a favor of anyone, never! In my eight years of knowing him, not once has me asked me for anything. Not even a donation to his party or to his election campaign. If at all, he has only given, given with full heart. He is a self-made man, like me. He started as a TV mechanic, became a cable operator, and then a corporator. Look where he is today! He wields such influence, such power. And he is so protective of his friends, he will do anything for them. Also, he has a great sense of values." He looked at me intently. "You don't believe me, do you? Then listen to this. When we first became friends, RP said to me, 'Ramakant, if you ever commit a murder I will save you. You can kill anyone for all I care, because I know you will have a damn good reason. But should you place your hands on a woman, should you touch her without her consent, I will not spare you. I will personally destroy you.' That's how principled he is."

I was about to protest the logic of this when the door opened and a youth entered. He was dark-skinned, broad-chested, and athletically built, wearing a midnight blue T-shirt, skintight jeans, and long, brown boots. "Gentlemen!" said the builder. "My son, Shashikant Kedia, the brains and driving force behind Kedia Constructions."

Pramod jumped to his feet and handed Shashikant his visiting card with undue deference. I made a mental note to chide him about this later.

Shashikant sat in a chair beside his father and said, "Nice to meet you fellas. Shashikant was a tactless error on the part of my parents. I assure you I have nothing of the cunt in me. So call me, Shashi, okay?" He smiled at us, as though – like his father – he was proud of his opening lines. His accent was unmistakably American; it had that slight drawl.

"Your father was just telling us ..." I began.

"About how he worked in temperatures of 45 and 50 degrees Celsius, about how he had shared a room with eight colleagues, sleeping only when there was a bed vacant, because there were only five beds in the dorm?"

"Well, no," I said. "We haven't come around to his life yet. Your father was talking about you, mostly. Your initiation into the business here. And how you are making things happen."

"Dad!" said the young man, turning to his father. He spread his hands out in a gesture of resignation. "This meeting is not about me. This is about *your* book, *your* story."

"We haven't started talking about that yet," I said. "First, we will have to see if there *is* a story. A story strong enough to tell." At my side, I could feel Pramod's exasperation; this was not the way he'd have wanted to play it. This was not the time for writerly integrity. Clearly, we were there for the moolah. To enrich ourselves.

"*I* will tell you what that story is," said Shashikant, crossing his legs. He certainly had the confidence of a leader, I thought. I could picture him in boardrooms, taking important decisions, defining goals, setting targets, mapping out a strategy. I wondered how he had coped with the babus at the municipality, who were known to test every grain of patience.

He continued. "This is about a guy who came from a village with twenty rupees in his pocket. A guy whose mother sold her jewelry to get him to Dubai. Who, once there, could not speak to his parents because he could not afford a phone call home. And when his mother died, he did not know about it for weeks. He wasn't told, lest he chucks up his job and comes rushing back. This is about a guy who could not marry till he was forty because he was too busy building an empire, which, incidentally, is now valued at 1.2 billion dollars. That's what his story is. And wait! You should know that the same guy is going to build the Mall of the World. Now chew on that, guys."

We must have looked blank, for Shashikant proceeded to explain. "The Mall of the World will be the world's first climate-controlled city. Spread over fifty million square feet, it will have a glass dome and a cool climate nine months of the year. The dome will open only in December, when temperatures drop. Till then, the tourists won't even need to venture out. There will be enough for them to do. It will have the world's largest shopping center, a hundred different hotels and restaurants serving the best cuisines, a skiing lodge made out of artificial ice, and a cultural district designed along the lines of the West End in London, Broadway in New York, and Las Ramblas in Barcelona. You guys have been there, right?"

Pramod and I shook our heads. We felt small, ignorant, and inadequate.

"Okay," said Shashikant, sitting up in his chair. "So here is the story. *We* are the guys who are going to be in charge of this project. We, as a company, will execute the super-luxury, high-end parts of the project. We will appoint other contractors of course, bring in partners from the UK and Europe, but it will be Dad who will be the final decision-maker. The sheikhs have left it to him. Imagine what this means: building the world's first climate-controlled city. It's like creating history, inventing the future. It can't get any bigger than this."

"I agree," said Pramod, turning and looking at me. "This is as big as it gets. This is a story that needs to be told." He looked at me for approval, for endorsement. But I was poker-faced, noncommittal.

Shashikant leaned forward with his elbows on his knees. "Money is no problem, guys," he said softly. "Only, we need to get the book out in time for our company's twenty-fifth anniversary. Which is six months away, on December 3rd. Think you guys can manage that?"

"We shall certainly try," said Pramod eagerly, but I stayed him with my hand and said I would think about it, let them know in a couple of days. "Pramod will call you," I said, swigging back the last bit of my coffee, which had gone cold by now.

"Wait!" said Ramakant Kedia, as I got to my feet. He opened a drawer in his desk and drew out a wad of notes. There must have been at least one hundred thousand rupees there. He pushed this toward me and said, "Here is something to help you think. It's not an advance, just a small token. To say that I am happy to have met you and would like to meet again." He smiled at me warmly, with fatherly benevolence. I could see that he meant it. But before I could say anything, Pramod had reached out and pocketed the wad. He thanked the father, thanked Shashikant, and then we made our way out.

"I am not going to do it," I said to Pramod firmly, on our way to the railway station. "You can return the money. I don't need it. I have no doubt that he is genuine and that he has a story to tell. But his logic sucks. His opinion of RP, for instance, and that bullshit about murder being okay but not rape. That kind of thinking is seriously warped, it's totally fucked up. Also, I don't see myself getting excited about this Mall of the World business. It is absurd to think we can manipulate nature, that we can replicate climate as though we are gods."

A flush of anger appeared on Pramod's face. "What the fuck is wrong with you, bro?" he cried. "An opportunity like this drops in our laps and you want to blow it. I could tell the guy liked you. You can have him eating out of your hand. And this could be the beginning of something big, a nice profitable venture for us. I bet Ramakant Kedia has friends in high places; I bet he is hugely connected. Give him three chapters of the book and a structure and he will be all over you, wanting to open doors. Why, you might even get to write Sheikh Mohammed's biography. Think what a coup that can be! Think about it, Gussy, seriously. Sleep over it. You will see it differently tomorrow morning."

"I might, but my answer will still be the same," I said.

I felt sorry for Pramod, for I knew he needed work, needed the money. He had lost his job at the bookstore, and did not have any options. It was not his fault. Independent bookstores were just not doing enough business, and real estate, costing what it did in Mumbai, did not justify the investment. Pramod also had family problems. He lived with his parents, wife, and kids, in a two-bedroom apartment in Kalina. And he had stopped getting along with his wife, who frequently fought with his parents and abused them. She had also turned the kids against their father, and while the girl (the older of the two) still came to Pramod, the boy (who was only ten) viewed him with hostility. It was totally fucked up, you could say: Pramod's life. They had talked about divorce, had considered it, but she wanted the flat and fifty lakh rupees as a settlement. She was the reason for his diabetes, his hypertension, his anxiety attacks. And it did not help that she was always ready to remind him that he was a loser, a born loser, who preferred to escape into the world of books rather than deal with the reality of his own life. And she would say this in front of the kids and his parents, which broke Pramod and drove him into depression. If it weren't for his elderly parents and his kids, he'd have killed himself. I genuinely wanted to help him, but could not see myself writing about a man who was bosom pals with the insidious Mr. RP. That went against my grain.

Seeing that I was not prepared to listen, Pramod shifted tracks. He said that he would keep the money for a few days and, if I did not change my mind, he would return it. He sounded crushed, crestfallen. I knew he was thinking about his commission, the twenty grand he'd have to return. He walked away defeated, his shoulders hunched, a man going back to nothing. I felt bad for him. Felt I had failed him.

Over the next few days, I pushed further into my novel and made some progress. In between phases of writing, Ramakant Kedia kept creeping into my mind. I don't know what it was about him that had made a bigger impression on me than his son had. The boy was bright and ambitious but impractical. He had no idea what it took to write a book, to track a whole life and make it meaningful. It was not like building a false ceiling and creating a phony climate. It was not as though you could keep people trapped under a dome. Your intentions have to be genuine, your efforts sincere, your narration lucid, your conclusions precise. You have to get under the skin of your subject and blow people's minds. Blow their jocks off.

A week later, I got a call from Pramod. He was excited and speaking rapidly. "Have you seen the papers, man? Have you—? Check out *The Times*. The front page. Read and call me back."

I opened the newspaper and there it was. "New City Development Plan Foils Builder's Plan," screamed the headline. The article went on to say how an overpass would now go past Kedia Celestial and how the residents' views would be blocked. The overpass would be at two levels: one for incoming traffic, the other for outgoing; six lanes, either way. This would decongest the city and provide a long-term solution, said the municipal commissioner. So much for the terrace gardens, I thought. So much for those villas in the sky.

My thoughts turned to Ramakant Kedia. He was a non-resident Indian, accustomed to a reliable way of life. He had made his fortune under a system that recognized his talent and hard work, that had rewarded him for his ingenuity and given him a story worth recounting. What would he do now, what would his next move be? Would he ask RP for a favor? Pull strings in the corridors of power? Or would he contemplate a long delicious thought murder, as all of us citizens do, when our plans are thwarted? When something unexpected looms up in our lives. Like a skyscraper that blocks our air and sunlight or metro line work that disrupts our peace and schedule.

I began to feel sorry for this self-made tycoon and, particularly, for young Shashikant, who might have thought his education complete when he had waited outside the building proposals' department, waited endlessly at the mercy of some junior clerk with an itchy palm. I thought, perhaps, I could be a friend to them. Perhaps, I could make something of their lives. Give it flesh, substance, meaning. In the bargain, I could help Pramod, too. Get him a job with Kedia Constructions, help him move to Dubai, make some money, and gain his freedom.

Thus inspired, I called up Pramod and told him that I *would* be doing the book. I would like to document the builder's struggles, his quest for an easier life.

The Lady at the Bank

I DON'T KNOW WHY I hated her the way I did, but I did. Maybe it was because the first time I approached her, she was feeding a cat out of her lunch box. What was a cat doing in a bank? I wondered. And why was the lady having lunch during banking hours? All I wanted to do was collect a new checkbook and she was in charge of issuing that. But instead of attending to my request, she seemed more inclined to feed the cat, who sat at her feet with a bored, haughty expression. From time to time, the cat would open its mouth in a yawn, and the lady would bend down to feed it, then use the same hand to scoop food out of her lunch box and eat. God, it was disgusting! I thought, feeling the first stirrings of dislike.

The United National Bank was where I'd had an account ever since I started working. Yes, it was ten years since I had begun my life as a content writer and seen my savings grow, diversifying into investments like fixed deposits and mutual funds. It was my grandfather who had opened the account for me, depositing a princely fifty-one rupees. "Good luck be with you," he had said, handing me a passbook, a checkbook, and smiling in that knowing way of his. I was very close to my grandfather, a tall regal man of remarkable dignity, who advised me to always live within my means. By minimizing his needs and keeping himself free of anger (what he called "toxic emotions"), my grandfather had lived till the age of ninety-six. So my relationship with the bank wasn't based on service, more on sentiment, I should say.

There were no great reasons to prefer this bank over any other. Its interiors spoke of neglect, the paint on the walls had faded, the plaster showed in places, and it hadn't changed its furniture in years. There was an automated teller machine that seldom worked. And the old printer squeaked plaintively while printing out passbook entries in a faint, almost illegible type. The print quality was so poor that every year my accountant would throw up his hands in exasperation and exclaim, "How am I to discern these entries? How am I to prepare your tax returns? Why can't your bank provide you a decent printout?"

I would bring this to the attention of the manager, who would be contrite and apologetic. "What to do, sir?" he would say. "I am asking the management every time for a new printer, but they say there is no budget. And I am giving them deposits worth sixty crore rupees every year. You tell me, sir, what am I to do?" His eyes would dim with shame, and he would look at me beseechingly. Poor man, I would think. The understanding he cannot get from his management, he expects from me.

The manager's cabin had a glass partition that was covered with posters of various schemes. In loud splashy colors, the posters invited customers to purchase new homes, new cars, to apply for education loans, small business loans, health insurance, and loans against shares. "The one-stop bank for all your needs," said one poster. Another claimed: "We don't build assets, we build relationships." The worst thing about this bank was the queue at the cash withdrawal counter. Invariably, long and slow-moving.

I really don't know why I hated her with the intensity I did, but I did. Maybe it was because she gave the cat priority over me, an old customer short on time, shorter still on patience. Maybe it was something about her appearance and manner: her dowdy sari; her languid walk; her attachment to her lunch box, which she carried in a possessive sort of a way; her look of sullen boredom when speaking to customers; and her delight at chatting with colleagues. Still, that did not give me the right to feel the way I did.

One day, I came upon her at the cash withdrawal counter discussing, with a colleague, the events of a popular TV serial. Behind me, senior citizens and other customers waited. There was no air-conditioning where we stood, no place to sit, either. In between chatting with her colleague and attending to customers, she would nibble at a vada dipped in a thick, white chutney. Then, she would wipe her chutney-stained fingers against the rim of the plate. When it was my turn to collect the cash, I saw her raise a forefinger to her tongue, lick it, and squeeze out rupee notes from a tightly packed bundle.

That was it! I lost control. Raising my voice, I screamed at her, "You are abusing Laxmi, the Goddess of Wealth. You are being disrespectful to the Goddess who resides in these notes, she who sanctifies them!" I repeated myself twice and enjoyed seeing her discomfort. I continued to berate her till someone in the queue suggested that I should let it pass, she had learned her lesson. But I was not so sure. Under her lowered gaze, I saw her resentment, and knew that my hostility was now mutually reciprocated.

On this particular morning, I arrive at the bank in a tearing hurry; I had to make an urgent cash withdrawal before leaving for work. And, pray, what do I see?

The "deposits" and "withdrawal" counters are empty. The women are seated at their desks, with their backs to their computers. The men are standing or leaning against their desks. From the center of the bank, in an open space, the manager is addressing his staff, who have stopped working and are listening to him, enrapt.

The manager is all charged up. He is a short, stocky man with a delicate swell of belly. His clothes are neat;

his shirtsleeves are buttoned all the way down to his wrists. His tie, a vivid red and green, stands out, like a table napkin, against the white of his shirt. At the side stands a tall, hefty security guard holding a raised cell phone, filming the manager as he speaks.

The manager, it seems, has attended a meeting with his bosses, the details of which he is sharing with his staff. "So the management speaks to me about customer service," he says. "They want us to be number one; among all banks we should lead. And I say to them, why customer service? That is the right of every customer. The minute you become a customer, do you not automatically have a right to service? I say to them, now the time has come to talk about 'customer delight' and 'customer retention.' Because why be number one, if we are not going to stay there?" His eyes gleam with achievement and, on cue, his staff applauds.

Satisfied, he continues, "They, the management, tell me that they want to appoint relationship managers in every branch, and that I should decide who among you will make the best relationship managers. And I say to them, sorry, I can't do that, because in *my* branch every employee *is* a relationship manager. He or she knows the value of every customer; we make every customer feel special, feel at home." Suddenly, he raises his hands and says to the customers present, "Come, sir, madam, tell me, am I not right? Do you not feel this is *your* bank? That *you* are the owners, and *we* are your humble servants?" The customers nod politely, and the manager beams proudly. At this point I look around, and my eyes fall upon her, my pet aversion. She is standing a few feet away, chewing on a paratha roll. Edging closer, I whisper, "Madam, I need to make an urgent cash withdrawal. Can you please do it for me?"

She stays me with wrinkled fingers while she finishes chewing. Then she looks at me distastefully and says, "Hush, can't you see? Sahib is speaking. He is saying important things. We cannot interrupt him. We cannot be rude. Let him finish. Then I will help you."

And then I knew. It was not so much her I disliked as it was the bleak apathy that had settled into the face and body language of every person who had worked too long in our sahib-dominated culture, who took their bosses as their gods, their customers as their burden, and their jobs as an imposition that threw up their shortcomings. It was a face I would see often. At the police station, where I went to report loud blaring street music and ear-shattering fireworks on Diwali. At the electricity board, where I went to protest illegal connections in my neighborhood or an inflated bill. At the municipality, where I went to bemoan a water problem or an illegal encroachment, and where I was advised to tolerate, to adjust.

"Adjust" was a word that crept up with alarming frequency in my overpopulated country. It would forgive every aberration, soothe every inconvenience, take the conflict out of every dispute, and build bridges where none could exist.

Having understood that now, understood clearly, I nodded at the lady with conspiratorial ease. And she: she looked at me as though she was sizing me up, deciding whether I was worth her next move. Then, she dipped into her lunch box, rolled up a paratha, daubed a little pickle onto it, and held it out to me, saying, "Come, have! You will like it. I made it myself."

I looked at her stained fingers and hesitant face and said, "Thank you, madam. But I have just had a bumper breakfast. I am very full. Thank you."

She thought for a moment, then said, "You are lucky. I can never eat bumper. Not allowed to. I have diabetes, you see. Very high sugar. Insulin twice a day. Sometimes thrice. So I have to eat at regular intervals. Only small amounts. Every few hours."

Mental About Mumbai

IT WAS AN ANGRY woman, Kitayun Alwa, who stepped onto Marine Drive, seeking relief from an issue that had played on her mind all day. Her beloved Mumbai was threatened by an underground metro which would strip it clean of five thousand trees. From flowering gulmohars to sturdy banyans, some of these were a hundred years old and as much a part of the city's heritage as its Gothic and art deco structures. By removing the trees, the underground water table would be affected, the risk of floods would increase. Had the city planners gone mad? she wondered. Had they forgotten that terrible flood of 2005, when the city had received, over two days, ninety-four centimeters of rain? The highways had been flooded, the airports had been closed, railway platforms and tracks had disappeared underwater. In parts of the city, the water level had risen to fifteen feet. Trees had fallen, walls and fences had come crashing down, cars had turned turtle, and a landslide had swept away a hundred lives: slum-dwellers, living in shanties, at the foot of a hill. The city planners should know, when it came to floods, Mumbai had a history, or rather, a propensity.

She had brooded all day, thinking, if it had happened before, it could happen again. And she had called to mind that poet who'd said: the great tragedy of human existence is not that we suffer but that we forget. Truly! Truly! The amputations were there for all to see. Hapless stumps and spidery roots, evidence of daylight murders, extending from Princess Street to Churchgate, all the way up to Cuffe Parade.

She had hurried past the stumps, aware of a growing lump in her throat, aware of a rising bilious rage. Heart pounding, she had stepped onto Marine Drive, hoping the sea breeze would assuage her anger. The promenade had never failed her. It was here that Kitayun walked every evening, in track pants and sports shoes. Daily she would clock three kilometers, noting the different walking styles of people, and trying to figure out, by their manner of stride, their state of mind. *Were they stressed or relaxed? Disgruntled or happy? Insular or friendly?* This was one of the games she played with herself, and it was childishly liberating. At other times, she would eavesdrop on passing conversations, trying to gauge, by the pronunciation of the speakers, their community.

The promenade was, perhaps, the only place in Mumbai where life ceased to be agitated, where you were reminded, instantly, that nature could prevail over concrete, regardless of what was happening in the city. Walking here had been Kitayun's routine for years, and despite the pressing duties of the day, it was strictly non-negotiable.

Sometimes, she would pause and watch the sunset. And just the sight of that bright flaming orb taking its leave of the city was enough to inspire deep feelings of awe.

And today she was in good time. Turning onto the drive, she saw the blazing ball of fire in the sky. And then, before her, the sadhu lying naked on his back. Yes, brazenly naked.

She looked around, her eyes craving support. This can't be possible, she thought. But there he was, spread out shamelessly, along the parapet, his palms over his chest, his nunu hidden in a fuzz of gray. Did anyone share her outrage? she wondered. Did anyone feel as furious?

Looking around, in the same line of vision, she saw two cops, a man and a woman, both very young and relaxed. Seated on the parapet, they were laughing and chatting; for all you know, they could have been romancing. And farther down, standing on the parapet with their backs to the sea, were a group of boys and girls posing for selfies.

What was this selfie mania? she wondered. People were taking pictures all the time. They couldn't walk a few steps without taking a snapshot. She had been seeing this for months. Friends hugging like lost-and-found siblings. Families posing like exuberant tourists. Girls pouting like debutants in a movie. And, oh, the one she hated most: people crouching and sticking out their fingers in a "V". V for vanity, V for validation, she would snicker in her mind.

Come to think of it, she was glad she wasn't growing up in these times, glad that she had missed it by thirty-odd years. But, strangely, what she felt now was the black, heaving anger of youth. Walking up to the cops, she said, "Hello, don't you see that naked man? Don't you see how he exposes himself? Don't you think you should be doing something about that? This being a public place, you know."

The male cop glanced sideways, then said, "Madam, he is a sanyasi; he has renounced the world. How is he affecting you by being there? If you don't like what you see, don't look, no. See those youngsters. Are they bothered?" He pointed to the selfie gang who were posing ecstatically.

The lady cop said, "I too am a woman, madam; so I know how you feel. But he is not misbehaving, he is not doing any harm. If he were, then we would take action. *That* we won't tolerate. You be assured, huh."

The male cop said, "You just take your walk, no, madam. Enjoy the breeze and this view. Why you bother your head with such mad people? You should just ignore …"

"Yes," said Kitayun, "we should just ignore. But, sometimes, the real mad people are not the ones we see, and yet they do us great harm. They cut our trees and take away our shelter. And they don't think what this does to our city, our climate, our health. And we should just ignore, you say. How? Tell me how. By not seeing, not caring!"

"*What* are you saying, madam? Why are you talking to us like this? We have not cut any trees. All that is decided by people in the municipality and in the government. We have no say in that." The male cop looked at her incredulously. His fingers tightened around the stick he was holding. He felt uncomfortable in the presence of this fair, middle-aged woman, who was looking at him with hard, accusing eyes.

"So, how is it that you have the authority to stop us when we try and protect our trees? But you don't stop politicians when they hold processions and block the traffic. Or when they put up illegal hoardings, when they plaster their faces all over bus stops, bridges, and walls. But, when we try and save our trees, you arrest us … treat us like common criminals."

"See, madam, we don't know anything about that. We are here for your protection, to see there is no pick-pocketing or bag-grabbing. But, if you like, we will go and speak to the sadhu. We will request him to go elsewhere."

"The only place he should go to is prison. Such a man should not be allowed to roam free. That is the problem with our society. In the name of religion, anything goes. Nudity-fudity, building of illegal temples, shouting and dancing on the streets, and putting up mandaps and hoardings on a whim. Now, are you going to do something about this pervert, havildar, or should I …?"

Reluctantly, the male cop got to his feet, and the lady cop followed him. Approaching the sadhu, the male cop banged his stick hard against the parapet. "Kai re, baba, people here are getting upset with you. Don't you have something to cover yourself? Why are you sleeping naked, as though you are in some forest?"

The sadhu turned his head away in the manner of an affronted child. Gazing outward, at the sea, he said, "What is wrong with how I am? How does it concern you? Go away, I say! You are disturbing my meditation."

Seeing the cops, some of the walkers stopped in their tracks and watched with interest.

Kitayun pushed forward and stood over the sadhu. "Why, you scoundrel, you besharam!" she glowered. "You think we have come here only to look at your private parts? This is a public road, not your father's house. Are you going to be on your way or should I ...?" She grabbed the stick from the cop's hand and started prodding the sadhu. She poked him in his stomach and ribs and was surprised to find how soft and spongy his flesh was.

The sadhu lay still, very still. He closed his eyes and began to mumble; he mumbled rapidly, as though it was some mantra he was chanting. The sun was almost at eye level with the walkers; it glowed and dispatched its last rays of the evening. At the side, more youngsters jumped onto the parapet and took pictures with their cell phones. They posed happily, this way and that way, oblivious to the ruckus that was happening.

Suddenly the sadhu sat up, erect. Kitayun recoiled. She averted her eyes from his nudity and stared into his face. She was amazed to see how young his face was and how large and clear his eyes. His body, she noticed, was lean and sinewy, with shrubs of gray, scraggly hair.

"Look, madam," said the sadhu, rubbing his thighs. "I understand that you women like to dress up and look elegant. But to me, a man of God, clothes make no difference. And if you think this natural state is vulgar, then it is you who have an impure mind. I will have you know that I am not a slave to society but a creature of God. I am made in his image. Naked – like the sun, the sky, and the trees." Raising his body, he drew an orange cloth from under him and, flicking it open, wrapped it around his waist with astonishing speed. Then he continued.

"Now that I am decent enough for you and your society, madam, let me tell you something. It is the face that wears a thousand masks, and lips that utter a million lies, and yet, it is the body we must cover up. What logic is that? What sense does that make? I am sorry to have ruined your walk, madam. That was not my intention. I am not a besharam, nor am I unkind. I was only being one with nature, looking at the sky, when all others are busy looking at themselves." His eyes wandered to the selfie gang. Then he bowed stiffly to Kitayun and, turning his back, began to walk away; he walked so rapidly that his feet barely seemed to touch the ground. The onlookers looked at each other and shrugged. What was all that about? They had expected some action, some drama, something to carry back home.

The male cop turned to Kitayun and said angrily, "I told you, madam, he is a holy man. See how decent he was. And it is not good to disturb a sadhu, madam. Not good to upset him. He might have blessed us. But now, instead, he has cursed me. You saw how he mumbled. He was saying something under his breath, something that will make me suffer."

The lady cop placed a hand on his shoulder. "Don't worry," she said gently. "If your faith is strong, then nothing can happen. No curse will stick to you. Just recite the name of God and all your fears will vanish." She snapped her fingers and smiled at him with warm, reassuring eyes.

Kitayun, who was thinking about the sadhu's words – *the face that wears a thousand masks and lips that utter a million lies* – remembered how many letters she had written to the government. To its various departments, its ministers, its undersecretaries. *Dear Sir, trees are the veins and arteries of Mumbai. They allow us to live, to breathe; it is our God-given duty to protect them.*

And then some reassurances had followed. *Dear Ms. Alwa: We are in receipt of your letter dated ____. Thank you for bringing this to our attention. We have forwarded it to the relevant department and expect to hear from them shortly. Meanwhile, we request your patience.*

And that was the only response she got. Each time. Every time. And what had followed was an indiscriminate felling of trees, muscular trunks brutally cut. They had been cut even where it was not required, where there were no tracks to be laid. She had stared at them disbelievingly, these fallen sentinels of the city, and had labeled the crime in her mind. The "hacksaw murders" she called it.

She tapped the lady cop on the shoulder. "Which God is that?" she asked smiling. "Which God will take away your troubles by simply uttering his name? Tell me, too, so I can ask him to save our city." Then, without waiting for an answer, she began to walk away. Like the sadhu, she too had made her point.

She walked for about forty minutes. Past the beautiful art deco buildings, past the cricket stadium that would resonate during matches with cries of frenzy, past the sweeping flyover and the tranquil manicured lawns of the gymkhanas, till she came to the aquarium and the yoga center, and then she turned back. The sun had set and the sky was filled with a dark orange light, and under its canopy, young couples snuggled and kissed, and older couples sat in well-adjusted harmony, or they fiddled with their cell phones, numbly engrossed.

On the main road, the traffic had slowed and congealed, and a breeze had started, a cool, soft breeze that ushered in the night. And then she heard the sound of a bugle, a long-drawn-out wail that ripped through the silence.

Heads turned, and she, too, stopped. And what she saw filled her heart with wonder.

Coming up the road was a procession of Victorias. There might have been twenty to thirty of them in a row: silver carriages pulled by horses, each horse wearing a crest of feathers. And in each carriage stood a trumpeter, blowing a bugle, and a horseman, holding the reins, turning, from time to time, and bowing grandly to the walkers.

Oh, what a sight, what a joyous sight! And what pain, too! thought Kitayun, for this was the Victorias' last ride. The carriages had been banned by the High Court. They had been banned on grounds of animal cruelty and would never ply again. And maybe it *was* a mercy. The horses would not have to breathe in the traffic fumes, would not have to endure the sharp, startling horns of speeding cars.

As the procession approached, Kitayun had to stop herself from crying out. Already she held her hands before her face, palms clasped, fingers entwined, prayerlike. It was prophetic that she should be here; she who had once celebrated her birthday in a Victoria. Her parents had made her cut a cake, and her aunts, uncles, and cousins had cruised up in an open car, beside the Victoria, singing happy birthday darling Katz. It was a different city then: her Mumbai, her Bombay (God, how she missed that name!), a more encompassing, nurturing place. And now, it was almost like the city was saying goodbye to its history. To its trees, its traditions, its heritage, and its neighborhoods, which were fast disappearing under the roar and rumble of earthmovers, the glitter of gated communities. Where had the sparrows of her youth gone? she wondered. And where were the butterflies? And how long before I, too, am a part of the city's history? Before I too am effaced? she thought.

But this was not a moment to miss. It was a proud moment, a historic moment, and it just begged to be captured and frozen. Drawing out her cell phone, Kitayun moved to the curb and pushed her way through the groups of youngsters who were crowding with their cell phones. "Come on, guys," she said, spreading out her arms like a traffic cop. "Make way for a lady. Show some respect for age."

Black Friday

FRIDAY, SEPTEMBER 29, 2017. I am trying hard not to gaze at my cell phone and read the flood of Facebook posts talking about the stampede in Mumbai. Twenty-two killed, thirty-six injured, even while 7.5 million people rode those tracks in order to get home after a harrowing commute. It was inevitable, the tragedy – the bane and curse of a city that had failed to protect itself, failed, perhaps, to even anticipate its needs – and I, the writer, the brooding, pensive chronicler, far away in distant California, seated in a plush leather armchair at Union Station, Los Angeles.

Here, the ceilings are reminiscent of a Roman cathedral. Here, giant chandeliers emit their light like evening lamps in a Jaipur palace. Here, a young pianist taps exuberantly on his piano while children stand around mesmerized. Here, electronic signboards gleam with designer fonts and change their faces every few minutes to signal the status of arriving and departing trains. Here, firm-bodied policemen stand in pairs, maintaining an alert vigil.

I wait in the lobby, which is spacious. The ceilings are high, the seating is comfortable. All of us get leather armchairs with broad flat armrests and ample legroom.

I look at the people seated.

On my left, a cherubic girl with thick lips and tight plaits speaks excitedly into her cell phone. Her legs hang loosely over the sides of her chair, and the ruptures in her jeans reveal glimpses of her knees. It is apparent by her expressions that she is speaking to her boyfriend.

She is filling him in on events he might have missed and, in between, she laughs heartily.

To my right, large-bodied Mexican women gorge on burritos, on chips, on Subway sandwiches, while their children frolic in a sort of running game that disturbs no one.

Stations are more than transit points, I think. Phases of stocktaking, points of introspection and reflection, beginnings and endings seamlessly interwoven, to bring a certain continuity to life. But, back home in Mumbai, stations are all about survival. A vast influx of human need. An outpouring of human life. And, now, not even that, I think. They had become death traps.

I take in a deep breath. My thoughts wander to the good doctor who had plunged into an open manhole when the city had flooded. This was a month ago. He was a well-known gastroenterologist who consulted at two reputed hospitals. He had treated complex cases, saved numerous lives, but that didn't guarantee him anything. He had been swamped and sentenced by the filth of the city. He had met his death in a brown watery grave.

A woman stretches her legs. At first glance I think she is Chinese American, but soon I realize that she is Jamaican. Her skin glows like a tropical sunset. She is tattooed all over. Without those tattoos, she might have been attractive. Her body is firm, there is youth in those limbs, but her skin is defaced with tattoos. There is something interesting about her face: it is pensive and scholarly and cupped by two large earrings. Her hair is matted and caked against her scalp. She sticks out her feet, and I notice her toes. No toenails and, in their place, was a thick layer of dark, chocolate-colored nail polish.

My eyes are drawn to this black kid, a teenager, sprawled leisurely in an armchair. He is tall and lanky, around sixteen years of age, and at his feet is a duffel bag of soft black leather. On the armrest of his chair, he has placed three one-dollar bills in a row. He looks at me pridefully. Am I intrigued by this? Of course, I am, but I don't show it.

I observe him in a way he doesn't notice. His eyes are large and clear. His face is slender. There is something tragically handsome about him.

He picks up one of the dollar bills and flings it to the floor. Then he looks at me defiantly. Slowly, he flicks another bill, then another. I pretend not to notice any of this.

He reaches into his pocket and pulls out a bunch of keys. He flings these to the ground as well. He then starts tapping his feet, hoping to draw attention to the fallen objects. But no one says anything, no one cares. I see he is wearing heavy boots, which are old and faded. Even without them, he'd be tall.

He brings his feet over the dollars and the keys and grinds at them, round and round, in a circular motion. I decide it's best to avoid looking at him. Maybe he craved attention; maybe he was working to a plan; or maybe he was just following some crazy impulse. I choose to look at the Jamaican woman, instead, her tattoos, and wonder what it was that led a human being to inflict such savage incisions on herself. I think of the underground metro coming up in Mumbai. My city of seven interconnected islands would have a roaring, thundering beast of steel tearing through her sinews. I wonder if the islands could take that, and if the old art deco buildings in the business district could withstand the tremors. I was sure that no one had done a structural audit of those buildings. I was sure – almost certain – that they were death traps in waiting.

My eyes return to the black kid. He is having a conversation with the floor. He is looking down and speaking to it. Like he was negotiating with it.

Druggie! my aunt Rosa in Mumbai would have said.

No, something more complex, I think. *Something not out of choice. Like: the homeless.*

Then, suddenly, he scoops the objects off the floor and shoves them back into his pocket. Rising, he shuffles over to me and says respectfully, in a voice that is trying hard to sound grown-up, "Excuse me, sir, do you have a dollar to spare?"

"I wish I did, brother. But no!"

He nods acceptingly and returns to his seat, where he taps feverishly on the armrest.

Just then a fat security woman comes up and hollers, "No loitering here! Only passengers traveling on the Metro can sit here. All others should leave, right away." She looks warily at the boy, who says, "My Dad laid these floors. Spent a year doing that. I have every right. Every right … you know." He tries his best to look angry and menacing. But the woman says gently, "All right, son. He done a mighty fine job, your dad. But, now, you git on your way." Something in her voice makes him leave.

My thoughts shift to the homeless in Mumbai: the gypsy women outside Grant Road Station, cooking, washing clothes and utensils, or yelling at their children, snot-nosed and half-naked; the gypsy men, playing cards or sleeping or fighting in loud, angry voices. And the railway policemen, who have been positioned there since the 2006 bomb blasts and who – going by their nonchalance – were convinced that what had happened once wasn't ever going to happen again.

My train arrives, I take my seat, the compartment is almost empty.

Suddenly my thoughts are interrupted by a low rumbling sound that gets louder and louder in my ears. I see it is the kid. He is on a skateboard. The duffel bag is strapped to his back. He stops at the entrance of the compartment, then hoists himself in skillfully, and skates past me, without as much as a glance. My ears follow him all the way down the corridor. But my mind is back in Mumbai, where I am on a local train and I can't find a way to disembark, can't make my way through the crowd at the exit. I am pleading, imploring, but people only laugh at me. *Where, where is the space to move?* Then the train starts and I watch helplessly as my destination whizzes past. The diamond signboard, the wooden benches, the food stalls, the newspaper stall, the shoepolish-wallas, striking at their boxes, and the overbridge: all this flies past. I watch with a sinking heart and a sense of desperation that I had lost control over my life. Seeing my distress, my fellow commuters console me. There was no use trying, they say. This is Mumbai, the peak hours. People were not ready to yield an inch of space. Not because they didn't want to but because they couldn't. Look! There were people standing on the footboard, hanging by a finger. People riding the rooftops, seated on their haunches. People balancing on the connectors, between bogeys. I should consider myself lucky, so very lucky! Among 7.5 million commuters, not everyone had a comfortable pass.

But this is different, this shiny tubular train. No one looks at me, no one gives a damn where I am going, or where I want to get off. I extract my cell phone and open my Facebook page. Scrolling down, I read: "The stampede occurred due to a panic, because people thought there was a short circuit. The railway authorities had been warned that the bridge was too narrow for the kinds of crowds it received. The chief minister has declared that there would be a five-lakh-rupee compensation for the victims' families and an inquiry."

I scroll down further and take note of the outrage. People are angry, livid. "Enough is enough," they are saying.

"Must we wait for a major disaster? Must we wait for a catastrophe?"

I want to write: "The catastrophe is already in the making. It is rumbling below our feet, striking at the hinges, removing our green cover, and tomorrow we will come apart at the seams."

I want to post this, but, instead, I set off in search of the black kid. I want to give him a few dollars. I want to tell him what a fine job his father had done. And maybe I would persuade him to skate in places that are built for it.

The History Lesson

ANURADHA SINGHAL (ANU HEREAFTER) stepped out of the Chhatrapati Shivaji International Airport and combed the faces at the exit. He would be easy to spot: her Jai. Not because he was six feet two inches in shoes but because he was her darling man, the undisputed owner of her heart, father to the warm bundle of joy she held in her arms and who was now asleep, thank God, for that! The flight from Dubai had not been easy. Although they had traveled business class, it had made baby cranky; she had cried for over an hour, much to the discomfort of other passengers.

The flight attendant – a fair, stocky, wide-hipped woman in her late thirties – hadn't been much help. Anu thought she looked the kind who saw her job as a chore. The excitement of flying had long dried in her face. You could see she had been through it all: the thrills of sightseeing, the frenzy of shopping, the joys of savoring gourmet cuisines and premium wines. She would have furnished her home with the latest gadgets, and bought expensive gifts for her family. She would have been on disaster dates with pursers and fought off advances from same-sex colleagues, with whom she would have shared a room. She would have received her share of propositions from drunken passengers, for whom she would have felt nothing but pity, and she would have known heartbreak, searing, wincing heartbreak, in her trysts with the dashing, unwilling-to-commit pilots. And that heartbreak would have changed her. It would explain to Anu why she now wore a sullen face, the makeup failing to hide her disappointment. It would also explain to Anu why this heavy-shouldered, wingless angel in the sky would shove so roughly a rubber nipple under baby's chin, saying: "Hush, take this, and be quiet." There was no kindness in that tone, no professional courtesy either, and first it angered Anu, and then it saddened her, saddened her that baby would have to grope her way around in this unfeeling world of service attendants and poseurs.

But awaiting her, right now, was the thrill of homecoming. Dirty, filthy Mumbai, with its veneer of slums, rushing to meet the slow-descending aircraft, had the power to stir her heart. It did not matter what the city looked like from the sky. Something in it had the tendency to raise in her a leaping excitement. She felt like this after every single vacation. Felt excited beyond words.

Now, wheeling the bags' trolley with one hand, baby in the other, Anu sallied forth, a slim, elegant figure in a trouser suit.

"Oh, Trimbuksh!" she called to Jai's chauffeur, who was craning his neck to be seen above the swarm of faces and, as though spurred by her presence, Trimbuksh indicated to her with a motion of his fingers that he'd get the car, she should wait there. He shuffled his way toward the parking lot, a bulky, anxious figure in his forties, wearing a starched white uniform and a crisp white cap.

"Hotel, madam?" a tout at Anu's elbow offered. "Very nice. Very comfortable. Close by! And safe for baby."

"No thank you," said Anu. "I am from Mumbai. I reside here." Her fingers tightened around the trolley handle and her eyes fixed onto the bags. One, two, three, four … yes, all there!

The car swept in. Jai's Audi. Sleek as a panther, dark as the night.

Anu strained her eyes to see past the tinted windows. Could it be possible? she wondered. But, no, he wasn't there.

Trimbuksh sprang from the driver's seat. With thick, brawny arms, he heaved the luggage from the trolley into the trunk of the car. He knew which suitcase should go on top and which at the bottom. Baby's hamper, he placed up-front, on the seat next to him. Then he opened wide the door for Anu, so that she could slide in without disturbing baby.

The car slid over the overpass and Anu breathed a sigh of relief. This was home. The cool comfort of the car. The enveloping softness of the seats. The familiar back of Trimbuksh. The neon lights, frozen, as though to welcome her home.

Glancing at her in the inside rearview mirror, Trimbuksh asked, "How are Pratap Sahib and Roma Memsahib? They must have been thrilled to see baby, no."

"They are fine," said Anu. "Sahib hardly went to work while we were there, and memsahib had friends over daily, to see baby. They will be coming to Mumbai more often now. What we haven't been able to do in years, this little one has achieved without a word."

"A child changes things, madam. It can change the toughest human beings. I know how my parents were when Karambuksh was born. They took hundreds of photographs and couldn't stop boasting to all the neighbors. Of course, my parents were excited because it was a boy. In our community we believe that if the first child is a boy, then God is pleased with you."

"Tell me about Jai Sahib," said Anu sharply. "Has he been working late? Taking his meals on time? Going for his yoga workouts?" She glanced at baby sleeping in angelic composure.

"Madam, you know sahib. His work is his life. Meetings and more meetings! That is all he has been doing since you went. It is good that you are back. Now he will come home early."

Anu suppressed a sigh. That man of hers was incapable of looking after himself. And to think he had promised her he would. This was just before she had entered the departure lounge and the doors had closed behind her. There was no point pressing Trimbuksh for details, which she could use to chide Jai. Trimbuksh was fiercely loyal to his boss. He had known Jai since Jai was a boy. He had seen Jai through his feisty pub-hopping days, which Anu had heard about from Jai's friends. She had also heard about his numerous girlfriends, who clung to his every word, aspired to his bed, and to whom Jai would commit no more than a few nights of pleasure.

"He was a real a hound in heat till he met you," a friend of Jai once told her.

"He still is!" she had replied. "Only more focused," she had laughed.

Now she couldn't imagine Jai like that. There was nothing of the rake left in him. He was, instead, the closest thing to an ideal husband. Sweet, lovable Jai! Always so attentive, so caring! Anu could hug Fate for what it had delivered to her.

Initially, she did have some doubts about their relationship. She would wonder if they would survive the differences in their backgrounds – he from a family of affluent builders, she from a middle-class family. Her father was a doctor with a small private practice; her mother was a teacher. There was never any scarcity, but no abundance, either. From an early age, she was taught to respect money, to understand the value of every rupee spent. But, here, in her marital home, huge amounts were discussed with nonchalance. The figures would send her mind reeling.

A ring!

At last! she thought, fumbling in her handbag.

"Darling!" said the voice at the other end. "Where are you?"

"We have just left the airport. We are on the highway. But why aren't you here? Kiyomi is sleeping right now, but she gave me a frightful time on the flight. Bawled throughout. It was our good luck that no one complained."

"Something must have disturbed her. It must have been too cold. Or maybe her ears were blocked."

"Darling, I love your faith in your daughter. But you must accept there are times when she can be a perfect terror, for no other reason than the fact that she *is* one."

"As long as she is fine now," said Jai doubtfully. "I am with the Americans. I excused myself to call you."

"Will you be late?" she asked.

"I think so. They have big plans for India and want us to partner them. Us, out of all the builders in this country. Listen, sweetheart, is all well with you? I need to return to the table. I just wanted to hear your voice and know that Ki is fine."

"Yes, all good. But *where* are you? You didn't say." Her heart was heavy with longing. She couldn't bear this distance, now that she knew how close he was, available to her in the same city. Those fifteen days in Dubai had seemed like a lifetime. All she wanted to do was slip into her husband's arms and stay there.

"We are at The Rooftop. Having drinks ..."

"Ok, I won't hold you then. Take care and see you soon. And good luck with the Americans. Tell them that my man *is* the best. They needn't look beyond."

"Love you, precious," he said, and hung up.

She dropped the phone into her handbag and leaned her head against the headrest. Suddenly she felt tired; she felt her body go limp. She should sleep, she thought. She could now afford to.

The car raced along a road which was full of potholes, but she did not feel them. The Audi was, clearly, a superior vehicle. And Trimbuksh was an expert handler. Anu knew that, Jai knew that. Which explained why Jai, from all his drivers, had chosen to send Trimbuksh to receive his darling wife and child. His family was in safe hands. And they were being returned to him. Now he could focus on business at hand. Business which could not wait.

As Jai sat down, the fat American at his table leaned forward and said, "You see, Mr. Singhal, the way we see it, there are only three things permanent in the world: the sun, the moon, and America. And what we want you to understand is that America is ready to invest in India and in you. We like you, Mr. Singhal. More than any of the other builders we have met so far. You've got style, you've got taste, *and* you've got history, which is the most important thing of all. History is what the others lack. And America is a country that respects history, it respects lineage. Because lineage spells continuity; it tells us you are here to stay. Now let me tell you one thing, Mr. Singhal, strictly between us. Whoever partners with us is going to be the next Olly Baba. He is going to make a fortune."

Olly Baba? Oh, he meant Ali Baba from *The Arabian Nights*, thought Jai, suppressing a smile. Ali Baba, who had stumbled onto a cave of treasures belonging to a band of thieves and helped himself. Looking at the American, Jai said, "Let me assure you, I am equally excited about your plans. I don't know about being the next Ali Baba; Singhal Constructions is doing well enough. But to create American-style cities in India and build a new India: that would be any builder's dream."

The second American spoke. He was an older man, and more sober, with a pockmarked face and silver-rimmed glasses. "Timing is everything, Mr. Singhal. The way things are right now, we have investors interested in India. And India, we know, is interested in building smart cities. So we need to work fast. We need to get Delhi involved. Which is where you come in, with your reputation and contacts. Once we have created an American-style infrastructure here, we will back you in every way. We will show you how to make it profitable and sustainable. You should know one thing about America: we never let down our friends."

"I *am* aware of that, gentlemen," said Jai, reaching for his glass and raising it. "To two of the greatest democracies in the world! What can we not achieve with a shared vision?" The word "values" also came to mind, but for some reason he did not say it.

Sipping his whiskey, Jai felt pleased. In school he had suffered from stage fright. But now he was eloquence itself. Must be the whiskey, he thought. It was making him glib, giving him ideas. He was already thinking where the new cities should be built. Along the coast. Coast to coast. Yes, Indians loved beaches. They loved the water. Any place where they could dip their feet without getting their bodies wet. That's why the hill cities had failed. Indians hated seclusion. And the hills isolated them. Besides, there was a lengthy coastline just waiting to be tapped. The fisherfolk could be rehabilitated. He would make them stakeholders in the new cities. Give them a share of the profits. Look at Alibaug, Kihim, Mandva, and Goa: how these places had boomed. Were still booming. But, God, where was his family? Where had they reached? He was missing them like crazy. Especially Ki. That daughter of his was something. She had played hell into her co-passengers. Well, she was a princess, and royalty does that: it makes its presence felt.

The third American leaned forward. He was slim, bald, blue-eyed, and clean-shaven. To Jai's mind, he looked like a robot, an inscrutable robot. He said, "We have thought everything through, in great detail. We will get professional companies to do the research. If it's music people want, we will give them a city with music. A Memphis, a Nashville, or a San Francisco. If it's entertainment they want, we will create L.A. If it's architecture, we will build Chicago. If it's art and fashion, we will replicate New York. And if they want eco-friendly, we will do Portland. That's how we will bring America to India." He smiled at Jai through thin lips, without showing any teeth. It all sounded very simple, thought Jai, but what was in it for them?

The American continued. "We will replicate the whole American system here. We will create American-style offices and American products. Set up American universities and American malls. So what you will get is the infrastructure, knowledge, and expertise of a superpower."

He paused and looked at Jai expectantly. They all did. They were expecting him to say something. To express surprise, pleasure, even gratitude. But all he could manage was a nod.

The fat guy reached for a roll at his feet and spread it out on the table. Jai was surprised to see it was a map of Mumbai. Holding it down with a pudgy palm, the fat man pointed to the east side, where there were salt pans, mangroves, and oil refineries. "This is a part of Mumbai we could exploit," he said. "We could develop a township here. A model township, which could become the norm, the gold standard. We could set up offices, malls, parks, cinema houses, gated communities, a high-tech hospital, international schools, colleges, a university. There is enough land, I am told. More than five thousand acres." Wow, thought Jai, these guys were prepared. They had come prepared to do business, to move in.

Now, for some strange reason, he remembered a history lesson from school. It came to him out of nowhere and he welcomed it, because it filled him with a sweet euphoria, a sensation like honey poured onto an outstretched tongue.

It was the start of a new academic year. He was in grade six, still in half pants. The Jesuit priest, Father Fredrick Noronha, had walked into the classroom, drawn the map of India on the blackboard, and said, "Boys, *this* is your country. A beautiful woman, a hauntingly beautiful woman, surrounded by hostile neighbors. There will be some countries that will lust after her from a distance and be content with that. But there will be others who will want to possess her, even steal her beauty." And then he had gone on to explain how it had always been that way. Century after century, India had been prey to the invaders. First the Moguls. Then the Dutch. Then the Portuguese. Then the French. And, finally, the British. For seven hundred years, the invaders had feasted on India's beauty, they had bled her dry. But now she must rise on her own, said the priest. Because she had been set free by the bravest of souls. They who cared neither for their lives nor for their careers. Nor for any of the fame their struggles brought them.

Jai looked at the faces before him. They were smiling, waiting for him to say something. Anything that would further their plans, reassure them that the meeting had paid off.

"Gentlemen," said Jai, "I don't think you have been correctly informed. The landmass you speak of is the water catchment area of the city, it is our green cover against floods. The land that is being considered for development is barely a thousand acres. Which would make no sense to you as a business proposition. No sense at all. Besides, you would do well to remember that this is salt pan land and the soil here has been greatly weakened by the continuous production of salt. This means whoever builds here will have to drill very deep, till they hit bedrock. Which means your cost of construction is going to be extremely high and not without risks. I am sure you wouldn't want that. Any more than you would want to violate the environment, at a time when climate change is staring us in the face, breathing down our necks. That would be most un-American. Now, gentlemen—" he rose to his feet. "If you will excuse me, my family is on its way back from the airport and I must be home to receive them. I haven't seen them for two weeks. Which is way too long for a family man like me. The restaurant staff has been instructed to look after you. Please eat and drink to your heart's content. Please feel free to order anything you want. I am traveling from tomorrow but will discuss your ideas with my board, on my return. You will appreciate that something as big as the creation of a city will need the approval of the board; I am unable to commit to it on my own. Meanwhile, I thank you for considering us and for giving us so much importance. I am sure we will always be friends, good friends, and that you can count on our hospitality whenever you visit India." With that, he bowed and walked away swiftly, feeling like a king who had protected his kingdom. Feeling lighter and more powerful, somehow.

The first thing he did when he got into his car was call his wife, his darling wife. She would be pleased to know he was on his way back.

But she did not pick up her phone. It just rang and rang and rang.

And then he called Trimbuksh, who responded right away. "Yes, sir. Madam is here. But she couldn't hear the phone because we are stuck in a procession. There is too much noise, and they are diverting all the traffic. No idea, sir, when we will reach. Yes, baby is awake, wide awake, and watching. No, she is not scared. In fact, she is very much enjoying the music." In the background, Jai could hear shouts, screams, drums, a keyboard wailing, and trumpets blaring.

Trimbuksh gave the phone to Anu, who rubbed it a couple of times against her trouser before bringing it to her ear. "Darling!" she said. "This is madness! Sheer madness! It is not even the festive season and they are out on the streets, dancing and bursting crackers. No, I have no idea what they are celebrating and Trimbuksh doesn't know, either. Seems like some local event. They have taken over the entire road and the cops are doing nothing about it. I am sorry, darling, but we are going to be late. I can't say how late. You know how these processions are."

And of course Jai knew. He knew well enough for him to chuckle at himself of a few minutes ago, sitting at the city's premium restaurant and planning the future of the country. To think that you could build an American-style city in India; to think that you could change the culture of this country; to think that you could stop a five-thousand-year-old civilization from pouring out into the street and expressing itself: that was sheer impudence, sheer delusion.

He swung his car onto Marine Drive. The seafront stretched before him like a giant smile, a dazzling, twinkling smile that seemed to say: I know what can never be corrupted in this city; I know what will always heal and refresh.

God, thought Jai, how he loved this city! This space-squeezed city that had no option but to go vertical. Sometimes he felt like a predator, looking for spaces to build: a slum, a defunct mill, a municipal compound, a public garden. Then, getting permissions by paying off politicians, bureaucrats, and civic officials. The worst were the slumlords, who cleared the decks for him. He had to visit them, eat with them, attend their daughters' marriages, provide employment to their sons and nephews. What a life! thought Jai, that it trapped you in unholy alliances, forced you to work with people you disliked. He wondered if it would have been the same working with the Americans. Would he have to swallow his pride? Play ball? Compromise? Here, at least, he was feeding the domestic demand for survival. He was giving back to his own people, hoping that one day their stomachs would be full. Their stomachs and their pockets.

A bus hooted at his rear and he promptly gave way, darting to one side, then slipping into the slow lane. Fumbling in his glove compartment, he pulled out a CD and slipped it into the player. Then, as the familiar song came on, he drummed on the steering wheel and hummed: *I'm an alien, I'm a legal alien; I'm an Englishman in New York.*

Neighbors

I WALK OUT OF my building – a fifteen-year-old high-rise – and greet the neighbor who hasn't paid his maintenance dues since we moved in. I am surprised to find he is walking. Usually he drives a black 4-seater Mercedes Cabriolet, which can barely accommodate him, his three daughters, and his wife, an extraordinarily fat woman with a perpetually haunted look. Under normal circumstances, I would have ignored him; but it was just the surprise of seeing him on foot that led me to deliver a terse, civic nod. Not that it gave me any pleasure. There's something revolting about this man: his eyes are long and narrow, his lips are thin, almost invisible, his deportment, like a giant reptile, unctuous and bloated. I know I am not being biased when I say he looks like one of those slimeballs you'd never want to do business with: he's got that kind of a look. The defaulter nods back gratefully, or, rather, shamelessly. Each time he is asked to pay his maintenance dues (this would be at our building society meetings), he would have some excuse: he had all his money locked up in some venture; his bank accounts had been frozen by the income tax department; his business partner had cheated him and the matter was in court, sub judice, till then, he was financially incapacitated. The funny thing is, he would be smiling when saying this, as though he enjoyed stretching our sense of decency. At some point he ran out of excuses and the committee members exhausted their patience and demanded that he pay up. That's when he would pull out his cell phone and ask if he should dial a politician who was notoriously powerful. Apparently, the politician and he were on excellent terms. They worked as a team, in cahoots, and had each other's back.

Leaving the gilded gates of my building, I take a right. To my left is a lovely old Shiva temple, sculpted out of black stone. At the side is another temple that houses the guardian deity of our neighborhood. A few hundred years ago, people weren't taking chances: they would insure the neighborhood against natural disasters – floods, fires, and plagues – by installing a guardian deity and praying to her. I like going to this temple and seeing my sleepy neighborhood unite in worship. Rows and rows of women, seated before their gods (Lord Shiva, Lord Ganesha, and Lord Hanuman), chanting melodiously in sync, while their menfolk stand respectfully at the side, their heads bowed, hands folded.

The temple has a courtyard and a well and is reminiscent of a village square. A proud rooster struts around fearlessly. Dogs sprawl in reproachful slumber. A black-and-white coated goat, tied to a water tap, gnaws at a bundle of grass. In the evenings, people assemble here and chat. The peace and devotion show on the faces of the residents; no one is in a hurry, no one has an axe to grind. They have left their fates to the guardian deity. Besides, time itself seems frozen here – as though nothing bad can ever happen.

Outside the temple, locals loiter in shorts. They rib each other. A family of gypsies work together, threading garlands. A large truck hands out newspapers, free, to those who wish to read. Another truck, a food truck, gleams with fresh vegetables. An elderly man with thick glasses and a four-pronged walking stick stops and stares at the sights before him. He smiles blandly: ah, yes, nothing has changed, nothing! All is peace and harmony, peace and camaraderie.

Turning into a side lane, I greet the barber standing outside his shop. He is a short, dark man with thick foggy glasses. There is admiration in the way I greet him. Because where else, these days, can you get a haircut for a hundred rupees? I had discovered this quite by chance, during the pandemic, when my regular salon had closed down. But this man, he had kept his place open, teaching jobless youth to navigate scalps of thick, unruly hair.

I feel a glow of warmth in my heart, a kindred peace in my mind. Sights of old Bombay do this to me: stir my sense of belonging, my love of heritage. And there is one such example right before my eyes: a circular art deco building, now in disarray but still bringing depth and character to the neighborhood.

The barber calls out to me; he has a piece of gossip he wants to share. I wasn't, frankly, interested, but didn't want to offend him, so I draw up close. That fancy new salon which has opened up down the lane is not a decent place, he whispers. They give male customers a massage and a happy ending, he adds disapprovingly.

I express surprise, consternation, shock. I say to the old barber that I am very sorry to hear this but the male residents would surely object and take strong measures to close down the place. "Hah!" he spits. "Object? You should see some of them sneak in. While their wives are busy making dinner or when they have gone to visit their mothers. When these men get their salaries, the first thing they do is go there, to that den of vice!" He says he had complained to the authorities, both the police and the municipality, but they said they had no evidence of wrongdoing, hence, were unable to take any action. He is sure the cops are getting a piece of the pie, if not that, at least a piece of the action. I say, "Yes, yes, quite possible," nod sadly, and take leave of him. "Wait, wait," he says. "You also complain. You call the police station, without giving your name, and tell them there are wicked things happening inside that place. Tell them how upset you are and how you are planning to approach the newspapers." I stare at him and recognize the seeds of professional envy. Even a hundred-rupee haircut faces competition these days.

I come upon a stretch of land that has been cleared for a gated community. I am told there are to be two towers constructed here, both fifty stories tall and revealing views of an ocean shrunk and depleted by the coastal road. There would be twelve levels of parking, a clubhouse, a swimming pool, a jogging track, a supermarket, a pharmacy, a business center, and a gymnasium. And tall ornate gates that would make the community impervious to outsiders. "Dogs and Indians not allowed!" was once the admonition of the English sahibs. But we were doing this to ourselves now, I think. Imposing limits on those who could enter our lives. Our own people.

I look at the long art deco building, where vendors go about their business.

The tailor huddled over his sewing machine, the tip of his tongue clenched between his teeth.

The ironing man working out of a dimly lit hovel, pressing down on his iron. Behind him is a soft, fragrant mountain of washed clothes.

The grocer making packets of flour, grain, pulses, rice, and spices whilst taking orders on his cell phone.

The stationer feeding his photocopying machine with blank sheets of paper, while handing out batteries, pens, notebooks, and erasers.

The snack-bar owner frying jalebis and samosas and bhajiyas and pakodas in large hissing pans, then wrapping them in old newspapers, which turn greasy from the oil that seeps through. And customers reaching eagerly for these packets.

The sweetmeat vendor churning milk in a large aluminum vessel; he'd scoop and churn with the dexterity of a juggler.

The cobbler threading soles that gaped like fish; then hammering them into submission.

And the pharmacist handing out medicines with the airs of a doctor.

Where would all these people go once the gated community was up and running? I wonder. Once everything was available in-house. And its inhabitants were too lazy and too pampered to venture out for their shopping. They would simply order online. Or get their kids to do it.

I stare at the construction site which is cordoned off by blue corrugated sheets of tin. And above that I see the necks of earthmovers, lurching forward and pounding the earth, scooping out vast mounds of debris.

During the pandemic, the earthmovers had fallen silent and a whole mangrove had sprung up at the site, a gossamer forest, tall and swaying, needing no other water than what lay below, than what the city was originally built on. I was amazed to see the mangrove spring up, before my eyes, unasked, uninvited; nature asserting itself, nature breaking through rocks, stones, and concrete. And then mankind had swept in and hacked away the grass, burning the shrubs that remained, sending smoke signals all over the neighborhood. No trespassing will be tolerated – not even by the rightful owners of the earth: that seemed to be the message.

On one side, the gated community; on the other, the single- and double-story wooden structures, painted yellow and blue, with latticed balconies, shingled roofs, and small shuttered windows that open like accordions. You are meant to look out onto the street, meant to see the life that swirls below: familiar faces going about their daily routine with habitual efficiency. “Inclusive” and “exclusive” were just words that crept into our vocabulary later, which split our society and divided us.

And now the city is in a rush to reconstruct itself – out of thin air! And the vendors and small traders are on the receiving end. This is happening all over the city. Uniformly. Unsparingly. Even in the lane where Gandhi had lived and where tourists visit daily, in droves. There, too, old houses are being torn down, flowering trees are cut, gaudy buildings rise like birds of prey, and wood and stone are being forced to live alongside glass and metal, surfaces that can dazzle but never impress. Impossible neighbors.

I think about the defaulter. At last count, he owed the society five million rupees. He lived in a 4000 square foot apartment; he had three domestics, a driver, and a cook, and yet he held his neighbors to ransom; for fifteen years, he simply refused to pay. In a sense, it was we who were paying for his lifestyle; we, the residents.

My other neighbors are good, kind people. They had refused to send the defaulter an eviction notice, to move the courts and take tough measures against him. It is not that they are afraid of the politician but are reluctant to put a man out of his house. A man with a grossly overweight wife (probably diabetic and unwell) and three daughters of marriageable age. In India, you can beat a man or humiliate him, but you just don’t go near his family. That – we don’t do.

And talking about families! Every year, the defaulter and his family went on vacation. We would see him in the foyer, dressed in a flowery beach shirt, shades, shorts, and boat shoes, ordering the security guards to load their luggage into a black SUV. His three daughters – skinny, giggly twenty-year-olds – would pose before the SUV, pout, cuddle, and take pictures with their cell phones.

His wife, dressed in a churidar and sports shoes, would be lounging on a sofa, fanning herself with a magazine. If we were to pass by, she would stare at us (that stricken look would vanish), her face alight with hope that we would ask where they were going and when they'd be back. We could see she craved a bon voyage, a touch of neighborly affection, which, regretfully, was not hers to enjoy.

Walking down the lane, I pass a Swachh Hindu hotel with a small black stove at its entrance and a big tawa with a white leathery dosa mix sizzling on it, and, next to that, is a Gomantak restaurant, emitting the strong unmistakable aromas of fried fish. And I look above the eateries and see the billboards of two rival political leaders, and both have happy, smiling faces, as though glad to share a common territory, common ground. And from a two-story building, the windows of a public school, come the sweet, melodious voices of young girls singing. And below the building their mothers wait, with patient faces and shopping bags in their hands.

I have come to the end of the lane now, where a big defunct telephone exchange wears all the signs of a failed enterprise. It had tried, by God it had! Offering special packages of LAN, Wi-Fi, and Data! But the private players had deep pockets and huge advertising budgets. With deals and discounts, they struck at its roots, brought it to its knees, simply did it in. And next to that are small shops selling cell phone accessories, cheap imitations that would shock the Chinese and give them a run for their money.

In a few moments, I will enter another universe, for which I must prepare myself. I must shake off this sense of reverence for the past, and I must brace myself – to become a survivor. For the benefit of my reader, I will call this new universe Mumbai mayhem, as opposed to Bombay bonhomie, which is the one I now leave. But the distinctions have to be clear, very clear in my mind. Because here, in the new universe, an overhead skywalk has made crossing hazardous, driving chaotic. The skywalk snakes out in all directions, as though its planners had changed their minds several times during the construction, choosing to experiment with the heart of a city, its hub. The skywalk scrapes past buildings with balconies, making the opening of windows impossible. It balances on fat ugly columns, it curls over whirling eddies of traffic, and lets itself down on narrow sidewalks, with loose, broken paver blocks and families of homeless people, sheltering, cooking. And it will stare at me insolently, this stale rotting octopus of steel, reminding me that my city, my beloved city, is imploding before my eyes. And that no guardian deity on earth is going to save it.

Scent of a Meal

IT WAS THAT TIME of the night when the city had hung up its boots, when the traffic had thinned out, when the signals blinked routinely, intermittently, arresting the night in a fog of yellow. It was that time of the night when pedestrians crossed cautiously, for drivers took their chances, speeding. Maneuvering his JCB under a tree, Sikander drew on his cigarette and exhaled slowly, watching the smoke disperse in the streetlight. The light illuminated the garbage on the main road, outside the bazaar that had long fallen silent. At the entrance to the bazaar was a bookstore, its blue wooden doors bolted. On the side wall of the bookstore was a blackboard, on which was written in chalk: Evil is truth misplaced. Below that: M.K. Gandhi, crediting the Father of the Nation. Parallel to the wall was a ledge on which young urchins slept. During the day, these boys would be rushing cups of tea to the vendors or playing coolies to the memsahibs who struggled with their shopping loads. But right now, they slept the thick dreamy sleep of the fatigued, their mouths open, their stomachs rising and settling.

Sikander's eyes fell on the pile of garbage before him. By maneuvering the JCB, he would crush and pulverize it, so that it made an easy pickup for the dumper that would follow. He had been doing this for years and would probably do so until he retired. As a crushing machine, the JCB was incomparable. Armed with a fender in front, a claw at the back, the bright yellow JCB could go anywhere it wanted. It could climb over piles, scoop with its front fender, crush with its back claw, and flatten mountains of debris with its huge, wide tires. Its motion was slow, awkward, and jerky, but the work it did was important. Which is why it was called the haathi, the elephant.

A bark! A yelp! The dogs had arrived.

Sikander liked dogs, particularly these ones.

The dogs were half-famished mongrels. They came sniffing at the pile, looking for leftovers. Most nights they got lucky; their excavations bore fruit. But when they didn't, Sikander would jump down from the JCB and, with a rake, would drag out what he thought was edible, pushing it toward them.

The white dog was Faltoo, the black one Kala Katta. These were the names he had given them. He told no one about them, and never called them out aloud.

Faltoo was half-blind, her eyes red, swollen, and reproachful. She barked a lot, straining her neck and raising her head skyward. She did this to mark out her territory, and would exercise this right each time a ragpicker came by, dragging his sack behind him, or each time a passing car would honk, or a motorbike would roar past. Sikander suspected that Faltoo got kicked around a lot because people thought her to be rabid. For that, he blamed those posters on the train which showed a red-eyed dog under a headline that said: *Rabies Kills!*

Faltoo was low on intelligence, but affectionate. As a pup, she could not even get her food from the pile. She would stand near the pile, looking at it with hesitation. Then Sikander would dig into his pocket and bring out a packet of biscuits, which she would wolf off his palm.

Growing up, Faltoo developed a special attachment for Sikander. After eating at the pile, she would come up and sit at the foot of the JCB, gazing at Sikander with doting eyes. Then Sikander would stick out a bare foot, and she would jump up and try to lick it. And he would dodge her playfully, until she managed to confer some of those licks.

Kala Katta, the black one, was a real matlabi. After he had eaten he would trot off, eyes and ears alert. But Faltoo would sit patiently, while Sikander rolled the JCB over the pile, working it down to a mash. Then she would scamper alongside the vehicle as it set off on its journey. She would accompany Sikander all the way to the traffic signal, where she'd leave off lest she encountered dogs from other territories.

Sikander pulled at his cigarette while the dogs probed their dinner. They were sure to find something, he thought. But he wasn't going to help them today because he had a long night ahead of him. He had to crush the garbage in several places before heading back to the municipal compound, where he would park the JCB. There, after a cup of tea, he would climb into a truck loaded with garbage and drive it to the city dump. He would drive with his foot on the accelerator, clattering over speed-breakers and potholes, the garbage in the back heaving like a giant omelet threatening to leave its pan.

A whistle!

Too loud, damn it!

Damn that watchman! Did he have to do this every night, as though his job depended on it? The watchman had it easy. All he did was keep watch at a construction site where a tall residential tower was coming up. He stood at the gate, blowing his whistle each time a truck came in or went out. Sikander was sure that the watchman had fun with the female workers. Well, why not? He was a pleasant-looking fellow, young, and full of energy.

In comparison to the watchman's job, his own job in garbage collection appeared dull and monotonous. What future did he have? What respect? He earned out of waste, out of kachra. He helped clean the city when no one was looking, no one was even aware. Often he felt his own life was a pile of waste that could be crushed by anyone, even a stranger in the dark.

The gloom of the hour settled on his shoulders. Well, thank God at least the JCB was a fine-looking vehicle, he thought. Sitting in it, he felt some status.

The ragpicker Hyder Ali approached. He was the filthiest creature Sikander had ever seen, and on his shoulder he carried a sack. The ragpicker had a limp; with difficulty, he dragged his right leg behind him. His right foot was swollen, and on his ankles were pink pussy sores. "*Kya re*, Sikander," sneered Hyder Ali. "Slacking in your job because your pets must eat?"

"What's it to you, O' gardaloo?" said Sikander.

The ragpicker's eyes narrowed. "Don't call me gardaloo," he said. "I don't like it."

"What else are you but that?" said Sikander. "You are addicted to that drug you take. You live only for that dose of poison that keeps you alive, and then you wait for your next dose, and your next, and you go on like this, day after day, with no respect for life. Just look at yourself! The very face of death you are."

The ragpicker pretended not to have heard Sikander. A sly look crept into his face and he said, "You haven't heard then, have you? No, it seems not. And perhaps it is better I don't tell you. Why should I do you any favors? Who are you to me, Sikander? Not my brother. Not my relative. Not even my friend."

Sikander threatened as if to get down, and the ragpicker fled some distance, then came back, laughing. "If you pay me, Sikander, I might share some important news," he said.

"Nice try, Hyder Ali, but I will not be the one to fund your habit and rush you to your grave," said Sikander firmly.

"Ah, then, perhaps you will bury your pets soon," said Hyder Ali. "When you hear how your pets have been put to sleep, you will wish you had listened to me. I am told it takes only a few minutes for the injection to work."

"Who ... who would dare do that, Hyder Ali? There are laws against that kind of thing. And, besides, there is that minister in Delhi who will kick up a ruckus. She will bring the skies down if something like this happens."

"It seems you haven't heard, Sikander; so I had better be the first to tell you. One of the strays, it seems, bit a minister's son, a young boy who forgot to tell his parents. After some time, the boy began to act strangely. He began to act like a dog, barking and snapping at people. At first, they thought he was just trying to draw attention, and they weren't surprised, for his father, too, was like that: he craved attention. Then one day the boy bit off a part of his father's ear. And that's when they realized that he was ill, very, very ill. So an order was issued that all strays had to be rounded up. It had to be done quietly, not through the municipality but through a private party, who has asked us, ragpickers, to help out. And for this they will pay well."

Shuffling in his pocket, he brought out a packet of biscuits wrapped in a transparent film. Holding it to the light, he squeezed the packet and said, "See this, Sikander. See the liquid oozing from these biscuits. You know what this is? The liquid that will put your dogs to sleep. Just long enough for the vans to come and collect them."

Sikander jumped off his seat. "Give me that!" he roared.

"Not so fast, Sikander," said the ragpicker slyly. He considered Sikander. A man of average height and strong build. Good-looking, yes, in a rough sort of a way. Couldn't have been more than forty. Married? Probably not! Otherwise why would he be so crazy about those dogs?

"Twenty rupees to see the packets, and two hundred rupees not to feed the dogs. I promise your dogs won't be drugged by my hands, Sikander. I won't have that on my conscience."

Sikander dug into his pocket and brought out two tenners. The ragpicker grabbed them with greasy hands; then he handed over the packets to Sikander.

Holding the packets, Sikander squeezed at them; at once an oily liquid oozed and smudged against the transparent coverings. Sikander brought one of the packets to his nose and sniffed at it. A strange smell! Not floury, not biscuity, but sickeningly fragrant.

"It will cost you two hundred rupees if you want me to spare your pets," said Hyder Ali. Sikander noticed how black and swollen the ragpicker's gums were and how yellow his teeth.

He had no problem about paying, he thought. He earned well enough, more than what he'd have imagined. Being a bachelor, his expenses, too, were limited; he always had money left over at the end of the month. But how could he be sure that Faltoo and Kala Katta would not stray into another neighborhood and meet some other ragpicker who would drug them? He said to Hyder Ali, "Let me think," not quite sure what he wanted to think about. He knew he was buying time; but then the dogs were everything to him. He could not afford to lose them.

But how could he trust the ragpicker? How could he believe him? The ragpicker was, after all, a gardaloo, a brown sugar addict. He would do anything to get his gard. He would lie, cheat, steal, even kill, if necessary. What if this was one of his tricks to fund his habit?

Sikander struggled with himself, then said, "Okay, Hyder Ali, you win. I will give you the money. But, by God, if I find these dogs missing, I will come looking for you, and then you know where I will send you. To your grave!" He fished in his pocket, brought out a wad of notes, and handed two hundred-rupee notes to the ragpicker, who said, "I don't know why you care so much about these dogs, but this I can say: You are a good man, Sikander, a better man than me, and may the moon be witness to that." Waving the notes in midair, he hobbled away, singing: *Pyar hua, ikrar hua....*

He is mad, thought Sikander, clearly, clearly mad. All that gard has affected his mind.

The next day, Sikander reached the spot earlier than usual and waited for the dogs to arrive. Meanwhile, he distracted himself with the street life. To his right was a chemist shop with its shutters down. Through a small window, the chemist gave out medicines. Sometimes, cars and cabs would cruise up and women would emerge – ladies of the night, in tight jeans or in low-backed saris – and the chemist would attend to them. The ladies would be pleased with their purchases. They would return to their vehicles with a bounce in their walk.

Farther up, a giant skywalk curled between buildings, its steely facade gleaming against the night. Below it, a chaiwalla on a cycle poured glasses of tea for waiting cabbies. On jagged pavements slept families of gypsies, the men snoring loudly, the women frowning in their sleep, the children half naked, snot running down their noses, congealed on their lips.

Sikander loved the night. He always had! He could work quietly and efficiently at night. But tonight he was tense. Could he trust that gardaloo? Where was he, and where were his dogs?

He waited. He could not swing the JCB into action lest the dogs arrived, craving their dinner. A fearful thought entered his mind. Perhaps the ragpicker had drugged them and sold them to a kebabwalla. Sikander had heard such stories, about dogs disappearing and ending up as dog meat. But no ... he hoped not!

An hour passed and yet there was no sign of the ragpicker or the dogs. Now a wild panic set in. Leaving the JCB, Sikander started pacing. After some time, he crossed the road, walked over to the watchman, and asked him if he had seen the ragpicker.

"No," said the watchman. "And, anyway, I wouldn't have noticed him because he is such an insignificant fellow."

Then Sikander asked about the dogs, and the watchman looked at him disbelievingly and said, "You are pulling my leg, aren't you? Why would I keep track of stray dogs? You think I have all the time in the world?"

And Sikander said, "Yes, yes, I am pulling your leg. But if it was one of those female workers I had asked about, you would have known, wouldn't you?"

The watchman glared at him. "You had better watch that tongue of yours," he said.

And Sikander said, "Sorry, brother, I meant no offense. In truth, I envy you. It's a fine job you have." He smiled at the watchman, who said gravely, "Fine, yes; but I can't slack. Can't go talking to fellows like you. I have to guard the site and all the construction material. Now buzz off, I say!"

And Sikander walked away....

Shortly after, the dumper arrived, and Sikander had not yet crushed the pile. The four boys who alighted from the back of the dumper found him scraping at the pile with a rake. From it, he had extracted a small cluster of meat bones.

One of the boys spoke tenderly. He said, "What's wrong, Sikander? Not well or what? Tell us, so one of us can take the JCB and finish your round for you."

But Sikander did not answer. He simply stared at the empty sack he had just drawn from the pile and which was dangling from the rusty prongs of his rake. Then slowly he lowered himself to his knees and said, "Yes, I am not well, my friend. I am feeling sick, very sick. Please take this round for me. I will be obliged." This was the first time in his life he would be handing over his haathi.

All through the week, there was no sign of Hyder Ali or the dogs. On his rounds, Sikander would stop and inquire of other ragpickers, but each time he drew a blank. "Hyder Ali? No, I haven't seen him. And not that I care. Maybe he is dead, fallen in some gutter. I hope so. The bastard owes me money. He is a liar and a snake."

By the end of the week, Sikander was convinced that he had been duped by the ragpicker. From his friends in the municipality he had learned that there was no campaign against strays, no plans to eliminate them. In which case, *where* were his dogs? Surely, if they were safe, they would come to him. They, too, would be miserable without him.

One day, when he was at the spot, about to raise the JCB onto the pile, he heard a voice from the pavement ask: "Would you be Sikander, the crusher of garbage and a lover of dogs?"

He was startled. It was more than two weeks since the dogs had disappeared. Every time he would see a dog, he would slow down and stop, his heart racing; then feel dejected. Now someone was reminding him of his loss.

He reversed the JCB and the owner of the voice came into sight. A pleasant-faced man, plumpish, middle-aged, wearing a white shirt, dark gray trousers, and chappals.

"Would I be right in thinking you are Sikander?" asked the man, and Sikander replied, "Yes, but who are you? And how do you know about my dogs?"

"Sikander is a fine name," said the man. "It has great meaning, great importance. I was looking forward to meeting you. I believe you are looking for your dogs, and might, also, be looking for Hyder Ali, in whose possession you left them."

Sikander jumped from his seat and stood before the man. "Yes! I am looking for my dogs. Where are they? As for that gardaloo, when I get my hands on him, I will … I will make him remember his mother."

The man shook his head gravely. "I am not sure you will do that. You seem to be a good man, a kind man. But right now you are angry. And right now you also have work to do. And duty before pleasure, I say. So I request you to meet me later. Once your work is done. You see, I am like you. I work nights. At that hospital down the road. Where I look after patients who can't look after themselves. And I get no time to eat. Which is why, I must eat now. Then later we can meet. And, by the way, my name is Vishwas Kharade, and I am here to relieve you of your tension. If you will trust me, that is."

The face before him was calm and composed, devoid of guile. Looking into it, Sikander said, "Where would you like to meet, Vishwas Kharade? And will you promise to tell me about the dogs? I need to know, please." He was surprised at the desperation in his voice.

"We will meet on that skywalk, right in the center. It is a good place. We can sit there and talk, undisturbed. It is eleven o'clock now. So let's say we meet at one. That will give me enough time to eat and you – you can finish your work."

After Kharade left, Sikander worked furiously. He slammed the claw of the JCB on pile after pile, not caring that the sound would wake up people. Later, he drove the truck like a man possessed, so fast that some of the garbage spilled from the back and fell onto the road. Not my fault, he shrugged. How often had he requested his bosses to close up the backs of these trucks! And how often had he drawn their attention to the stench and the pollution! But had they listened, had they taken any steps? "Why do you want to disturb the system?" they would say.

"The citizens are not complaining. So why you want to create unnecessary work?"

The skywalks were a new addition to the city, and this one ran from the railway station all the way to the crossroads, where it branched out into a series of exits. Already its sides had rusted, Sikander noted, treading in silence. Along the way, he saw figures sleeping, huddled under blankets, and he wondered how long before the whole skywalk turned into a dormitory.

Vishwas Kharade was there already, seated in the center. He looked very comfortable, like one presiding over the city. As soon as Sikander sat, he said, "Brother Sikander, you have come here for a reason, out of great concern for your dogs. So I will not prolong your agony; I will give you the answers you seek. But you must give me a patient hearing, and you must not judge or condemn Hyder Ali until I have finished speaking. This you must promise me."

Sikander nodded, and Vishwas Kharade began. "Hyder Ali was once a boy like any other. There was hope in his eyes, joy in his actions, and goodness in his heart. He was born in the village of Rawalgaon, to a family of modest means. His mother was a housewife, his father worked at an arms' factory in Sankheda. He was the youngest among four siblings, all sisters.

"When his father retired, he got Hyder a job at the arms' factory. The boy, who was only eighteen, moved to Sankheda. He would return to Rawalgaon once a month to see his family. Visiting, he would give half his salary to his mother; for his father he would bring gifts like shirts, shoes, and razors; and for his unmarried sisters, he would carry saris and perfumes.

"Then one day, a gun went missing from the packing department of the factory and the suspicion fell on Hyder. His bosses called him and grilled him. They claimed that someone had seen him take the gun, which he flatly denied. They asked him to confess to the theft, which he refused. He felt they were accusing him because he was a Muslim. He felt someone was framing him, was out to get him. But who? He could not say.

"Not knowing what to do, he called up a friend of his in Rawalgaon – Shaukat – who advised him to get away as soon as possible. Shaukat advised him to go to Mumbai and stay there for a few months. If the police were called in, he could be jailed and beaten.

"So Hyder left for Mumbai that day itself. But before leaving, he transferred all his money to his mother's bank account and asked Shaukat to explain the situation to his father. His father might be able to speak to his bosses and convince them, he said. Maybe then he could return.

"He came to Mumbai with five hundred rupees in his pocket. And no sooner had he arrived than two men approached him and asked him if he wanted a job. They said there was a job available with a recruitment agency that sent people to the Middle East. If Hyder proved himself, in a few months he would find himself on a plane to Bahrain or Dubai.

"His new friends made him fill up a form and even helped him with the details. And they sympathized when he told them how he had to run away from the factory. They said they knew the moment they had seen him that he was an honest man who was in trouble and that they should help him. They asked him for two thousand rupees. Not for themselves, they said, but for the manager of the agency who would have to be softened.

"When Hyder told them how much he had on him, they laughed and said he was very brave, coming to Mumbai with so little money. They said they would put in the rest but he would have to repay them from his first salary. They took the five hundred rupees off him, promising to return in an hour or so.

"But they never did, and Hyder had to spend the night at the railway station. He said the station stank like an unclean toilet and that the announcements kept him awake all night. He did not have the money to call home or to call Shaukat and, for the first time in his life, he felt afraid.

"The next day he wandered around outside the station, wondering if he should return home by traveling in the toilet of a train. His head hurt from the noise of the traffic; he felt he was drowning in a sea of people. He stopped some strangers and requested them for some money, but they just recoiled and moved away.

"Toward afternoon, some urchins befriended him and shared with them their food. And they told him where he could get a regular meal and where he could find himself a job, pointing to an eatery called 'Sadanand Thali.'

"The eater owner interviewed him, then hired him. He would be a table cleaner, a waiter, and a washer-boy, all rolled into one. No pay for three months, during his probation period, but he would get two meals, two cups of chai, and a place to sleep. For that, he would have to put in twelve hours of work daily.

"The owner's name was Suresh Babu. He was a religious man. He did puja three times a day. At other times, he had a foul temper. He would not hesitate to abuse the boys or to cuff them or to pull their hair until tears ran from their eyes. And every night he would make the boys massage him, for two hours nonstop.

"The eatery was just outside the railway station, and it so happened that, one day, Hyder spotted the two men who had cheated him. Great anger came over him; he ran after them, and brought one of them down. He began to punch his opponent, even while the other rained blows on him. He ended up breaking the nose of his adversary, who began to bleed profusely.

"Soon, a railway constable arrived and pulled them apart. Hyder's shirt was drenched with blood. The constable wanted to take Hyder to the lockup, but Suresh Babu settled with him for Hyder's release.

"Having paid off the constable, Suresh Babu refused to pay Hyder his dues. He said Hyder would now have to work for free for another three months. Hyder pleaded with him. He said he needed to call home, needed to speak to his parents, who would be sick worrying about him. But none of that served to move Suresh Babu.

"And then Hyder did something he shouldn't have: he abused Suresh Babu and called him a cheat, and he cursed him and his family.

"Seeing that a crowd had gathered, Suresh Babu started shouting. 'Look, brothers, look! What an ungrateful fellow this boy is! I give him a job; I give him food, clothes, and a roof over his head; and what does he do? He abuses me and my family. He says he will teach me a lesson. Arrey, what lesson can I learn, when I have seen such ingratitude from him?'

"Hyder began to protest. He began to say what a liar Suresh Babu was, when he saw something in the faces of the people that made him realize they weren't going to believe him. And then he felt a hand on his shoulder and he heard a voice at his ear say: 'Come! It is time to leave. Before things get out of hand.' And because that was the only kind voice in the crowd, Hyder obeyed him. His well-wisher turned out to be a man named Idris.

"Idris Khan gave Hyder a place to stay. He gave him food, clothes, and money to call home. Speaking to his parents, Hyder learned how bad things were. His father was driving an autorickshaw but had to stop on the road often because he was diabetic and had to pee. This would upset his passengers. Daily, they'd quarrel with him, and daily he'd come home in a foul mood. His sisters had stopped getting proposals – there was no money for their marriages. His mother wanted to take on small tailoring jobs but his father wouldn't hear of it.

"His father felt that Hyder shouldn't have run away, he should have stayed and cleared his name. He said that Hyder had shamed them by running away; the police had visited their home and questioned them before all the neighbors. Hyder realized he couldn't return now, and his parents, too, agreed with him.

"And now our Hyder does what most boys of his age do when they come to Mumbai: he falls into temptation. With Idris and his brother Bilkis, he embarks on a life of crime.

"The brothers were engaged in a fraud called Double Dollar. They would approach a man outside the railway station and, pointing to a woman, any woman, ask him if he would be interested in a few hours of pleasure. If the man agreed, one of them would walk up to the woman and speak to her; then, returning, he would tell the man that she would meet him at a certain hotel. Of course, he would have to pay them in advance. As it turned out, this Double Dollar con was foolproof, because the men who got cheated wouldn't take their complaints to the police. They'd be too embarrassed …

"Traveling on the late-night trains, the brothers would steal the luggage of sleeping passengers. And they would also steal from those who would be sleeping in the station foyer. Soon, Hyder and the Khan brothers were joined by a man named Shamsher, who had earlier led a gang from Madanpura.

"Shamsher was a history sheeter. He had spent a few years in prison, which had made him hard and cynical. He had no sense of right and wrong, and had very little patience with those who did not think like him.

"With him, the gang took to larger crimes. Hiring motorcycles, they would go to the Borivali National

Park, where they would threaten and rob couples and picnickers.

"As the money poured in, they developed new habits. They began drinking, began visiting brothels and gambling dens, and began to dress flashily. In all this, Shamsher took the lead.

"The first time they took Hyder to a brothel he felt shy and refused to go with any woman. Then Shamsher said, 'If you don't go, it will spoil my mood,' and Idris and Bilkis too said he shouldn't act like a spoilsport, they were brothers in everything, after all.

"And so began our Hyder's corruption. Many times he thought of breaking away from this gang but did not know how. He sent money home but did not visit his family. Not because he was scared of the police, but because he could not look his father in the eye.

"He began drinking heavily and smoking hashish from a chillum. He also began to see a young prostitute called Rashmi, to whom he had lost his heart.

"Rashmi, too, liked him. But she had seen more of life than Hyder and did not want him to waste his youth. So even while entertaining him, she would urge him to marry a *decent girl* and settle down. When she saw he had no intention of staying away, she lay down with Shamsher, just at the time when Hyder was about to visit her.

"Seeing them together, Hyder went mad. He abused Shamsher and threatened to kill him. He told Shamsher that it was he who had led them into sin; he was the Satan in their lives.

"Shamsher was not the kind to take insults lightly. In prison, he had held his own against dreaded gang lords. He whipped out a knife and ran it down Hyder's chest. Then, while Hyder was rushed to hospital, he gave Idris and Bilkis a warning – they could either continue to work with him or go their own way.

"By now, the brothers had a lavish lifestyle. They liked stylish clothes, good food, and throwing money at bars and brothels. And there were expenses, too. Idris had to pay sixty thousand rupees to an agent who had got his nephew a job in Oman. As for Bilkis, he was trying to get his mehbooba out of the sex trade, for which he needed a lakh of rupees. Idris had also developed a liking for the races. And Bilkis had his eye on a 350cc motorcycle. Yes, the brothers had their weaknesses, which mattered more to them than their relationship with Hyder. Besides, Hyder had been foolish, he had been ungrateful. For the sake of a prostitute, he had endangered a friendship.

"And so, again, Hyder found himself alone and homeless. The fool that he was, he had not saved a rupee. He would send half his money home and spend the rest on Rashmi. Now he began to take up daily wage work, like washing the pier at Chowpatty Beach or washing vessels after a wedding. Some days he would join the workforce that paved the road leading to the Haji Ali Dargah. There, he remembered his father's words from the Quran: *He who is saved from his own greed, Allah deems him most successful.*

"But, alas, it was not possible for Hyder to tread the path of righteousness, for desperation had clouded his judgment and made him angry and bitter. Besides, he still craved Rashmi, he still visited her, running up huge debts at the brothel.

"After a while, the pimps forbade him from coming, and yet he would show up, drunk and out of his senses. Rashmi, fearing for his life, told him she did not want to have anything to do with him, he should stop coming. That's when he went crazy. He started doing gard, and in no time got addicted."

"But why are you telling me all this?" cried Sikander, rising to his feet. "I am not interested in Hyder Ali and how he went to his ruin. All I want to know is where my dogs are."

Vishwas Kharade reached out and caught Sikander by the wrist. "You promised, friend," he said, and reluctantly Sikander sat down.

Vishwas Kharade continued. "Why did he do it? Take to that vile habit? I think it was because he wanted Rashmi's sympathy. He wanted her to tell him to stop. He wanted to hear that she would do anything to make him stop. He wanted to know that she would fight the pimps and all her customers just to be with him. Sometimes, Sikander, a man needs to know how important he is to the world and how far the world will go to save him. That is what happened to our friend. He had pledged his life to Rashmi, not realizing that she wasn't in control of her own, and that whatever little control she had, she was using it to save him.

"The pimps, meanwhile, spoke to Shamsher, asking him to do something about his old friend, who, by his loud drunken rants, was ruining their business. Besides, he owed them a few thousand rupees.

"When Rashmi heard about this, she begged the pimps to transfer her to another brothel. She said she would earn and pay them off, but they should spare Hyder's life.

"But nothing could save our friend now; he had made a pact with the devil. To feed his habit, he would steal road signs and gutter tops; he would go into the railway yard, at night, and take whatever he could find: brakes, cables, handgrips, sleepers, taps, window shutters, and he would sell these and buy gard. Soon, smoking and inhaling wasn't enough; he took to injecting himself. He would mix the gard with lime juice and water and shoot it directly into his veins. And sometimes he wouldn't find a vein, and then his flesh would burn and rupture. And sometimes he ran out of gard and would get severe stomach pains, convulsions, runs, and vomiting.

"One night the police waited for him in the railway yard, and they caught him and cut a nerve at the back of his foot. They warned him that the next time he would not be so lucky. They would book him for peddling drugs and put him away for ten years.

"His career in crime was over; his right leg was useless. So he took up the goni, the sack, and became a ragpicker. In the waste of the city, he lost himself. After all, he had so much to forget: his family, his friends, his home, and the fact that he would never attend his sisters' marriages or see Rashmi again. The only thing that kept him going was the thought that there were others like him, the stray dogs, who also rummaged and scraped for their meals. And he enjoyed his nightly skirmishes with you, Sikander, and the fact that you fed your dogs before going about your work. He felt you had some decency, some kindness. You were everything human.

"And now, Sikander, let me tell you why I am sharing all this with you. Our friend was dying. He knew that, and he knew, also, that he had to do one good deed before he was gone, so that one good man would remember him kindly. And that man was you. He wanted *you* to know about his life, wanted *you* to think well of him. So, from the money he took from you, he took your dogs to the animal hospital in Parel, where the white one's eyes were treated. And he did not want the white one to be alone, and so he also took the black one. And having done that, he came to us at the hospital and got himself admitted. But before that, he gave up his goni. He knew, that in the place where he was going, he would have no need for it.

"Oh yes, and in the days that followed, he suffered, really suffered, and when he was conscious he would tell me about his life, making me promise that I would narrate it to you.

"So come, Sikander, join me in saying a small prayer for this hapless man, and let us wish a better life for him. Either in heaven, or the next time here, on earth."

With that, Vishwas Kharade gripped Sikander by the shoulders and helped him to his feet, and Sikander felt something leave him. A cloud of anxiety, of doubt. All that the city had built up and accumulated, all that it had thrown up.

Auntie Elena's Revenge

THE DOORBELL RANG WITH piercing intensity. It made Auntie Elena wince. She knew who it might be; or rather, she suspected. Not again, she thought, wondering, should I tell her off? But, no, it was not in her nature to be offensive. All her life Auntie Elena had lived by the holy book, had taken its commandments to be the guiding lights of her life. And now, at seventy-five, she wasn't going to ruin that. She wasn't going to be rude to a neighbor.

Wearing a patient, impassive face – the kind she'd worn when she had taught English to a class of rambunctious schoolboys – she opened the door and said, "What can I do for you, Mrs. Shah?"

The short, stout lady before her smiled. "Some family members have come … I was telling them about your *boootiful* kitchen … Can they see it, please?"

Auntie Elena felt the muscles in her throat tighten. Her tongue readied itself for a retort; the refusal would come easily, like a whiplash. But then her late father's words swam into her mind: "When dealing with people who are inherently annoying, remember, they might not have had the same upbringing as you, the same good fortune. The Lord has willed differently for them."

She swallowed her annoyance and said, "Please come in. I *am* a bit busy. But feel free to look around …"

Four women entered and went around the kitchen. They gasped at its interiors. They stood before the jade-colored platform and exclaimed how clever it was to have the stove in the center, with enough space to move around and the storage so accessible. They marveled at the cabinets, their Scandinavian-style decor. They even went to the extent of opening the cabinets and looking inside. They spoke among themselves in whispers; then asked if they could take photographs; to which Auntie Elena said no, a flat no. They looked at her sulkily, as though she had spoiled their plans; and then one of them asked what it had cost to create this beautiful kitchen.

She knew where this was coming from, who had primed this woman. She shot Mrs. Shah a glance, but her neighbor's face showed no sign of guilt, no trace of complicity. Auntie Elena shrugged and said, "I have no idea; it was my brother Carl who paid for it. He lives in Toronto. He made all the payments from there."

"Can you ask him?" said Mrs. Shah sweetly. "I want one like this. Not for me – what would I do with a big kitchen? – but for my daughter, Sejal." She lowered her voice. "Seju is getting married soon, to a rich boy from Ahmedabad, and we must show his family that we have modern thinking. That is why we want to take a photo." She looked pleased with herself, as though she could not have proffered a more satisfactory explanation.

"Yes, but sorry," said Auntie Elena firmly. "You should look up some catalogues or get onto the internet. You will get ample ideas from there."

That ended the conversation. The ladies trooped out.

After they left, Auntie Elena got back to what she was doing before the interruption: churning the batter for a Christmas pudding. Next to her, on a plate, was a pile of candied peel, cherries, raisins, and sultanas, which had been soaked in rum for the last six months. With strong, bony fingers, now dark and wrinkled with age, Auntie Elena stirred at the bowl in her hand, pausing, from time to time, to dip a finger in and taste the batter. She would do this until she got the consistency right.

Truth be told, in all of Bandra, you wouldn't find a kinder soul than Auntie Elena. Even when she was teaching schoolkids, when she had those added responsibilities of setting test papers and correcting exam papers and arranging concerts, plays, and inter-class debates, she would render community service with the zeal of a nun. She would take her students to orphanages and slums, where they would distribute old clothes and toys, and to homes for the aged, where they'd know the joy that comes out of giving books, free food, and free medicines to the elderly. She would teach the orphans and slum kids to feed stray cats and dogs and would motivate the elders to put up plays and singing competitions. "It is not just about giving them time and money," she would say. "But about raising self-esteem."

She now thought of her neighbor and the many annoyances to which she had subjected her. Mrs. Shah was a widow. She lived in a one-bedroom apartment next door, with her two daughters, Sejal and Tejal. As of now, the girls were pretty, but their hips were filling out fast. There was no doubt that in a few years they would resemble their mother. As a family, the Shahs were loud and noisy, and they left their front door open all the time, which annoyed Auntie Elena greatly. The girls fought with their mother in thin, shrill voices, and the mother fought back stubbornly. Their open-door quarrels made Auntie Elena uncomfortable; it made her miss her peaceful little cottage on Chapel Road, which she had to sell because maintaining it became impossible and the builder offered a price high enough to buy a three-bedroom apartment in a new building. Her brother Carl – bless him! – didn't want a single rupee from the sale. So Auntie Elena found herself with a substantial saving, and more comfortable than she had ever been.

Of course, it had taken her some time to get used to staying in a high-rise, a Bandra so altered from the place of her childhood, where she would play with her friends on the beach, collect crabs, go on midnight boat rides, and explore its orchards for mangoes, tamarinds, and peaches. The people then were different, too, she thought. More close-knit, more supportive, more community-minded.

Her thoughts returned to her neighbor. This was not the first time that Mrs. Shah had dropped in uninvited and, certainly, it would not be the last. Auntie Elena felt sorry for the widow, she knew she was lonely and did not deserve the way her daughters spoke to her. But, still, Auntie Elena liked her privacy, and her neighbor did not seem to get that; she was always bringing visitors to see her kitchen, and it had come to a point when Auntie Elena dreaded the sound of the doorbell. In fact, time and again, Mrs. Shah would ring the doorbell and say to Auntie Elena, "Why you don't leave your front door open? Why do you keep it closed all the time? It's so nice to see each other; we can chat when we want to." How to tell her that she, Auntie Elena, didn't quite relish seeing Mrs. Shah lounging in the living room, on her sofa, whale-like, in a loose cotton nightgown, remote control in hand, blaring her television serials. And she, Auntie Elena, certainly did not enjoy being a party to her fights with her daughters. She found it distasteful. No, something must be done to stop this invasion, thought Auntie Elena firmly. Something to drive home the message.

The Christmas Day lunch was, perhaps, the most important event in Auntie Elena's life. It had to be perfect, just perfect, because, well, all her favorite people would be there – the Vazs from Santa Cruz, the Pereiras from Khar, the Noronhas from Kalina, the Lobos from Byculla, and, of course, Dr. Chris de Souza from Holy Family Hospital and his charming wife, Rosemary. After the extraordinary meal which her guests would savor, Dr. Chris would bring out his guitar and Auntie Elena would get on to the piano, and together they would sing and the afternoon would stretch out like an exquisite soprano, well into the evening, assuring this little gathering that they had the Lord's blessings, silently and munificently, for the rest of the year.

Auntie Elena noted with satisfaction the spread on the kitchen platform – the roast chicken with mint sauce, the baked salmon with lemon sauce, the potato-and-ham salad, the asparagus mousse, the crispy spinach with garlic prawns, the bacon-and-sausage rolls, the tray of cold cuts, the fish vindaloo with rice, and the yakhni lamb pulao – and she felt a surge of achievement. It had taken her all of three days to prepare this, and she had to work so hard, cutting back on her afternoon sleep and her evening walks.

But it would be worth it, she thought, thinking of her guests' faces when they would see the spread. She wished Carl and Marie were here. She wished that her brother and his wife were coming down for Christmas, but promptly after the new year their granddaughter was leaving for the UK, for her postgraduate studies at the University of Leeds, and they wanted to spend time with her. Understandable, totally understandable! thought Auntie Elena. But at least she would send them photographs of the Christmas lunch, so that they would know what they were missing.

She reached for her cell phone and tapped at the camera icon. She tried this angle and that, and eventually settled for a top shot which captured the full array of her labors. The Christmas pudding, the almond soufflé, and the coffee liqueur mousse would not feature; but that was fine, she thought. Her brother was anyway forbidden sweet things; he would not miss those. Suddenly, a smile spread across her face. It made her look younger. Made her look as though she was a young girl contemplating some mischief.

She bathed, she dressed, she powdered; then daubed on a little rouge before the mirror. She was ready for her guests now. She stepped out and saw that her neighbor's door was ajar, not fully, just slightly. She knocked gently, and after a while Mrs. Shah opened the door. "Why, I was just coming to see you," she said with a look of delight. "Just now in fact. To wish you a Merry Christmas."

"Do come," said Auntie Elena. "I have some guests coming shortly, but do come and spend a few minutes with me. And bring your cell phone, so that you can take some pictures."

Mrs. Shah looked at Auntie Elena warily. "You don't mind?" she asked. "Really, you don't mind?"

"No," said Auntie Elena smiling.

The two of them entered the apartment. Auntie Elena allowed Mrs. Shah to walk ahead, through the passage that led to the kitchen. As they entered the kitchen, Auntie Elena snapped on the lights and said, "Go on, Mrs. Shah, take some pictures; feel free!" She smiled at her neighbor. The light fell onto the kitchen platform, illuminating the feast.

Mrs. Shah stared at the plump roast chicken with its stomach sewed up and its legs in midair, and she looked at the salmon, its clear black eye fixed and unblinking, and she felt faint, she felt dizzy. So this is what non-vegetarian fare looks like, she thought. Like death! Like murder! Fighting back the nausea, she said weakly to Auntie Elena, "It's all right, all right. I don't need any pictures. I will just explain to the designer how the kitchen looks."

"Are you sure?" asked Auntie Elena helpfully.

"Yes, yes," said Mrs. Shah. "I must go now. I am expecting a call … from Ahmedabad."

"I hope there is no emergency," said Auntie Elena.

"Something like that," said Mrs. Shah, clutching her nightgown and hurrying toward her apartment. She slammed the door behind her and, a moment later, Auntie Elena heard the sound of a bolt sliding into place.

There's still time for the guests to arrive, but there is no reason why I can't get started, why I can't celebrate my hard-earned privacy, she thought.

Moving to the bar, she looked over her collection of wines and reached for a bottle of Merlot. She poured herself a glass, right to the brim. "Merry Christmas, Elena," she said to herself, as the thick red liquid touched her lips. "May you never feel your age. And may the Lord forgive you your trespasses."

The Earth Shall Be Enjoyed by Heroes

THEY CAME FOR HIM after his clinic had shut, his secretary had left, and the neighborhood – usually bustling with activity – was a pale shadow of itself, stunned and frozen under the streetlights. There were three policemen and one policewoman, and among them an older constable, who was grim-faced but polite. "Sorry to trouble you, Doctor-sahib," he said from behind his whiskers. "You will have to come with us. There has been a complaint against you. Perhaps some mistake, surely some misunderstanding, but we have to investigate, you know." He avoided the doctor's eyes and stared at the floor unhappily. "Give me a few minutes," said the doctor. "You can sit in the waiting room; I will switch on the A/C for you." He knew what this was about. Or rather, he suspected. Those damn builders! Or was it those municipality guys? What did it matter? There was no difference between the two. Each was as insidious, as corrupt as the other. Look what they had done to his serene, beautiful neighborhood. Sent it under the hammer, sent it reeling, till it was disfigured. And Doctor-sahib, who had grown up here, could recognize it no longer.

Anyone else in Doctor-sahib's shoes would have been elated with the changes. Any other doctor, that is. Because more development simply meant more patients, and more patients meant more money. Also, people who bought new flats, costing upward of fifty million rupees, wouldn't crib about a hike in fees. If Doctor-sahib had been a shrewd man of progress, he'd be salivating at the changes, he would have braced himself to benefit from the boom.

The truth was: he didn't see this rash of construction as a boom. He saw it as an epidemic. The virus of greed, as he called it, which had gripped the city's caretakers and driven them mad.

Why else would they permit construction on small plots in narrow lanes?

Why else would they approve plans for residential towers that were twenty stories high, with seven levels of parking, when there was no road to take all that traffic?

Why else would they sanction projects, with no improvement to the infrastructure or to the sanitation?

Madness! Sheer madness! Doctor-sahib would think when walking to his clinic.

And not that he had kept quiet and been a passive spectator to all this random construction.

First, he had done a survey of the new buildings coming up in the lane behind his clinic. There were three 20-story buildings, cheek by jowl, with three apartments per story. That would mean a minimum of 120 cars per building, 360 cars rolling out every morning, on a road no wider than twenty-three feet.

Then, via a letter, he had brought this to the attention of the housing department, the municipality, and the road transport organization and, not getting a reply, to the chief minister.

When that failed to draw a response, he had written to the newspapers and moved the Bombay High Court for a stay order on the three other projects that were coming up in the lane. The high court had taken serious note of his objections and imposed a blanket stay on all projects in the neighborhood. That's when the phone calls had started, and the death threats. That's when they had vandalized his 1937 Jaguar Roadster, causing grievous injury to its sleek black body and to his disbelieving heart.

It was just as well that Doctor-sahib was a bachelor and had no family of his own. Otherwise, who knows, his adversaries would have harmed them as well. His single status emboldened him in his fight against his opponents. He was sure that the recent complaint was yet another ploy on the part of those thugs. Well, he wasn't going to back out now. Worst case, he would call his old friend Aditya Sharma to the police station. Aditya was an accomplished lawyer. His name appeared regularly in the newspapers. He was often appointed as amicus curiae, a friend of the court, in order to arbitrate on matters of dispute.

The police station was within walking distance of the doctor's clinic, but the inspector had sent a jeep for him. That much respect he had for Doctor-sahib. And why not? Everyone in the neighborhood knew what a good man he was. The fact that he never took money from poor patients, that he had a nominal rate for retired persons, that he never refused a home visit during an emergency, and that he gave free medicines to those who could not afford them. Clearly, Doctor-sahib was an angel. So what if he never wore a white coat and had no wings to show for it? He had a heart of pure gold, and it was impossible to imagine the neighborhood without him.

The police station had been recently refurbished. Its walls were painted beige, its columns white, the corridor leading to the senior inspector's office was tiled with slabs of gray polished granite. A queue of complainants thronged the enclosure in the center, where several constables sat. The complainants appeared hot and bothered, while the constables chatted away happily.

Senior Inspector Bedekar rose to greet Doctor-sahib. He was a tall, dark man, with a well-trimmed mustache. "Doctor-sahib," he said, "I feel so bad about this. I know you are doing God's work, but I had no choice, believe me." His voice dropped. "The matter is quite serious. You will understand when I tell you." He nodded to the others, who filed out quietly, except for the older constable with the whiskers, who moved to shut the office doors.

Doctor-sahib looked around the room; he had been here before. The first time was when a pavement dweller had stabbed his pregnant wife in a drunken rage, missing her belly by an inch. Then, when an urchin-boy, a brown sugar addict, had been caught stealing and been beaten so badly by the public that he could have died had Doctor-sahib not intervened. Doctor-sahib had gone to the police station to request that they send the boy to a de-addiction center. Then, of course, when his beloved Jaguar had been mutilated, and his heart was in so many pieces that he could barely file a complaint. But who could he file against? Who would have seen anything? Who would have the guts to testify against the culprits?

The last time he had been here was when a fast-food outlet had brought chairs onto a sidewalk and blocked it. Doctor-sahib had appealed to the owner. "You see, sir, this is a public walkway, and you are preventing free movement. I request you to remove these tables and chairs."

The owner was a short, vulpine-faced man, wearing white clothes and a gold chain around his neck. He had looked at Doctor-sahib warily and said, "How is it bothering you? You just walk around, no? As it is, people walk on the main road all the time. Where are there any sidewalks left in Mumbai! So many hawkers, and repair work going on all the time. All these people come from the villages and set up stalls anywhere. But I am from this area. So everyone knows me. Even the police. Even the municipality. And they don't interfere with my business. They like to see me prosper."

Doctor-sahib understood the threat and the nexus. Sometimes he felt older than his forty-odd years. He felt defeated by the resistance he faced each time he tried to do something correct. Illegal encroachments had been one of his battles, and it was a losing battle, he would admit to himself. He tried to explain to the man in white that if everyone thought that way there'd be no law and order, no public spaces. But he had looked at Doctor-sahib coldly and said, "So what you want to do? How far you want to take this?"

Then Doctor-sahib had snapped. He had said to the man, "You will see," and had turned and walked to the police station, where Inspector Bedekar had been most sympathetic. He had sent a constable with Doctor-sahib, who ordered the man to remove his furniture from the sidewalk. The owner had looked at Doctor-sahib with uncontained fury. But Doctor-sahib had chosen to ignore the hostile looks and said to him, "Sir, the Goddess Laxmi will respect you only if you respect others. What is in your destiny is going to come to you, anyway. But for that, you don't have to inconvenience others."

At once the goon's face had softened. He had reached out and pumped Doctor-sahib's hands vigorously. "You are a good man, Doctor-sahib, a good man," he said. "You *are* my well-wisher. You *are* like my elder brother. So I will listen to you." Doctor-sahib was not sure of the sibling honor conferred, but he was glad to have gotten his way.

Now Inspector Bedekar spoke. "Doctor-sahib, we all know your reputation. We know how much service you do and how highly people think of you. We know you are a man of honor and that you have a large and kind heart." He paused and leaned forward, his elbows resting on his desk, his palms locked. "But there has been a complaint against you, a serious complaint, and it is our duty to investigate. So I hope you will let us do our job. Without judging us or thinking too badly of us."

"My dear Bedekar, why do you think I am here? If there has been a complaint against me, it is my duty to respond. As a responsible citizen, I have to help you do your job. Now tell me, what do my enemies have to say about me this time? What is their complaint?" A light smile played on Doctor-sahib's face.

Inspector Bedekar cursed softly in his mind. Sometimes he hated his job. Especially when he had to investigate a complaint he knew was false. He was sure Doctor-sahib was innocent. But the complaint was serious, and he wanted to act promptly, before those presswallas got wind of it. Once that happened and the news broke, his hands would be tied. He would have to follow protocol; he would have to take Doctor-sahib into custody.

The inspector flicked open his cell phone and held it so that Doctor-sahib could see the screen. "Know this woman?" he asked. "And this man?" He swiped at the screen.

"The woman is Manju," said Doctor-sahib. "She used to come to my house to collect my laundry which she would get washed at the dhobi ghat. I terminated her services some time back, but I do see her as my patient. The man, I don't know. Can't say I have ever seen him."

The inspector realized that the constable was still standing, so he pointed to the chair next to Doctor-sahib. The constable pulled the chair to the side and sat down, such that the three of them were now in a triangle. The inspector pushed a notepad toward him and said, "Take notes, Dandekar. In detail, mind you." Then to Doctor-sahib: "I hope you don't mind?" And Doctor-sahib shrugged, to indicate that he was fine with it.

Reclining in his chair, the inspector said, "You say she is your patient. Since when? What do you treat her for, and when was the first time you saw her?"

"Well, let me see. The first time she consulted me was when she had some swellings on her feet. She was coming to my home to pick up the laundry then, and after I examined her I attributed it to her carrying heavy loads of washing and wearing cheap footwear. I remember asking her to increase her water intake and to wear comfortable footwear, and, of course, I prescribed an anti-inflammatory tablet. But why? What has the complaint got to do with her?"

"If you don't mind, Doctor-sahib," said the inspector, "I will be asking the questions from now on. Just so that we understand the situation better. And the faster we do that, the better it will be for you. I hope you trust me on that?"

"Yes, of course," said Doctor-sahib. He felt a bit uneasy and wondered if he should call Aditya. His lawyer friend would drop whatever he was doing and rush over. With him here, Bedekar would have to get to the point. He'd have to drop this cat-and-mouse game.

"So, when she first told you about her problem, her swollen feet, did it occur to you to call her to your clinic? To examine her there?"

"No, she just showed me the swellings, and I could see she had blisters. It was something very minor. I didn't need to make a big deal out of it, by calling her to the clinic and making her wait. It could easily be cured with a mild anti-inflammatory – and the right kind of footwear. Lots of water."

"And do you do this often? See patients at home and prescribe? Or was this a first?"

"It's not that she was a patient then. Or that I see patients at home. It's just that her feet were troubling her, she had come to my door with a problem, and I was in a position to help."

The inspector nodded and waited; he was giving Dandekar time to get all this down.

Then he asked, "And where were you when you examined her? In which part of your house?"

"Why, the living room, I think. That's where I would give her the soiled clothes, after taking stock of the clean ones she was returning."

"Please, Doctor-sahib, please think properly where you were when you examined her. It is important. I want you to be sure. Very sure. For your own sake."

"What do you mean for my own sake? And what do you mean you want me to be sure? What are you implying, Bedekar? I am not sure what you are getting at."

"Relax, Doctor-sahib. You are already misjudging us. We are only doing our job. This is our way of arriving at the truth. Please cooperate. It is for your own good. Trust me." He looked at Doctor-sahib and saw anger in his eyes. Anger born out of injured pride.

"You say you want to help me and get at the truth, Bedekar. But you are not being very truthful with me. You are not telling me what it is I am being investigated for. Don't you think I have a right to know?"

"Please, Doctor-sahib. If I didn't want to help you, I wouldn't be questioning you myself. I would have delegated this to some junior officer and gone home, to eat dinner with my family and watch TV. If I am here, beyond my hours of duty, it is to see that no harm comes to you."

"What do you mean harm? Who is trying to harm me? And what is this ridiculous line of questioning?" Doctor-sahib sprang to his feet and banged the table with his fist. "I want to know what the hell is going on. Or I am leaving."

Promptly, Dandekar rose to his feet, but Bedekar restrained him. He continued to address Doctor-sahib. "I must request you, Doctor-sahib, to sit down. Should you move from this room, I will have no option but to detain you. Using force, if necessary. You have been accused of rape, of molestation. By none other than your patient, Ms. Manju Kanaujia. Who, I believe, you saw this evening."

Doctor-sahib sank back in his chair. His legs felt weak, his arms numb; he could hear his heart pound. "Yes, I did," he said. "She and her husband came to the clinic. I didn't meet him, though." It suddenly dawned on him. "Is he the man in the photograph?" he asked.

"Yes, he too was at your clinic. But you insisted on seeing her alone. Because you wanted to examine her in private. Without anyone watching."

"Is *that* the accusation?" asked Doctor-sahib softly.

"Yes, that's the story we have been told. That's her statement in the first information report. Now we want to listen to your side of it. And we want to help you."

"What do you want to know? What precisely?" Doctor-sahib was tired and afraid now. Builders and civic officials he could deal with. Because they fought in the open and there was evidence of their crimes all over. Blatant, visible evidence. But this – a woman accusing him of misconduct, of rape – was unknown territory. Something like this could destroy him, destroy all that he had worked for. He would never recover. Never be able to face his patients again. Looking at the inspector, he said weakly, "I would never … never!!!" Bedekar leaned forward and said, "I know, Doctor-sahib, I know you wouldn't. So tell me everything you know about this woman. How you came to know her. How you treated her at your clinic."

"Yes, yes … but first, may I have some water, please?" asked the doctor.

"Of course. I am so sorry, I should have offered," said the inspector. "Tea or coffee? And something to eat? A sandwich or a sev puri? The man down the road is excellent. He might still be open."

"No, I am fine with water," said Doctor-sahib. "Just water will do."

Reaching for a jug, the inspector poured him a glass. And while Doctor-sahib drank, the inspector looked at his tense face magnified in the glass and thought, How frightened people are of the law, how they come apart at the seams; they just don't see us as friends.

Soothed by the break, Doctor-sahib started speaking. Manju Kanaujia had started coming to him two years ago, when he had gotten so busy that he did not have time to attend to his washing. His shirts and trousers he would give to the laundry, but the heavier articles – the bedsheets, blankets, curtains, and towels – he decided to give to a washerman, a dhobi. He had asked around and someone had sent her, saying she worked at the dhobi ghat, her husband was a washerman, and that she was quite prompt in her deliveries.

And so she would come every Sunday to deliver the washed clothes and pick up the dirty ones. This was around eleven in the morning, after he had returned from his club, where he would have played a game of squash and treated himself to a heavy breakfast.

She was a real chatterbox. Would talk about her husband and kids. Her husband drank too much. That's why she never let him do the ironing: he would end up burning the clothes. She would talk about the tough times the dhobis were facing: the water restrictions, the rising cost of detergents, the high electricity bills, and incidents of clothes being stolen from the drying lines. Her children had to make do with less. Their school uniforms were old and shabby and, unlike other kids, they could not afford to have birthday parties. He would listen out of politeness. And, at the end of her visit, would pay her more than he owed her, more than what she had actually earned.

"And how much more would that be?" asked the inspector, his eyes narrowing.

"Not too much. Thirty or forty rupees extra. If, say, I had to pay her a hundred and twenty, I'd give her one fifty and tell her to keep the change. Or if it was one sixty, I would give her two hundred. She said she wouldn't tell her husband about it; he would squander it on drink. Instead, she'd use it to give her children something special in their lunch boxes."

The inspector turned to Dandekar and said, "Please write that Doctor-sahib was always kind to her, he was generous, because she was needy and wanting extra money for her children." Dandekar noted this diligently, in a slow, methodical scrawl.

"Tell us about the time you examined her in your living room," said the inspector.

Doctor-sahib shrugged. "There's not much to say. She was seated on the floor, and I on the sofa, and, from time to time, she kept rubbing her feet and groaning. I realized that she wanted to draw my attention to some discomfort she was feeling. So I asked her what the matter was, and she stuck her feet out and showed me the swellings. Then, on the soles of her feet, the blisters."

"And did you touch her feet or feel the blisters?"

"Just the parts that were swollen," said Doctor-sahib. "To see how bad the problem was."

"Okay. Now please don't get upset and fly off the handle, but we need to know this. At any point, did you ask her to come into your bedroom, saying the light there was better?"

"Certainly not! Is that what she said, the little bitch? In fact, I did not want to say this, but let me tell you something, Bedekar. I felt, even then, that there was something strange about her. While showing me her feet, she raised her sari all the way up to her thighs. And I was embarrassed, greatly embarrassed. I can be shy about these things, even though I am a doctor. So I got up and moved away to write out a prescription for her. I even gave her a tube of ointment. How dare … how dare she say I invited her into the bedroom!"

"Arrey, Doctor-sahib, let her say what she likes. If you have done nothing, then why do you get so angry? Just relax. We will get to the bottom of this. We will catch out her lies."

"*Relax?!* How do you expect me to relax, Bedekar? This is my reputation we are talking about. I think I am going to call my lawyer."

"You are, of course, within your rights to do that. And it's likely that your lawyer will get you out of here in ten minutes. You have not been charged as yet. But then, we will have to request the court for your custody. Which they will grant, because this *is* a non-bailable offense. And that won't be pleasant, I assure you. You won't like staying in one of our cells. But why let it come to that? We are trying to help you. All we are asking for is some information, some clarity. Is that such a problem?" The inspector looked at Doctor-sahib gravely, reproachfully.

"I am sorry, Bedekar, I can see you are being patient. It's just that I am tired. It's been a long day. I've been seeing patients since morning. I've had three cases of dengue, two hospital admissions. I am tired. And hungry."

"Then this is the right time to have a sev puri. And wait, I am ordering a sandwich, too, for you. A toasted sandwich with cheese, tomatoes, and cucumber. You will like that, won't you? And how do you like your sev puri: sweet or spicy? Just tell Dandekar here; he will order it."

"Well, right now, I could do with a little sweetness in my life," said Doctor-sahib, smiling faintly.

"Wait!" said the inspector to Dandekar, who had gotten to his feet. "It is custard apple season. So get a nice big glass of custard apple juice for Doctor-sahib. Get it from that juicewalla down the road. And tell him it's for an important guest." Then, turning to the doctor, he said, "You have this juice, Doctor-sahib, and you will not forget the taste, I promise!"

Doctor-sahib smiled, but in his heart he felt a pinch of guilt. He knew the juicewalla, Babubhai, who had his stall at the end of the street. Babubhai had magic in his fingers. He made the juices to the right degree of sweetness. Doctor-sahib was a regular at his stall, and Babubhai had often told him how the policemen would come and fill their containers with his juices. All for free. That was the price he paid for doing business on the streets of Mumbai.

"Wait, I'd like to pay for this," said Doctor-sahib to Dandekar, who was about to leave.

"Relax, Doctor-sahib. You are our guest now. We can't let you pay," said the inspector. Besides, we too will be eating. He gestured to Dandekar, who promptly vanished, closing the door behind him.

The inspector leaned forward and said in a confiding voice, "Good that he is gone and that we are alone. I can speak to you freely now, Doctor-sahib. Not as one who sits in this chair but as one who is your friend and admirer." He paused, and Doctor-sahib waited. His mind was on the sandwich and sev puri. Not the ideal dinner for him – too high on cholesterol, on calories – but it would do.

"Do you know, Doctor-sahib, why I am here so late, sitting with you and trying to get to the bottom of this case? Earlier I gave you the impression that I was staying back for you. Yes, that is true to some extent. But there is another reason. A more important reason.

"You see these hands, Doctor-sahib? You see how healthy and strong they are? These are hands that have played many games – cricket, hockey, volley ball, badminton, table tennis – and they have helped friends during rock-climbing and mountain-climbing expeditions. These hands have served an ailing father, supported an elderly mother, and held the face of a newly wedded wife, to assure her that she will be looked after for her lifetime. But today these hands have blood on them, the blood of an innocent man. Let me tell you what happened this morning.

"Last night, it seems, there was an altercation between two drunken men and a taxi driver. The men wanted to go to the other side of Grant Road to do some mischief, but the taxi driver refused to take them. He was a young boy from Bihar who had just gotten his license, and had been advised by his friends to steer clear of that area. Anyway, he refused, but the men insisted. One thing led to another, and the men pulled him out of the taxi and began to beat him.

"Fortunately, two constables from our police station were passing by. They stopped the men and asked them what was going on, and the men said it was the taxi driver who had started it: he had gotten aggressive with them. The men insisted that the constables take the taxi driver to the police station and book him. These men, it seems, were the cousins of some minister. They pulled out their cell phones and asked the constables if they'd like to speak to the minister.

"Hearing this, my men got nervous and hauled off the cabbie to the station, where they detained him till morning, till I arrived. The men insisted that the station officer file a complaint of assault, but the officer refused. Instead, he filed a complaint for disturbing the public peace.

"Now, on my way to the station this morning, I get a call from the minister. I won't say who he is, but he *is* a very important man in the state cabinet. He starts some conversation about these 'outsiders' and how, if we weren't careful, they'd start to think they owned the city. Soon, they'd take our jobs and take over our city, he said. Every few seconds, he would stop and ask me, 'Am I not correct?

Am I saying anything wrong? You tell me.' And, of course, I had no option but to agree, because I didn't quite know where this was leading.

"Then he says these outsiders must be taught a lesson, they must be made an example of, and there was one such opportunity right there in my police station. He went on to tell me about the taxi driver who had gotten aggressive with his cousins, two men who meant more to him than his own brothers. 'What exactly did he do, sir?' I asked, to which he said, 'You will not believe: *daat dakhawale*. He showed teeth.'

"He then went on to say that his two cousins would be coming to the police station and that I should teach the taxi driver a lesson in their presence. It was important I did this personally so that the message would get through that no outsider should mess with the locals. He ended by saying he hoped I realized how important this was for our community and for our state.

"Hearing him, I felt repulsed, I felt nauseated. I had studied in a cosmopolitan school and college, grown up with outsiders, enjoyed their company, food, and hospitality. But now I was powerless. High command had spoken. The men came around noon. Their eyes were bloodshot from all the drinking they had done the night before.

"In their presence, we had to beat up the poor taxi driver. We first asked him to apologize to the men, but he refused. He asked, why should he since it wasn't his fault. Each time he said that, I would slap him, hoping that he would apologize and the matter would end there. I had barely slapped him a few times when he peed in his pants. He looked at me horrified, shaking with fright; then, slowly, he spurted blood from his mouth.

"I decided that he had had enough. I instructed a constable to take him to Nair Hospital so that he could get prompt treatment. The two men were disappointed.

They wanted me to beat him more, and seeing that I wouldn't, they abused him on his way out.

"The constable returned toward evening and told me that the driver had recently had oral surgery and that my beating had opened up his stitches. Thankfully, he could get treated in Nair Dental, which was just next to the main hospital. But he was very stricken, very shattered. He kept saying, 'Inspector sahib has been unfair to me; he did not even give me a chance to explain.'

"Now, Doctor-sahib, you might wonder why I am telling you all this. You see these hands? You see them before you? Well, tonight, if I had gone home early, my children would have come running up to me. They would want me to hold them, hug them, put them to bed. They would want me to take them in my arms and stroke their foreheads till they dozed off.

"But how can I do that? How can I touch their soft, innocent faces with these hands and pretend that nothing has happened? How can I perform tender acts of fatherhood with hands that have, in all probability, ruined someone's life, made him bitter – about the law, about justice, about our city, about life, and people in general?

"I was brooding about this and wondering if I should call home and make some excuse and then go to the police gymkhana and have a few drinks, when your washerwoman came in with her complaint.

"It was a serious complaint, saying you had molested her, penetrated her with your fingers in the course of a physical examination, which, under Section 375 of the Indian Penal Code, amounts to rape. The station officer immediately brought it to my attention. And because I know you well, and knew, at once, that this was bogus, I decided to stay back. Your case gave me a chance to stay away from home, away from the humiliation of having to face my children and pretend to be a hero. The truth is, Doctor-sahib, I am no hero. I am as much a victim of my circumstances as you are. But I would like to be one, and the only way I can do so is by saving you. Will you help me do that?" He looked at Doctor-sahib intently, and the doctor nodded.

A few minutes later, the food arrived, and the two men ate appreciatively, in silence, knowing that there was serious work to be done after this, work that would save them both a lot of heartburn. The sev puri was crisp and fresh, but the sandwich tasted a little leathery because it had gone cold while Dandekar waited for the juice to be made. Apparently, more sev puri and sandwiches were coming: two constables were bringing them. Doctor-sahib fretted about Babubhai; he knew the juicewalla was trying to put his son through college, he was saving up for that. Plus, Babubhai needed a new mixer, his old one was giving him trouble. As Doctor-sahib sipped the juice, relishing its creamy sweetness, he remembered that a pharma company would give him a gift every Diwali. Not that he ever asked. But the company would insist he name a gift of his choice, costing up to ten thousand rupees. This time, he thought, he would ask for a mixer for Babubhai, one of those heavy, professional models that work for a lifetime. Babubhai had given Doctor-sahib free juices all through his college days, and this would be his way of making it up to him. Pleased with this thought, Doctor-sahib rose and went to the washroom to wash his hands. Returning, he tapped a couple of oral fresheners into his mouth. Now he was ready to speak, ready to defend himself. Whatever it took to keep himself out of trouble.

A peon came in and picked up the plates, then ran a wipe over the table. Dandekar came in and took his seat. His belly seemed distended; he looked as though he had eaten well. From under his desk, the inspector drew a can of air freshener and sprayed the room. Clouds of vapor rose and faded, and the smell of spices gave way to a sweet lavender fragrance. Fed, sated, and convinced that he was now in the company of friends, Doctor-sahib began his story.

After he had treated her swollen feet, the washerwoman had started getting extremely familiar. She had asked Doctor-sahib why he hadn't married, why he didn't have a girlfriend. How do I tell her I am married to my work? he said, and, besides, I don't like anyone prying into my personal life. She had said to him that it was not good for a man to be without a woman, especially a nice-looking man like him. He had understood what she was getting at, but had brushed it aside, thinking, if he didn't give it any importance, she would get the message. But then he had noticed that the cut of her blouses was conspicuously low and that, whilst counting the clothes, she would show an undue amount of cleavage. He turned red even as he spoke, even as he told this to Bedekar, saying that he had begun to feel horribly trapped by that woman.

One day she told him that he was looking tired and that she could give him a good neck and shoulder massage. She smiled at him coyly and giggled, adding that her husband had taken the children and gone to his brother's house, so she was free to spend time with him. When he replied that he didn't need a massage, she had asked what he needed, if he had anything else in mind.

A cold fear had gripped him. He did not know how to reprimand her, how to sack her.

That evening, speaking to his sister over the phone, he had mentioned this and shared his anxiety and concern. She had promptly taken charge. She came over the next Sunday and, after taking stock of the washed clothes, had firmly told the washerwoman that her services wouldn't be required anymore, and she was not to come to the apartment again, ever.

The washerwoman had looked dazed and hurt. She had looked reproachfully at Doctor-sahib, who simply pretended to be busy, while feeling, in his heart, an immense relief. "It was as though I had been saved from a terrible danger," he said. "But how was I to know the danger would follow me, pursue me, all the way here?"

Thereafter, she had started coming to his clinic on some pretext or other. A cough, a cold, headaches and backaches, which he diagnosed as menstrual cramps. She would ask that he feel the parts that were causing her pain, and he would pretend he hadn't heard her.

At first, he didn't charge her; then he realized that asking for payment might work as a deterrent. When he'd ask, she would dig into her blouse, pull out a few rupees, and say that she would give him the balance the next time. And hearing this, he would flinch. He didn't want there to be a next time.

This went on for two years. She would come every month or so.

"But why didn't you simply tell her to stop coming? Say you weren't interested in being her physician," asked the inspector.

"How could I do that? I can't turn away a patient without a valid reason. If she came to me for some ailment outside my area of competence, then I could refuse. But all her problems were within my scope; I had no reason to turn her away. Till now, that is."

"So what happened this evening? What *was* her problem? And how did you treat her?" The inspector leaned forward on his desk.

"No, wait, Bedekar; before that, I have to tell you something. One day she arrived at the clinic in a distraught state. She said to my secretary, at the reception desk, that she wanted to talk to me and would wait till the last patient had gone. When, eventually, I called her in,

I left the door open and told my secretary that he should wait. I asked her what the problem was, and she said that she was having sleepless nights; she hadn't slept for four nights, so could I give her something to induce sleep. She kept pressing her forehead, saying she was going crazy without sleep, and it was all because of that husband of hers, who had brought ruin onto them. I did not want to probe into what looked like a domestic matter, so I thought I would give her a strip of sleeping pills and send her away, but she went on ranting. She said her husband was downright stupid and that because of him they would become homeless. She mumbled something about their ghat going in for redevelopment, and when the builder's men had come around asking how long they had been living there, that stupid husband of hers had told the truth: that they had been there for only seven years. That did not entitle them to a flat in the new building but only to financial compensation, which, knowing her husband, he would squander in no time. Hai Ram, she said, what had she done to deserve such a man? Anyway, this time she had no ulterior motive and had made no advances, so I allowed her to vent her feelings and leave. And I even forgot to ask for payment."

After that, he hadn't seen her for months – four to five months, at least.

"Then why today?" asked the inspector, frowning.

"Today she said she had been getting severe abdominal pains and some bleeding, too, from the vagina. I knew this was outside my area of competence. It was, likely, a gynecological problem. But since she mentioned the bleeding and the pains, I thought I should at least give her an external examination. That way, she'd know what to tell the gynecologist."

"What about the husband? Did he not accompany her in?"

"Now that is what is strange. My secretary asked him to go in with her, but he refused. Later, my secretary told me that the husband was reeking of alcohol. His breath was foul-smelling, overpowering, and maybe that's why he did not want to come in. He did not want to face me."

"Hmm ...," said the inspector. "Go on."

"I don't know if you know how an abdominal examination works, but we do it in four parts. The first part is the inspection, where we look for lesions, scars, and swellings, from the sternum to the pelvic bone. The second part is auscultation, where, with a stethoscope, we listen to sounds from the abdomen. We check for sounds of bowel irregularity and constipation."

Here, the inspector interjected. He said to Dandekar, "You needn't take all that down. Just say that Doctor-sahib gave the patient a thorough examination." Then turning to the doctor, he said, "Please, go on."

"The third part is palpation, and here we physically test the painful and non-painful areas; we check for things like hernia and enlargement of the liver and spleen. And then there's the fourth part, percussion, where we tap the abdomen for abnormal sounds."

"And what precisely did you find?"

"Well," said Doctor-sahib, "I am not an expert in this area. This is something only a gynecologist can confirm, but my hunch is that she has a vascular fibroid, which is stuck to some blood vessels, and these rupture and bleed each time there's an abrupt movement."

"At any point, did you ask her to remove her clothes? Her sari and petticoat? Her undergarments?"

"No, of course not," said Doctor-sahib. "We don't do that in an external examination."

"And, at any point, did you penetrate her with your fingers? Like, an internal examination."

"Certainly not!" said Doctor-sahib. He felt a dizzying heat rise to his face. His ears burned, and slowly the sensation spread to his neck.

"And what advice did you give her? Did you prescribe anything?"

"I asked her to go to a government hospital and consult a gynecologist. And I prescribed a drug, aminocaproic acid, to stop the bleeding. I even wrote out a note, detailing my observations for the gynecologist."

The inspector sighed. "Well, Doctor-sahib, I have no reason to doubt you. None whatsoever. But I must ask you again. Just for the record. Because all this comes under Section 375 of the Indian Penal Code, which is a non-bailable offense, punishable with ten years of imprisonment. I must ask you, Doctor-sahib: Did you, as a person in a position of trust, violate that trust and take advantage of your position as a doctor? Did you perform any kind of coercive, non-consensual act on your patient?"

"No, sir, I did not."

"Then, Doctor-sahib, I must ask you to go home and get a good night's sleep. You will need it. I am going to do everything in my power to help you. But if I am not able to get to the bottom of this by morning, you will have to get yourself a very good lawyer. Someone competent and reliable. Because the accusations against you are serious. Very serious."

"So, you are not arresting me?" asked Doctor-sahib wryly. He tried to smile, but his heart wouldn't let him.

"Not yet. And never, I hope," said the inspector. He, too, tried to smile, but didn't quite succeed.

Doctor-sahib took leave of the policemen. But at the door he paused, turned, and said, "I am not such a bastard, Bedekar, that I would molest a woman who had come to my door asking for help."

The inspector leaned back in his chair, his hands behind his head, and said, "I know. But what I think does not matter. It's the world and its opinion of you. I am sure you know that."

Doctor-sahib felt a chill run down his spine. He shut the door behind him and looked at his watch. 11:30 P.M. It was too late to call Aditya, too late to call his sister, either. He was alone till morning, alone with his thoughts.

The city he stepped out into was not the city of his birth. Everything looked different now. The streets looked bare and empty; the tall, gray buildings, under construction, looked like they were coming up only to devour the smaller buildings, to crush whoever dared to live there. He himself felt small, vulnerable, and dispensable. He felt as though one of the speeding cars would run him over, if he wasn't careful. And he *had* been careful. He had remembered to cover Manju with a bedsheet while examining her. Through all the stages, except the inspection, where he needed to check for signs of abrasion and growth. Damn! he had forgotten to mention this to the inspector. How could he let such an important detail slip? But then he had been so tense, so stressed out. He wondered if he should go back and clarify this. The bedsheet was still lying on the examination bed. Bedekar could send a constable to collect it. It would be strong evidence. Hope flooded his heart, but equally fast it dissolved into gloom, into despondency. What would that prove? Nothing, really! The washerwoman would lie and say that he had not covered her. She was a lying bitch, a cold-hearted slut. She had no clue what she was putting him through. She had no idea what this would do to his life and practice. His heart started pounding. He could swear it was trying to pound its way out of his body. Before him, the traffic signals blinked. Now yellow, now red; now red, now yellow.

What should he do? Go back to the police station, where a friendly voice waited, a voice that could, with equal poise, write out his arrest warrant? Or should he return to the loneliness of his apartment?

For once Doctor-sahib wished he were married. A man with a wife, anchored in a happy marriage: that would have amounted to something; it would have spoken for his decency.

At once he felt ashamed. Why was he thinking like a typical Indian male who needed a wife only to reinforce his social status? The truth was: he had never felt the need to get married. He was shy with women, a bit wary of them, too. He could never tell what they were thinking, or what they thought of him. There had been a girl in college. She was intelligent and reserved. He had taken her to the prom, where all they had done was sit and watch other couples dancing. He would meet her in the college canteen, after lab work, and they'd walk to the railway station, where they'd enjoy a Frankie and an ice-cream, before parting. Somehow, it was she who always paid, saying that she received a decent allowance from her father, a diamond merchant.

They would chat for a while before parting, and there'd always be some reluctance, a need to linger. He had felt that was love, or something close to it. He had thought of confessing his feelings to her and asking her to wait till he finished medical college, which would be five years later. But no, it would take him longer than that to pay off his student loans, he calculated. So he had kept his feelings to himself, and she had gotten married as soon as she completed her twelfth grade. Because that's what her parents wanted and that's how it was in her community.

Not that he had regretted it. His life's plan was pretty much laid out for him. He had lost both his parents early in life and had been brought up by an older sister, older by twelve years, who loved him dearly and had taken heavy loans so that he could go to medical college and become a doctor.

And he had! Forsaking all temptations and applying himself single-mindedly to his studies. His original plan was to do his postgraduate work in critical care medicine. But then his sister had gotten divorced. She had two young daughters to raise by herself, and Doctor-sahib had thought it prudent to start earning, paying back his student loans and his debt to his sister.

Of course, he hadn't told her that. He just spoke of an offer to take over one of the shops in the neighborhood, which was going for a song because the owner wanted to hang up his boots and retire to his farm.

The location was perfect for a clinic: it faced the main road, and there was no other doctor within a kilometer. Doctor-sahib had taken it, and from day one it was a success. Patients had poured in, and Doctor-sahib had attributed it to his late parents watching over him.

Right now, he could do with their help, he thought. But no, he was staring at an empty apartment and a silence that loomed like an unseen wall between him and his peace of mind.

I am not that kind of man, not that kind of man, he kept saying to himself. He did not remember when he changed into his pajamas, when he brushed his teeth – brushed so vigorously that his gums bled – when he went into the kitchen and poured himself a glass of water. All he remembered was falling on the bed, face down, between two pillows, and allowing himself to sink in deeper, repeating to himself: *I am not that kind of man. Anybody can see that.*

Outside his window, a train hooted, sending its long, sad refrain down the tracks.

Outside his window, pavement dwellers fought, the women haranguing the men and the men threatening violence.

Outside his window, a few meters away, a ladies' bar swung open its doors to customers: well-dressed men with money in their pockets and mischief on their minds.

And, meanwhile, Doctor-sahib suffered the sleep of the troubled, the sleep of a frightened child, clinging, with clenched fingers, to the starched white edges of his pillows.

No sooner had Doctor-sahib left the station than Inspector Bedekar leaned over his desk and jabbed at the intercom. "Send in Rupali Madam, please. Right away!" he said.

Minutes later, a smartly dressed woman in her late twenties walked in with a file under her arm. She had a high forehead, soft hair bunched up loosely, large, clear eyes, and dark, well-cropped eyebrows. Her figure was elegant, her shoulders firm and erect, her khaki trousers neatly pressed and fitted in the manner of a fashionable cut. She held the file close to her chest. She stood before Bedekar. The name tag on her uniform read: Rupali Karmakar.

"What have you got for me?" asked Bedekar, pointing to a chair opposite.

Dandekar straightened up in his chair. His face was grim, impassive, unsmiling.

Bedekar knew that Dandekar did not approve of women on the force and that he showed it. Well, he'd better get used to it, thought Bedekar. Sub-inspector Rupali Karmakar was one of his finest officers. If anyone could crack this case, it would be her.

Seated, Rupali crossed her legs. Her smooth, pudgy hands rested on the file. Her deportment brought strength and beauty to her uniform. "What would you like to know, sir?" she asked. "My findings or my opinion?"

"Opinion first!" said Bedekar. "We don't have much time."

"Well, sir, it's clearly a bogus complaint. The woman is lying through her teeth. As for her husband, his acting is so bad that even a child can see through it. If Doctor-sahib *had* molested her, as she claims, then would she not have screamed and gone rushing to her husband, who was waiting outside? But she did no such thing. She even asked Doctor-sahib's secretary for an appointment for the following week. Also, sir, if, as she says, Doctor-sahib *had* made advances to her when she had visited his home and shown him her swollen feet, if he *had* invited her into his bedroom – then why did she continue going to him as a patient? Her story makes no sense."

"Yes, but I am wondering what would she achieve by doing this? What *is* her game? Is it revenge or obsession? Or are we missing something, altogether? I am hoping, Rupali, you can find some answers."

"I am trying, sir; I am doing my best. But if it is revenge, why would she wait so long? Obsession? No, she wouldn't take her husband with her. I think she and her husband have some plan. Maybe it's extortion. And you need to know this, sir: while they have been here, giving their statement, the husband kept pleading and saying he needed to go out for a few minutes. He sounded very desperate. I think he is an alcoholic. He can't do without his quota."

"It's good to know this. Maybe *that* is something we can work on. What about the medical examination? Has it shown any injuries? Any signs of penetration, rough play?"

"Nothing, sir. I sent her to Nair Hospital, and the report has come back as 'normal.' No bleeding, no injuries. Nothing!"

"No bleeding, huh? That's a point in Doctor-sahib's favor. She had said that there was vaginal bleeding. Which is why she went to see Doctor-sahib, in the first place."

"Would you like to see the first information report, sir?" She opened the file and pushed it toward him.

He scanned it, then said, "It's what I expected. Her statement makes Doctor-sahib look like a pervert. She says he made her remove her blouse, then her undergarments. Then, there is this statement which the presswallas will love: 'He spent time inside me, probing with his fingers, despite knowing I was bleeding.' I think, Rupali, this woman knows what she is doing, she has come prepared. Do you think the husband has set her up? I would like to know your thoughts."

"If you ask me, sir, she is the one in charge, she is the one who controls the relationship. While filing the complaint, she was doing all the talking and he would only nod like a goat. Sometimes I could tell that his mind was far away, probably on his next drink. And at times he would shiver. Out of nervousness or out of withdrawal, I don't know."

"The addiction is an interesting angle. I would like to work on it. See if something turns up."

Turning to Dandekar, he asked, "Which is the adda closest to the dhobi ghat, where these Kanaujias stay?"

Rupali interjected, "Narang's den, sir. It is just around the corner from the dhobi ghat. Some of the dhobis go there to drink."

Dandekar scowled; clearly he was displeased with Rupali's interjection. And seeing this, Bedekar had to make an effort not to smile.

She continued, "With your permission, sir, I would like to go and make some inquiries at Narang's den. This might be the right time to get a few tongues wagging. I am sure many of them will be knowing Gopal Kanaujia. They might have some information for us."

"Sir, I don't think that's a good idea. Madam going to such a place—"

"Hold your tongue, Dandekar. No one's asked you." Rupali's eyes blazed with indignation.

"Dandekar is just trying to help," said Bedekar quickly. "He is right. Your presence will make the men uncomfortable. They are not used to seeing a woman there. They will clam up."

"Well, I know how to unclam them," said Rupali firmly. She narrowed her eyes and pursed her lips, her anger adding to her attractiveness.

"That won't help," said Bedekar, smiling. "We want to win them over. We want them to give information willingly. I think I will speak to Narang myself."

"Well, I will take your leave then, sir," said Rupali. "What do you want me to do with the Kanaujias? Should I continue questioning them or let them go?"

"Let the woman leave. The man should stay. Say we want to ask him a few more questions. She will probably kick up a fuss, but you can say it's only routine. That way no one can accuse us of being unsympathetic to her."

Rupali bowed and left, and the inspector dismissed Dandekar as well.

Moments later, he punched at the intercom and asked the operator to get him Narang.

Two minutes later, she called back. "Sir, Narang on the line."

"Put him through."

"What can I do for you, Inspector-sahib? Don't tell me you are about to raid me."

"I might, Narang, if you don't cooperate. I am looking for some important information."

"Anything, sir; tell me what you need. You want me to come over?"

"That won't be necessary. First, let me tell you what this is about. But this is strictly between you and me. Don't go opening your mouth to anyone. Otherwise, I will close down your adda."

"Don't worry, sir; you can trust me. I am always on the side of the law."

"See, Narang, I want some information on a dhobi who might be your customer. He is here right now, and I think he is lying to us. He is trying to frame someone who is known to me. Now this dhobi thinks he is smart, that he can fool us. We will, sooner or later, get a confession out of him. But for that I need your help."

"Tell me his name, sir. Most of the dhobis drink at my adda. They have running accounts with me."

"His name is Gopal Kanaujia. Does that ring a bell?"

"Of course I know Gopal; he is a regular here. He is a meek sort of a fellow, not robust, like some of the other dhobis. He usually comes alone, orders half a bottle, which he finishes in about three hours. Then he goes off staggering. Once or twice it seemed like he wouldn't make it back home on his own. So I sent one of my boys to help him. What does it take, sir, to go out of your way for another human being?"

"If I know you, Narang, you were only protecting your debt. Anyway, tell me about Gopal. Who is he friendly with? Anyone we can speak to at the adda whom you might know?"

"Well, I could ask my manager, Manohar. He is the one who knows all the customers. Keeps a close watch on them. Let me ask him and call you back."

"Yes, but call on my direct line … you have my number?"

Half an hour later, Narang called, and the two of them spoke for over twenty minutes. At a certain point, the manager Manohar also came on the line and spoke to the inspector, who kept nodding and saying, "I see, I see … This is interesting. Go on!"

After putting down the phone, the inspector rang for Rupali, who came in promptly. "Have the Kanaujias gone?" he asked.

"Sir, the woman left most reluctantly. But I told her she needed to get back to her children, which seemed to convince her. I could make out she was worried about leaving her husband behind. It's as though she does not trust him. As for him, he is quite nervous, keeps saying he wants to go home."

"He is the weak link in their plan," said Bedekar. "Now, if we play it right, we will have a confession by morning. But let's do this right, Rupali. Listen to what I have learned."

Rupali sat down, and the inspector began. "It seems our friend Gopal has come into a lot of money of late. He has not only repaid all his debts to Narang but has also been drinking and bragging about how, in Mumbai, one needs to be smart, needs to look out for oneself, because no one else cares. What is strange is that he was very depressed some time ago. He would drink heavily and curse his luck, and now, suddenly, he is very cheerful and social."

"Sir, any idea what exactly he was depressed about? Maybe there is some clue there."

"Well, it appears that he was going to be homeless, because the ghat, as you know, is going in for redevelopment, and many of the dhobis will be accommodated in a new building. The builder is also giving some compensation for the loss of livelihood, in addition to giving them a 325 square foot apartment. But Gopal Kanaujia is not eligible for that; he has not lived the required number of years at the ghat. This had made him very angry and bitter. He was drinking heavily. To the point that he would pass out, and twice or thrice he had to be taken home by one of Narang's boys. Now all that has changed, suddenly. He doesn't talk about being homeless anymore. He says, instead, a man needs to be smarter than the city so that it doesn't defeat him. I wonder, Rupali, where this new attitude is coming from. What has changed in the last few days? And if it has any connection to their complaint."

"It *is* very strange, sir. But if he has come into money suddenly, then that would rule out our extortion theory."

"Not quite. Perhaps he has discovered that extortion is one way to make easy money. Perhaps, husband and wife have started some kind of a racket. The question is, how do we find out? And we don't have much time, Rupali."

The two lapsed into silence, thinking hard. Then the inspector said, "I have an idea. I am not sure if it will work, but it's worth a try. But for that we will need Narang's help, again."

Leaning across, he spoke to Rupali for a good fifteen minutes, and she listened attentively. Then he called up Narang and explained, saying, "You understand the importance of this, Narang? It has to be done right. We can't afford to make even a small mistake." And Narang said, "Don't worry, sir; just leave it to me. Between Manohar and me, we will get this done."

It was an elated dhobi who left the police station, bowing and thanking the lady inspector who said he could go. She cautioned him to go straight home, to not stop anywhere on the way, and he nodded eagerly: anything to get out of here. Walking him out, this kindhearted lady inspector lowered her voice and told him not to speak to any press reporters about what had happened. "You understand why I am saying this?" she asked. "It will look bad on your family, bad on your wife, and worse for your children in school. You know how people are: they will not blame the doctor. They will say: What kind of man are you that you could not even protect your wife? So if anyone asks you anything or contacts you about this, you just say nothing. Is that clear?" He listened to her and nodded vigorously.

He hurried along, cutting through a back lane that led to the dhobi ghat. At one point, he pulled out his cell phone and thought of calling Manju to tell her he was on his way back. But no, she would ask him to come straight home – and he didn't want that. What he wanted was a drink. Maybe two, maybe three. His lips were parched, his nose was running, he was getting cramps in his stomach. Besides, his head was all muddled. What had that lady inspector said? That the world would think of him as a coward. They would say he was unable to protect his wife. Yes, his brother-dhobis would do that. They would snicker at him, laugh at him, run him down. He had seen how some of them looked at Manju. With eyes of desire and inflamed mouths. They thought he hadn't noticed, that he didn't know. Well, he did!

At once he felt shame. It was his fault, really. He hadn't been much of a husband to her. How long since they had slept together? He couldn't remember, couldn't say. It was the alcohol that came between them, it made him numb to everything else. But things *would* get better once they had that flat, their very own flat. Once he had done what he had to. Besides, he wasn't doing it for himself. But for her and for the children.

And so, along the same route where, an hour or so before, Doctor-sahib had walked home heavyhearted, where the weight of his humiliation had made every step difficult, here Gopal Dhobi trotted along, joyous in the realization that life was about to get better. The police *had* believed their story; there *was* money in his pocket; his wife *was* pleased with him; and soon, very soon he *would* be the owner of a flat, his very own.

But what would he do with a flat if he didn't have work? Ah, but theirs was a shrinking business anyway. The washing machines had made sure of that, and those municipality chaps who increased the rates of water and electricity. Being a dhobi just didn't make sense anymore. If he had his way he would sell the flat, take the money, and go back to his village. There he would build a house, a grand house, which people would want to visit. And he would keep a few cows and buy a tractor and a motorcycle. What about his drinking? He would have to give that up. Otherwise, people would laugh and say, "Gopalbhai, what happened to you? You went to the city sober and came back a drunkard."

But right now, while he was rich, he might as well indulge. He was approaching Narang's adda, where it might be crowded; he might have to stand and drink, but that was okay. Anyway, he did not want to spend too much time there, just a few quick pegs, a few doubles. But first he had to shut off his cell phone. He did not want Manju calling and disturbing him. He did not want her to pester him to come home. Not until he had had his fill.

But a man who has never seen money before doesn't know when enough is enough. It is so easy to forget once the first few glasses have gone down. Especially when Narang was being so hospitable and Manohar himself was serving. What big pegs Manohar was pouring! It must be because they had recognized him as an important customer. After all, in one swoop he had cleared all his debts. He had gone and thrown three thousand rupees at them – just like that! That would have told them who he was. And what he was capable of.

And while he drank, he was joined by some others. People he knew and others he had only seen before.

There was Bheem Singh Bahadur, who once worked as a maalishwalla on Chowpatty Beach, but had been forced to quit when they cleared up the beach. Bheem Singh now worked as a handcart pusher, transporting heavy loads to Cotton Green, Ray Road, and Masjid Bunder. When his day's work was done, Bheem Singh rushed to Mumbai Central Station, where he worked as a coolie till midnight.

There was Varun Paoli, who once ran a matka den and an extortion racket but, having fallen on hard days, worked with Narang as a bodyguard. Paoli still had criminal cases against him, he couldn't leave the city, which is why he needed Narang's hand of protection.

And there was Jamal Haddi, an out-of-work sweeper, addicted to the bottle. Jamal was dying of a terrible wasting disease, the poor fellow! You could see death in Jamal's face: in his gaunt cheeks, his sunken eyes, his black, inflamed gums, the bulging veins on his neck.

And together they drank and spoke, and drank and cursed their fate, and they all agreed that this was one haraami of a city. How it pushed them, tested them, made them into something they were not. "This city will make you sell your own mother if you are stupid," said Gopal. "But if you are smart, like me, you will know how to play it."

"What do you mean, brother?" asked Manohar solemnly. The manager had lingered at their table after serving the last round. "You have obviously understood something that we haven't."

"Ah, forget it; I don't give away my secrets so easily," said Gopal slyly.

"And yet you call us brothers," said Manohar. "I thought you meant it."

"I do! But these days you don't know who to trust and who not to."

"Why treat us like enemies, brother?" asked Bheem Singh. "We have told you our situation. Hidden nothing from you. Then why can't you trust us?"

"It's not me, it's my wife, she won't like it. It's her secret, too."

"Ah, so you are tied to your wife's palloo," said Jamal Haddi. "Then say so, we understand." The men broke into laughter.

"It is you who are tied to your wife's palloo, Jamal Haddi," replied Gopal angrily. "We know where you get your money from. Your wife's dhanda, which is to entertain other men."

"That is a terrible thing to say, Gopalbhai," said Varun Paoli quickly, seeing the color drain from Jamal's face. "You know Jamal's wife needs to support them. You know how much it costs just to keep our friend alive. I don't think we should blame her for that."

"Yes, if you don't wish to tell us your secret, that's fine, Gopalbhai," said Manohar. "But you don't have to condemn our brother for what life has done to him."

A tense silence followed. Jamal's eyes filled with tears. His hands shook, his lips quivered. In a broken voice he said that perhaps he should leave, he hadn't come here to be insulted.

"I beg your forgiveness, Jamalbhai," said Gopal unhappily. "I didn't mean to hurt you. It just slipped from my mouth. Maybe I've had too much drink. It is I who should leave."

"Well, you can always make up, Gopalbhai, by sharing your secret with us," said Manohar. "That will prove that you trust us. That you consider us your brothers."

And then Gopal spoke while the others listened, and at some point Manohar gestured to the table boy and ordered another bottle, and he filled all their glasses, Gopal's glass to the brim.

And then they drank and confided some more till they were all slurring. And in the midst of it all there was laughter and teasing and hopes and dreams drawn from the deepest corners of their hearts and placed on the table for all to see, all to know. And in this way they proved they were brothers.

It was 2:00 A.M. by the time they left. They had to leave Jamal behind, snoring on a bench. "One day, just like that, he will pass away," said Manohar sadly. "It's only a matter of time."

"It's okay if he goes like that," said Bheem Singh. "He shouldn't suffer. That's all I ask."

"How to avoid suffering, brother?" asked Gopal. "To live is to suffer, and especially for us who have neither a privileged birth nor education in our favor."

"Poor wretch!" said Varun Paoli. "I hope he enjoys a better life in his next birth."

They walked on a road lit by a cold, bright moon. Barely had they walked a few meters when Gopal lurched. Bheem Singh caught him before he fell and Gopal went limp in his arms.

"Our friend has drunk too much," said Manohar. "And maybe it's just as well that he sleeps it off, for tomorrow his life will change."

"Yes," said Bheem Singh. "After what he has done, it's a wonder he can sleep at all. Nobody ever prospered from making someone else unhappy. That's what I have come to believe."

"Quite true, brother," said Varun Paoli. "I have learned that the hard way. And our friend here is about to learn that, too."

Sitting in her shanty, surrounded by mounds of unwashed clothes, Manju felt a wave of panic. Where was that fool? And why was his cell phone switched off? She had called twenty or thirty times at least. And each time she got a message saying that the cell phone was switched off, please try again later. She sat on a chair while her children slept. The room was in darkness, except for a tiny red bulb which glowed and illuminated some pictures on the wall. There were pictures of Lord Shiva, Lord Ganesha, Lord Hanuman, and Mother Durga on a tiger, fiery yet benevolent. Her eyes darted around the room – to the blue peeling walls; the thick wooden shelves holding tins of rice, pulses, and spices; the black wall-mounted fan that whirred and swung its neck from side to side, then settled on her children. The little ones slept so soundly, their stomachs rising and falling rhythmically. Manju wished she could be like them. As innocent. As carefree.

Her mind flew over the events of the day. She had done exactly as she had been ordered. She had gone to the clinic and played out her little drama. And then to the police station, which was the tough part. And she had excelled in both places. The only problem was that her fool of a husband might spoil it now. She wished she hadn't left him behind. But what to do? The lady inspector had been so insistent, saying she needed to return to her children.

But now something was wrong: she could tell. His cell phone was switched off. A thought crossed her mind: Could he have gone to Narang's adda. No, he wouldn't dare! Not when he knew she'd be waiting. She made sure the kids were sleeping soundly; then, wearing her slippers, she closed the door and stepped out onto the moonlit path. Behind her, the ghat rose against the dark, velvet night sky. The next morning it would erupt in a profusion of colors, brightly colored clothes fluttering on drying lines, while the sun poured its magnificent rays on them. But right now it looked like a sage in meditation, pondering his fate.

Covering her face with her sari, Manju started in the direction of the police station. She took the main road and set off at a brisk pace.

When she arrived, the first person she saw was Narang. Next to him was Manohar, and beside them were two other men, both strangers. She did not know why, but suddenly she felt sweat breaking out on her neck. The men were sitting with the station officer, who smiled at her and said, "Welcome, madam, welcome. Sahib has been waiting for you. We were wondering when you would come."

"I am here to see my husband," she said stiffly. "I don't know what business you people have with him. We have already said what we had to. There is nothing more to add."

"Yes, madam, but we just want to make sure. You sit on the bench outside. Sahib is busy. He will see you in a while."

"I don't want to see your sahib; I want to see my husband. Where is he?" She was now panicking, for she sensed – and she knew she wasn't wrong to feel this way – that there was something terribly wrong in the way the station officer was speaking to her. It was like he was mocking her. Like she was some insect on the wall. Not to be taken seriously.

"You just wait, madam," said the station officer firmly. Then turning to Narang and the others, he began speaking in a low voice, pausing, from time to time, to note something in a book.

She waited for a long, long time. Two groups of youngsters came in and filed complaints against each other. It appeared that they had been in an accident and both groups were enraged. It took several constables to calm them down. This was followed by a woman in a burqa, who came with her brother and complained about her husband, who, it seems, was sleeping with another woman. Her brother was sure that the husband had married the other woman; he had stopped giving his sister money, and some of her jewelry was missing. The woman was hysterical; she wanted the police to arrest the other woman. Wasn't there a law against bigamy? she demanded. And what about her jewelry? Could she file a complaint for theft?

Hearing the commotion, Sub-inspector Rupali came out of her office and spoke to the Muslim woman. It was a domestic matter, she said. The police couldn't get involved. If her husband had beaten her or she had proof of the theft, they could do something. But adultery was no longer a crime; the law had been repealed. She advised the brother to handle the situation with maturity. His sister should go and meet with the other woman and appeal to her good nature and conscience. The sub-inspector leaned against a desk, speaking to the complainants in a kind, soothing voice, and Manju could not help but admire her. How smart the inspector was! And how confident in the way she dealt with the situation!

As soon as the Muslims left, Manju rose from her seat and approached the lady inspector. "Madam, madam!" she said. "Please help me. These men are not allowing me to rejoin my husband. I am worried. He should have been home by now."

Rupali Karmakar stared at her. "You and your husband might be here a long time," she said. "I hope you have someone looking after your children."

She turned and walked away, toward an office at the end of the corridor, and after the men had finished speaking to the station officer, they, too, went into the same room. On their way, the men gave Manju a peculiar look. Something between pity and cold revulsion.

Seeing that the station officer was free, Manju approached him. "Please, sahib," she said. "Please let me see my husband. I just want to know he is fine."

"What is the hurry, madam? You will get your chance. Just be patient, no?" He smiled without looking at her.

It was 4:30 A.M. by the time she was called in to the office at the end of the corridor. They were all there: Senior Inspector Bedekar, Sub-inspector Rupali Karmakar, a senior constable with long, stiff whiskers and an unsmiling face, Narang, Manohar, and the two other men. They were all seated, and appeared to be so united that she found herself trembling under their gaze.

"Speak, madam. You have something to tell us," said the inspector from his chair.

"My husband!" she said. "He hasn't come home. I am worried. He was here when I left."

"Ah, yes, but he is in no state to talk right now. And whatever he had to say, he has said already. Now it's your turn. Perhaps there is something you want to tell us. Like why you think us to be such fools. Why you have wasted our time with your false complaint."

"What do you mean, sahib? I have told you the truth, everything that happened. I swear on my children that I would never lie to you. Never!"

"Shut up!" said the lady inspector wrathfully. "One more false word from your mouth and I will make sure you never see your children again. You are an insult to women, to motherhood. You know very well what you have done. We have proof, solid proof."

Something in her face reminded Manju of Kali, the Goddess of Destruction. Tears rushed into her eyes. She covered her face with her hands and sobbed into them. Her whole body shook and convulsed. Yet no one asked her to sit down.

Then Inspector Bedekar spoke in a kindly voice. "Look, we know about your plan. We know you've been offered a large sum of money and a flat in the new building, in order to frame Doctor-sahib, in order to shame him. It is best that you confess. Your husband already has! He has done so in the presence of four witnesses: these three men and one who is not here." He pointed to Manohar and the two strangers.

Manju kept sobbing. She could not help it; the tears flowed, as did the kohl from her eyes.

"Arrey, Dandekar. What is the minimum sentence for someone who gives a false complaint of rape? Can you tell us?" It was Kali speaking again, and the voice made Manju shiver.

"Why, madam, it is a minimum of seven years. But in that Azad Nagar case, the judge gave life imprisonment to the culprits."

"You hear that?" said the lady inspector to Manju. "You had better start talking, if you don't want to spend the rest of your life in prison."

Manju felt as though the ground beneath her had opened up and she was falling, falling. What had that idiot husband of hers told them? How could he do this to her and their children? A bitter taste rose in her mouth, her stomach tightened, and she felt sick, so sick that she wanted to throw up. She fought back her tears and said, "Sahib, please listen to me. I know I have done wrong; I know I have committed a big sin. But please let me tell you why I did it."

"Go on," said Bedekar. "But, first, have some water." Leaning across, he poured her a glass.

With trembling hands, she raised the glass to her lips and drank. Some of the water spilled and ran down her neck and into her blouse, but she did not care.

She kept the empty glass on the desk and began. "Sahib," she said, "you know our ghat is going in for redevelopment. We are going to lose our livelihood, the only means of earning we have. But that would be okay if we at least got a flat, like our brother-dhobis. In our case, however, there is a problem. We have lived here for only seven years, but only the dhobis who have been here for ten years will get a flat. We pleaded with the builder's men who came to check who is eligible, and we met with the municipality people and begged them as well. Please help us, we said. Somehow fit us in. But they would not listen.

"Sahib, I have three children: two girls and a boy. Right now, we stay in a small eleven-by-fourteen-foot room. In that, we work, cook, bathe, and sleep. The light is not enough, and often, because of the poor ventilation, my children fall ill. Once, my younger daughter got dengue, and we had to get her admitted to the hospital. Now you might say that *that* is life in the slums and it can't be helped. But what mother doesn't dream of a better life for her children? After all, dreams are all we have.

"Sahib, when I heard that we would not be getting a flat, only some money, which my husband would spend on alcohol, I became afraid. Not for myself, but for my children. What would they do, I thought, if we became homeless? I know my husband. He would like to leave the city and go back to the village. And what would my children do there?

"You see, sahib, I want my children to be educated. My older daughter is so clever, she wins prizes, and my younger one is smart, too; her teachers like her. The boy: he is playful, but good in sports. Here, in Mumbai, there is a chance they will become somebody. They will study and get degrees. But if we move back to the village, our elders won't let me send my daughters to school. They will say it's a waste of time, a waste of money. They will say that a woman's place is at home, in the kitchen. And I will have no say in my children's lives, no say in their future.

"Yes, I know what I did was wrong. I pleaded with the builder's men to help me, and they took me to meet their manager, a man named Mohite. He said he could help me, provided I did them a favor in return. He then told me about Doctor-sahib, how he was making life difficult for them, had got their project held up. He wanted to teach Doctor-sahib a lesson, and when I mentioned I knew him, he said that would make it easier for them to put their plan into motion. I know it was wrong, very wrong, but you, too, might have children, sahib. You, too, might have dreams for them.

"There is one more thing, sahib. I want you to know that this was my idea. My husband is innocent. He will do whatever I tell him. I beg you not to punish him for my sins."

She fell silent. The morning light pressed against the window and entered through the blinds, overpowering the harshness of the florescent lights. Manju stood with her hands folded, her fingers entwined. Inspector Bedekar leaned back in his chair and looked at her as though he was making up his mind about something. The washerwoman's face was stained from the kohl that had run from her eyes and mingled with her tears. She looked lost, he thought, like a girl who had committed some grave error for the first time and was dreading the punishment that would follow. He would like to forgive her, he thought. For the sake of her kids. But he was not a judge; he did not have that luxury, nor that power. He was bound by the law, and that would have to run its course.

All eyes in the room were on him. He would have to speak, have to choose his words carefully. "You have been foolish, sister," he said. "Your greed could have sent an innocent man to prison. It could have destroyed him."

"I know, sahib; I realize that. What will happen to my children if we go to jail?" Her voice trailed off, and she fought back her tears. That Mohite: she wished she had never set eyes on him; she wished she hadn't believed him and his promises.

"I don't know," said the inspector. "I can't say what the court will decide. You will have to wait here for now. We will send somebody to look after your children. And get you some clothes."

The lady inspector rose to her feet. Dandekar, too, closed his notepad and stood up.

"Come, sister," said the lady inspector, her voice kinder now.

"Let her rejoin her husband, and give them some time together, so she can explain to him what has happened," said Bedekar to Rupali.

"That is if he has woken up," she said.

Dandekar held open the door for them, and Manju went out first.

Inspector Bedekar fell back in his chair. He looked at the men before him and said softly, "It worked. It was a long shot, but it worked. And, Narang, I have *you* to thank for this. You and the others. You handled it well – as well as a policeman, in fact."

And Narang replied, "Don't say that, sahib. You are embarrassing me. It is my duty, my God-given duty."

The grandfather clock on the wall showed six fifteen when Doctor-sahib's phone rang. The sun had come up over the railway yard and lit the art deco arches of his building. He had woken up twice during the night. The first time, he had imagined his sister's voice: "Cutlet, what have you done, Cutlet? You have got yourself into trouble. How often have I told you not to trust people? Why did you take that woman as your patient? Why, why, after I went through such pains to get rid of her?"

She never called him by his real name, and he did not mind that. He quite liked Cutlet in fact. It had come about when he was around seven or eight, because whenever she would ask him what he wanted in his lunch box to take to school, he would say "cutlet." It was always in the singular, which seemed to amuse his sister no end. She, of course, could prepare a whole range of cutlets: chicken, mutton, fish, prawns; and these she served with a rich, spicy tomato gravy. It became something of an addiction for him, and the nickname spoke of the bond he shared with his sister: the fact that she knew him so well. Perhaps even better than a mother, he'd sometimes think. Twelve years his senior, she had taken charge of him after their parents had died. She had held a secretarial job during the week and would take catering orders over the weekend. Then there had been that disastrous marriage of hers, and the divorce, which had brought them closer. It made him shiver to imagine how she would take the news of the complaint. How badly it would affect her.

He went to the kitchen and drank a glass of water, then buried himself between two pillows and tried to sleep again. It was as though he was trying to shut out the world outside and the voices in his head. "What, Doctor-sahib, just because you are a doctor, you think you can take advantage of some poor woman?" And: "Saala, he is a predator and a pervert. Who would have thought he would turn out like that … after all these years?"

When at last the voices had faded and he had been overcome by sleep, he had a nightmare. He was standing on a large, empty floor, in a large, empty room, and there were tigers circling around him. They were just circling, eyeing him and drawing closer and closer, and each time the circle narrowed, they would stop and snarl at him. Their eyes glinted and made him shiver, made him sweat. In one hand he held a briefcase – his only weapon against them.

When the first tiger sprang at him, he managed to shove the briefcase into its open jaws and save himself from a mauling. But the weight of the beast knocked him down, and he sank to his knees, drained of strength and numb with fear. As he fell, the other tigers moved in on him. One went for his face, another for his torso, a third for his stomach. He screamed and punched at the pillows, which flew off the bed. His mattress was soaking wet, his heart was pounding, his throat was dry, his lips were salty, he tasted his own tears. Then he woke up.

He was reluctant to turn the light on. The darkness felt like a safe place to him, a tent into which he had retired after a long and exhausting journey. Lying in bed in the dark, he did some stretches. To get the blood flowing in his veins. To calm his mind.

He rose, thinking he would make some tea for himself; that would make him feel better. Then the phone rang, and the name Bedekar flashed across the display, sending bolts of fear through his heart. It must be bad news, he thought. They were coming for him. Coming to get him.

But the voice was light, chirpy, and teasing. "Doctor-sahib, I hope you've had a good night's sleep, because I have some good news for you. Our night-long investigations have paid off. That woman has confessed. It seems you have upset some of our builder friends with your stay order, and they were trying to get even with you. Clearly, Doctor-sahib, you have made some bad enemies, and they almost destroyed you this time. I am the last person to discourage you from doing what is right, but you must think whether this issue is worth all this trouble. This time your enemies did not succeed. But the next time you might not be so lucky."

And, suddenly, Doctor-sahib felt alive, he felt normal. "So what happens now?" he asked.

"You will have to come to the station and file a counter-FIR, and the sooner you do this, the better."

Doctor-sahib said he'd be there in half an hour. Forty minutes, at the most.

"Not so fast, Doctor-sahib," said the inspector. "I don't want you to come empty-handed. I want something from you."

Doctor-sahib flinched. So here it comes, he thought. The catch, the pay-off! His relief turned to disappointment, to anger. Had the system spared no one? Not even a fine man like Bedekar?

"You see, Doctor-sahib, I don't take bribes personally, but I will have to take something for my missus.

Some sweetener, to pacify her for my not going home last night. Now, close to your house is that Irani bakery, which makes the most delicious mawa cakes. I know they bake fresh batches every morning, from five to seven. So if you can, you go there and get me a dozen cakes, I will be able to avoid some fireworks at home. And, of course, I will reimburse you. No two ways about that! But you will have to hurry, lest they sell out."

And Doctor-sahib said, "Of course, of course! It will be a pleasure." He felt like laughing, he felt like shouting. Damn those tigers! Damn those builders! They were not getting him yet. Not when there were men like Bedekar around. Unsung heroes, who deserved to have their kids rush at them. Who, crossing their threshold, deserved the best welcome a man could get.

He walked across to the balcony, threw open its doors, and welcomed the sun on his face. Below him, a newspaper vendor was busy making lots on the pavement, a flower vendor and her daughter knitted garlands of marigolds, a municipal worker swept moodily at the garbage, while young male cleaners, in shorts, scrubbed vigorously at the bonnets and windscreens of cars. A milkman passed by on his bicycle, pedaling slowly and striking at the large shiny vessel that dangled from his handle. A vegetable vendor set up his cart, arranging the vegetables neatly in rows. Ah, thought, Doctor-sahib, it's nice to see people work and toil under an open sky. People who can't be accused of anything other than an honest day of labor.

Acknowledgments

The birth of a book is never easy—it calls for several hands on deck; some overt and palpable; others silent and invisible. I am grateful to have drawn the strength and support of friends who have made this birth possible, even pleasurable. To them, I submit my heartfelt thanks.

To Bahram Vakil, for his magnanimous and spontaneous support.

To Riddhi Tulshian, for her professional acumen, her sharp insights and her punctilious care.

To Vikram Gaikwad, for the strength of his talent, matched only by the strength of his generosity.

To Vistasp Hodiwala, who continues to write the book on friendship.

To Porus Pardiwalla, for his sagacious advice and his comforting presence in my life.

To Chris de Souza, for taking my family concerns as his own.

To Kanishka Gupta, my wonderful agent, who shepherded me through the knotty corridors of Indian publishing.

To Chirag Thakkar, my publisher-editor, whom providence brought to my door, and who created the ideal room for my work to thrive.

Last but not the least, my profound gratitude to my parents, my mother Jeroo and my father Fali, whose faith, conviction and love drive my work and who remain the terra firma on which I pursue my life's goals.

About the Author

Murzban F. Shroff is a Mumbai-based writer. His fiction has appeared in over seventy-five literary journals in the United States and the United Kingdom. He is the recipient of the Bacopa Review Fiction Award and the John Gilgun Fiction Award. He has garnered seven Pushcart Prize nominations, among the most honored short story prizes in the United States. His story collection *Breathless in Bombay* was shortlisted for the Commonwealth Writers' Prize in the best debut category from Europe and South Asia, and rated by the *Guardian* as among the ten best Mumbai books. His novel, *Waiting for Jonathan Koshy*, was a finalist for the Horatio Nelson Fiction Prize and was published in India, China, and the United States. His India collection of stories, *Third Eye Rising*, won high praise from five renowned American authors and featured on the *Esquire* list of Best Books of 2021. Shroff has been a speaker at several international literary festivals and universities.